SACRED
COWS
SILENT
SHEEP

ISBN: 978-1-907593-53-6

Author: Simon W. Kennedy
Editor: Michael Freeman
Sub-Editor: Helen Ashdown
Research: Paddy Whelan
Cover design: Sin É Design
Media: Peter O'Connell
Author's Photograph: Ger Hore
Printed by Naas Printing, Naas, County Kildare

Published by Three Sisters Press, Galbally, Enniscorthy, County Wexford

Distributed by Gill & Macmillan Distribution
Hume Avenue, Park West, Dublin 12
T: +353 (1) 500 9534 | F: +353 (1) 500 9595 | E: sales@gillmacmillan.ie

This book is a work of the imagination.

TWELVE STORIES–SIX DECADES

SACRED COWS

SILENT SHEEP

SIMON W. KENNEDY

With Michael Freeman (Editor), Helen Ashdown
(Sub-editor), and Paddy Whelan (Research)

THREE SISTERS PRESS

Contents

Before you read the stories in this book you should know the following . . .

The stories in this book are contained within a time frame of the early 1950s to recent times. The book is dedicated to my family whose influence on me is profound.

These influences started with my father and mother who were both born British subjects, as were my older brother Phil and my sister Ann at the end of the first De Valera period in power. I was born an Irish citizen after John A. Costello declared the new Republic. So were my younger brothers Martin and John.

As you read this book you will observe the influences of my family and their perspective on mine during these periods.

When I married Lillian in the seventies, we had just joined the EEC. Before that decade was out Pope John Paul II visited Ireland and our first two children Sinéad and Patrick started school. The 1980s was a transition period for me because it established me as a young married man and a young professional lawyer. During this period Brian and Niamh arrived. At this time also my parents passed on. These events further broadened my perspective and deepened my awareness. This was the start of my mid-life.

In the 1990s Gráinne and Niall arrived to complete our family. The child sexual abuse scandals started to rock the Catholic Church.

In the next decade my daughter Sinead, my eldest child, married

Padhraig. At this time the country seemed destined for years of prosperity. It was then the banks collapsed but in the middle of the turmoil my first grandchild Ciarán arrived and as the next decade started, Cathal, my second grandchild arrived.

As the writing of this book reveals, changing attitudes over the timeframe coincide with these events and these people in my life. You will note that I am placed at the centre of this universe and it is from there I write. I summed this experience up in four lines of a poem which I wrote last year. They set out this perspective;

> I am the Isotropic Man
> In space all viewpoints centrify in Man
> Where mystery met itself one Christmas Eve
> To stem a dreadful exploitation

'The Isotropic Man'
Síomón Ó Cinnéide 15 March 2011

I wish to acknowledge all that my family has done for me and in particular how they have helped each other to survive and arrive at this point. It is now or never for us. In the name of the dead generations in my family and in the name of my own generation, I dedicate this book to the next generation in the manner of sovereign continuity because in the words of my grandson Ciarán, aged three, they are the winniest of them all.

I dedicate this book to Ciarán and Cathal Fox.

Simon W. Kennedy
The Spring Equinox 2012

Introduction

The operators of Ireland's monoliths, Church, State and society, have dictated the course and fortune and way of life and living of millions of our people for generations. Some of our people are still here. Some are part of our diaspora spread across the globe.

Politicians, priests, guards, teachers, bankers, lawyers and civil and public servants have served us well; and they have served us poorly. Some have served in our empowerment – those of them who fought for necessary change, who stepped outside the rules and bureaucracy from time to time to help a victim of the system, an innovator, a free thinker – someone who was prepared to help someone who deserved justice.

Some of our oppressors have participated in our destruction. They have exercised power, influence and authority over our lives, sometimes just for their own preservation. Collectively, they have failed us. They have given away our economic sovereignty – our control over our own debts and our own money. People have become units of production, numbers on giant computer systems that cannot be reasoned with and have become the subjects of cold inanimate authority. The enabling devices have become our controllers.

Collectively, we the ordinary people have given this ruling class of our own making and the systems they operate, also of our own making, the power to control us. They, our own, have with our acquiescence, arrogantly taken control of everything except, so far, our thinking. It is a human condition to seek power and then try to keep it. However, they became the untouchables, the people and systems to whom the compliant and the unquestionning genuflect. We have allowed them to keep power and control and perpetuate old and out of date systems. They have become our sacred cows.

Are they merely the operators of systems that we created and then gave them power to operate? Are they products of the monoliths? Are they now inculcated slaves to the 'invisible hand' and culture of the monoliths? That is a conundrum and a dilemma. Should we now take back some of the power that we the silent sheep have given them? Or, is it too late?

The stories in this book are each independent, but at the same time interdependent, each contiguous and part of a continuously emerging and developing bigger story – that of our future. They are representative of defining moments and catalysts of change in our culture and our economy and society in the last sixty years. The author, like myself , has been here for more than sixty years and knows through his rural village background, his training for the priesthood and the law, his expertise and experience, and his excursions in local, sporting and party and organisational politics, how the influences and levers of change work. He brings a lifetime of hard earned wisdom , and that of several others to his stories.

He uses metaphor, symbolism and mythology to tell us about repression, coercion, inculcation, indoctrination, manipulation and control; survival, cunning, creativity and authority of Church and State and how good people bypassed it, helped at times by good citizens, lawyers or even bankers; our cultures pre-EEC and post-EEC; our tribal dance on the GAA playing fields; our struggles, right and wrong; social prejudice, morality, the challenge that life, or is it God, asks us to transcend our normal 'at-rest' selves. His stories tell us about eventual collapse and ultimately, recovery.

The stories mature with the author over his lifetime through the sixties, the seventies, the eighties, the nineties, the oughts and the Crash and are about all of us – you, me , the neighbours, and our ruling classes. They are representative of our social history. The author shines a light and hopefully sets many souls free. The author has given us the gift of his observations and his experiences.

The philosopher Thomas Merton in *A Book of Hours* says:

> It seems to me that the basic problem is not political, it is apolitical and human. One of the most important things to do is keep cutting deliberately through political lines and barriers and emphasising the fact that these are largely fabrications and that there is another dimension, a genuine reality, totally opposed to the fictions of politics: the human dimension which politics pretends to arrogate entirely to themselves.

Merton says it so well. He urges us to challenge the operators of the political systems.

The personal challenge for all of us is to choose one of three options: to keep on doing as we have been doing in the past; to do nothing, or to purposefully end our passive stance of being obedient and silent sheep and engage actively in questioning, challenging, thinking, taking nothing for granted and creating our own future.

Michael Freeman (Editor)

I.

The Silence

This was the awfullest thing a schoolboy could do. He had looked up under a girl's skirt. It was more awful still because he had seen her knickers. But the awfullest thing was that she was dead.

He was out hunting rabbits and was coming back where there was a grove of trees before you come into the village. He saw her hanging. He did not mean to look up under her skirt. He simply couldn't avoid it. He knew from school though that it was a sin.

The frightful thing was that he did not at first think what he saw in the tree was a girl. South-westerly gales oftentimes robbed clothes line garments from village gardens. This was often mistaken for the banshee and, as his father called her, the *badbh* (pronounced 'bough'), by late-night drinkers. The stories were always explained away later by recovery of the lost apparel. He still did not like going there on account of the stories. Bad things were often explained away by other stories like this. The explanations did not always convince. He stood there frozen not knowing what to do. Then he recognised Maire Lynch. This was far worse than supposed apparitions from the otherworld.

He ran as hard as he could out of the trees to the village. The first person he met was Father Doyle and he blurted and stumbled and half caught his breath while he stuttered out to the priest what he had seen in the trees. The priest took him home.

They cut down the corpse of Maire Lynch, sixteen years of age, wrapped it in a blanket and took it to Donoghue's Public House until the Guards came.

Looking back on the matter it's difficult now to understand how nobody ever knew what was going on. It killed poor old Mrs. Lynch who took to the bed after her husband died. Her daughter, Peggy, who was married to Sergeant Thorpey lived with her and minded her. Maire had lived with them as well.

That Sunday afternoon was a rotten dark day. A pall descended upon the village when the hearse arrived and took the body of Maire Lynch away. Nobody went near the pub until very late that evening when everything was tidied up.

There was no Mass when she was buried. It was just a simple ceremony served by the finder of the corpse and presided over by Father Doyle. Only Sergeant Thorpey, his wife, Peggy, and her sister, Kathleen, who had arrived home from London, were at the funeral.

They said Peggy fell on her feet when she married the Sergeant. He supported not alone herself and her mother, but also Peggy's sister, Kathleen, who lived there before she left for England. That was back in the forties.

Kathleen arrived at the funeral with her twelve-year-old son. She had left for England when she was pregnant. It was the first time she was home since. She had not even come home for her mother's funeral.

The village was a fishing village of three pubs, a church, a school, a post office and a Guards' barracks. It was ten miles from the nearest provincial town of New Ross. It had been raining for most of several weeks and a few tall trees for several hundred yards outside of the village were limp and bedraggled on that miserable November afternoon.

After the funeral was over and the altar boy put away the candles, Sergeant Thorpey came into the vestry to speak with the Priest. It had a worn carpet and a stained-glass window facing to the east. This was where Father Doyle took off his vestments. Some of the wall was damp and the plaster was peeling. Whatever secrets were told in the vestry stayed in the vestry. It was difficult to know whether it was religious business or official Garda business. One thing was sure: it was very serious and very important. The boy kept his ear cocked and his head down – Guards and Priests were very serious and very important. They could also be very dangerous.

There were four phones in the village and the one in the Priest's house rang as the two men were talking. The housekeeper told the Priest that the Coroner was on the phone looking to speak with the Sergeant.

The schoolboy was sitting in the kitchen doing his home exercise that evening when he looked out across the farmyard and saw a big black car drive up the laneway to the house. The driver had a briefcase.

The boy looked at the big black car and knew it was a Ford Prefect. There were four cars in the village altogether but none of them looked as new as this one. The registration number read ZR 5259 and had silver numbers on the black registration plate. The registration plate was on the front bumper just to one side of where the starting handle would be put in through the chromium. His father had a car, but this car had little spokes near the edge of the wheel rim and shiny hub caps, and the running board was trimmed with chromium as well. The steering wheel had a cloth cover which was very fancy.

He knocked at the front door. The man was a solicitor and was Coroner for the county. He told the schoolboy's mother he wanted to speak to her son about what he had found in the trees.

The boy was afraid. He felt he had done something wrong. His mother told him not to be afraid. But that was all very well for her. He had not told her everything. He only told her that he found Maire Lynch in the grove. He did not tell her about seeing up under her skirt. He knew that was an awful thing because the nuns told him so in school. He didn't know why, but he knew you weren't supposed to do that in the same way as he knew Maire Lynch should not have hanged herself. He also knew from his Catechism class that she should not have been buried in the graveyard. Nobody wanted to go to the funeral because it was a bad thing that had happened. A community silence was blending into the pall of gloom. Nobody wanted to talk about it.

The Coroner told the boy there was no need to be afraid. But the boy thought that was all very well for him, he was a solicitor and the one who was asking the questions. The questions were going to be about Maire Lynch.

The Coroner wanted to know what time it was when he went hunting for the rabbits and what time it was when he was coming back. He wanted to know how often he went hunting for rabbits. He wanted to know if he always came back the same way.

It was only when the boy started to tell him about coming into the grove that he began to feel frightened. Then, strangely, the fear left him. He was the centre of attention.

She was hanging from the biggest tree, he said. It was the one that was the furthest in, in the middle, and he always came through there because sometimes rabbits would be hiding in the briars. He never set snares in there though, because of the briars. It would be too hard to find a track.

The Coroner asked him if he ever climbed trees. He knew he was not supposed to because his mother had told him so many times. His mother told him it was alright to say 'yes', so he said 'yes'. He said it was an easy tree to climb because the branches were low.

He never went there with anybody because the grove was supposed to be haunted. He didn't see anybody else there and when he was going to the village he didn't meet anybody either. He never said anything about looking up under the girl's skirt.

The solicitor asked him if he knew what a lie was and he said he did. He asked if he was telling all of the truth and he said that he was. He thought at first that the solicitor did not believe him. But then the solicitor said he was a great boy for telling the truth so he knew he was okay. The solicitor put his papers away. His mother told him to go out and play.

When the Coroner got back to his office in New Ross, an official brown envelope was waiting for him. It was from the State Pathologist who had carried out the post-mortem on Maire Lynch. In his dimly-lit office he turned up the paraffin wick on his oil heater. In the envelope was the State Pathologist's report, duly signed, and also a carbon copy of it. He composed himself as he usually did by lighting his crooked-shank meerschaum pipe and began to read the Pathologist's report slowly and carefully, line by line, as was his fashion.

In the manner of Pathologists' reports, every detail of the deceased's body was explicitly dealt with and painstakingly and painfully detailed down to what the deceased had last eaten. Clinical descriptions were given of the bruising about the neck consistent with hanging from a rope. Details were given of each of the limbs in all of their technical detail with all of their medical names. The following is the extract that fogged the Coroner's eyes. It survives in the file to this day:

'*External examination – The body was that of a post-pubescent female appropriate to stated age showing pressure injuries to the skin consistent with the application of a ligature.*'

Ominously, the next paragraph read,

'*Genitourinal examination: Examination revealed evidence of a non intact hymen consistent with recent penetration of vagina suggestive of first episode penetration.*'

No one had warned him.

She was no longer a virgin – and maybe worse. Matters like this were not spoken about in public. However, he was the established Coroner and he should have been informed officially, if secretly. He could have walked himself clean into it.

The news arrived to him cold on the foolscap sheet over which he was now poring. Slowly he removed his horn-rimmed glasses and cleaned them having removed his pipe which he carefully laid in the ashtray on his roll-top desk. He blew the cold weather from his nose, stood up from his bentwood chair and looked through the rain-lined window pane out onto the evening street, reflecting the wet shadows scurrying along in the gathering November squall. He closed the shutters on the window and sat down once more.

Again he read it and looked in the envelope to see if it was accompanied by another statement. He retrieved the covering letter which addressed him as 'A Chara' and was signed by the Superintendent of the District who had sent him the report. He lifted the telephone on his desk and rang the Superintendent who refused to answer any of his questions while the Garda investigation into the demise of Maire Lynch was still ongoing.

Tom Lynch had never been to Ireland. His mother, Kathleen, brought him with her when she came over for his aunt's funeral. It was the first time she had been back in the village since she left for London when she was pregnant.

17

Tom had never seen his mother's homeplace. The only boy of his own age he had seen had served his cousin Maire's funeral. He only knew that because he heard his mother say the boy who found Maire hanging was specially picked to serve the funeral as they didn't want any of the other children involved who were younger, and that boy was his age.

He met him by chance at the shop. Tom wanted to see him but he did not wish his mother to know. He had not been brought to the funeral and was kept out of sight for most of the time. He had wandered around the Garda barracks and was shown the 'black hole' where bold boys were put. The only getaway he had was getting messages from the shop for his Aunt Peggy – mostly cigarettes. Though he was told the boy's name it meant nothing to him as he knew nobody in the village.

The Guards questioned a lot of people about who had last seen Maire. The Coroner was the only one to have spoken to the boy who found her. That was because he was young and it was an important case.

The shop was close to the church and was half of the street away from the Guards' barracks where Tom was sometimes brought by his Uncle Tom, the Garda Sergeant. His mother, Kathleen, did not like the Sergeant. It appeared to him they had a falling-out a long time ago as they never spoke and they avoided each other's company. It was awkward when they came home and got off the train and he met them at the station. His mother had been quiet the whole way over on the boat and on the train. She smoked a lot as well. The Sergeant wore a pioneer pin on his tunic.

By chance Tom Lynch met the boy at the shop when he was coming home from the Garda station. *The Dandy* and *The Beano* were as popular in Kilhile as Kilburn with twelve-year-olds. Common denominators facilitate easy introduction and common literary tastes make for easier invitation to conversation for young and old. They walked together up the long street that swept up from the seashore past the Garda barracks, the school and the church and out past the copse where Maire Lynch hanged herself.

It wasn't long before they were talking about it. They spoke in whispers in the open innocent way of children not yet fully inducted in the ways of their elders. The ruling social mantra was: 'Children should be seen and not heard'. Children had a habit of blurting out the truth.

The less children said the better. 'Less said, easiest mended' was another of these mantras, except when nothing was said nothing had to be mended. Tom told the boy his mother was very fond of both her sisters, the older, Peggy, whom she worshipped from childhood and her baby sister, Maire, adored by both from the cradle and now cruelly snatched from them.

Kathleen Lynch, Tom Lynch's mother had spent a lot of time with Peggy since she had come over. She consoled her that she had looked after Maire like a mother since their own mother had died. Peggy had no children of her own and had become very close to Maire since her mother's death. It was the main reason Kathleen had come home in spite of the intense dislike she had for Tom Thorpey, Peggy's husband, the main reason for her not returning even for their mother's funeral.

Before they knew it they were at the dreadful spot.

Where Maire Lynch hanged herself was quite close to the Lynch household. Tom Lynch stood for a while looking up at the tree trying to imagine his young aunt hanging there. He asked the boy who found her if he got a fright. He did. Tom never knew his aunt. He was staying around the place for a few weeks and would probably meet him again.

When they came back from the trees towards the street, the boy said that the Ford Prefect was outside of Lynch's house. He said goodbye to Tom Lynch and went home.

Later that same evening the Coroner called and asked the boy more questions about whether he was sure he had seen no one else after he found Maire Lynch hanging from the tree. He said he was sure. He asked him if he could remember seeing her with anybody in the trees or if he had met anybody before he came to the trees or when he was running to the village after he had found her. He said he met nobody. The Coroner was wearing a dickey bow. It was red with blue spots.

Nothing more was said by anybody about the matter until after Christmas

One January afternoon a Guard called to the boy's house and gave his mother a Summons. The boy was to come to the Coroner's Court to tell what he had told the Coroner. The Court was held in New Ross. His mother came with him. There was a big counter that they called the bench which was higher than every place else in the Courtroom. There was a high-backed chair and over the chair there was the emblem of a harp on the wall.

This was where the Judge usually sat and the Coroner sat there. Underneath this was a desk for a Registrar and below that was a table where the lawyers sat. Behind this table there was a partition which was chest-high and the public were not allowed to pass this. Everything was painted dark brown. This was the bar that divided the lawyers from the people. There was a jury box as well and some serious sober-looking men sat in it. The boy sat with his mother in the body of the Court and waited.

The lawyers read out all of the grim details. The two men and the woman from the newspapers took down notes. The boy noticed that everybody went quiet when the State Pathologist read out his report. The boy understood none of it. The jury returned a verdict of death caused by strangulation by misadventure.

When he got home, and over the following days, all of the talk was about how Maire Lynch was too shy to have a boyfriend. It was the first time he heard somebody whispering the word 'rape' to his mother when he was bringing in the coal for the fire and they had not seen him coming into the room. He did not know what it meant until he later looked it up in the dictionary and knew it had to do with sex, which was awful, and was also a crime.

Peggy Thorpey went to Mass everyday. She looked more and more gaunt. The skin was barely hanging on her. She wore a headscarf tightly tied under her chin and she fingered her rosary beads with her bony fingers all during Mass muttering 'Aves and Paters', as he heard his daddy say. It used annoy him when he was serving Mass because sometimes it put him off getting the Latin right when he was supposed to answer the Priest.

Sometimes it would distract him when they were all quiet coming up to the Consecration and he would hear her muttering and he might forget to ring the warning bell. When he held the golden paten under her chin, as the Priest placed the communion on her tongue, he noticed where her eyes met her nose was pinched and her tongue had red pimples. The Sergeant had a big tongue which was lumpy and had blue veins.

Kathleen Lynch came back just before Easter with her son, Tom Lynch. This time it was for another funeral. This time it was for another strange and awful funeral. Peggy Thorpey's husband, Sergeant Tom Thorpey broke his neck when he fell down the stairs of his house late at night.

Mrs. Thorpey was found the same night up in the grove of trees where Maire had been found hanging, keening and rocking in her night dress. The Priest and the doctor took her away to St. Senan's mental asylum.

Sergeant Tom Lynch's funeral was attended by his brothers and sisters. Kathleen Lynch was visiting her sister in St. Senan's when the funeral was taking place. There would be another inquest and another report from the Pathologist.

A week after the funeral, the boy saw the Coroner's car pull up outside Lynch's house. He saw Tom Lynch and his mother get into the Coroner's car and drive away. It was late before they came back because it was a Wednesday night and he saw them when he was coming back from serving the Stations of the Cross for Lent. He saw the lights of the car shining on the gable of the thatched house that was Lynchs'. He did not see them going in but he saw the lights going on. That was the last he saw of Kathleen Lynch. He never saw Mrs. Thorpey again. She was admitted to the asylum.

Next morning Kathleen and her son, Tom Lynch, left the village never to return. The house was put up for sale but nobody wanted to buy a house where somebody had fallen down and broken their neck and where a girl who had hanged herself had lived. There were stories that it was haunted and it was boarded up. After a while the roof became rotten and it fell in leaving nothing but the bare walls and the garden behind.

Forty years later, Mrs. Thorpey died in the asylum aged eighty-six. The village had come on in leaps and bounds and a number of housing estates had been built around the picturesque little village which was now a holiday destination for the new rich. Holiday sites were fetching big money and land was being sold at premium prices.

Most of the village had been renovated but there was one site that remained an eyesore throughout the years and that was Mrs. Thorpey's derelict house. Various people tried to buy it but, because she was in the asylum, nothing could be done about her title.

The boy who had found her sister hanging from the tree had become a solicitor and partner to the Coroner and was now working in the office of the Coroner who had long ago held the inquest into her death. The Coroner was long dead. About a month after Mrs. Thorpey died, he received a phone call from a Mr. Thomas Lynch, stockbroker in London. He was taken aback to discover that he was Kathleen Lynch's son whom he knew as Tom Lynch all those year's ago. He was further taken aback when he discovered that Mr. Thomas Lynch, stockbroker, was the sole surviving relative of Peggy Lynch, Mrs. Tom Thorpey. His mother, Kathleen, was long since dead and he was the sole surviving next of kin.

The solicitor asked Mr. Thomas Lynch to send over his birth certificate by post and when it arrived, the solicitor read it. Mr. Thomas Lynch's date of birth was given. The place of his birth was a London nursing home. In the place where it said mother's name, it read 'Kathleen Lynch'. In the place where it said father's name, it read 'Thomas Thorpey'.

The young solicitor was in shock. This was the most awful thing he had ever read. He read it again. Slowly he removed his glasses. He opened a fresh pack of Afton Major cigarettes and lit one. He got up in almost a jitter, placed the spent match in the ashtray which as sitting on the top of his former partner's roll-topped desk. He steadied himself. He opened the half closed shutter on the window to let in more light. He sat down and looked at the certificate once more as he inhaled heavily on his cigarette.

He was now privy to the darkest of dark secrets and the feeling echoed, and re-echoed, the frightened heart of a young altar boy who innocently looked up under a young dead girl's skirt all those years ago. He pulled on the cigarette, but more steadily and slower. He saw the bulbous tongue of Tom Thorpey receiving Holy Communion once more. He remembered the horn-rimmed glasses his former partner wore when he saw him first in the Ford Prefect with the cloth-covered steering wheel. And poor Mrs. Thorpey after Kathleen being ferreted off to England having to relive her habitual nightmare and keeping her mouth grimly and firmly shut by dint of the consequences of what might happen if she did not. And how she took to her rosary and the Chapel after Maire and all that happened.

In the swirl of the confusion and the mutterings of the 'Aves' and 'Paters' in the dizziness of all that was happening, who then could possibly be surprised that some night Sergeant Tom Thorpey might have been assisted to lose his balance at the top of the stairs in his own house, with nobody only his mad wife present, and accidentally fall down and break his neck?

He was not buried with Maire. And when it came to her turn, his wife was not buried with him either. She was put to rest beside Maire. All that survived were Tom Lynch who became a stockbroker and the boy who became a solicitor.

The solicitor walked back to the ashtray and the window. He closed the shutter on the world outside. He folded the birth certificate of Tom Lynch, placed it in an envelope, marked it 'Top Secret', and then placed it in a locked, secret compartment in his safe where it would remain unopened for generations to come. He retrieved the bottle of whiskey which he kept there for emergencies and special occasions. He poured a generous measure for himself and sat down once more. He sipped his whiskey slowly and reflectively. Silently he reopened the cigarette pack and withdrew another cigarette and lit it. Silently he sat there smoking in the semi-darkness. The Angelus bell roused him from his brooding. There were four cigarettes left in the pack when he left to go home.

2.

The Beating

I got to bed late that night. I could not sleep. My parents heard the noise of my twisting and turning from their bedroom. My mother got out of bed, took one look at me and went downstairs to get me a cup of hot tea. My father came to my door, stood there watching me and said he would never let me go to another film. But it was too late; the image of Frankenstein's monster on the white sheet screen of the parish hall cinema had already burned its negative imprint into my fourteen-year-old brain.

When I got up in the morning, I performed the usual rituals of washing my face and hands and putting on my shirt and shorts and eating my breakfast and getting my school bag ready. That week I was the morning Mass altar server in the Star of the Sea church but I was bothered and weary and missed the warning bell for the Consecration. Father Harpur looked at me for a long time but said nothing.

When I got back home for breakfast afterwards, I put the little silver toy aeroplane with its propellers on my saucer, and I put the teaspoon in my pocket. I really couldn't wake myself up. I had won the aeroplane in the Lucky Bag I bought on the way to the Picture show. It was now my prized possession above all others. My father remarked that between films and comics and toy aeroplanes and getting up in the night, I would turn into a fairy man.

By the time I got to the school, the sun was splitting the trees and was streaming through the classroom windows. I was wearing only a tee shirt and elastic-waisted khaki shorts. The other boys dressed likewise.

Sister Ignatius was in a foul mood as she paced up and down in front of the class. Her square-shaped headgear with black veil and her heavy black dress emphasised her severity as she stabbed the blackboard with the stick of chalk. Her countenance this morning revealed resentment. The dark furrowing brow of anger had not yet arrived.

She was in her mid-fifties. She was pale-faced but when she got excited, she flushed profusely. Underneath her heavy black dress coat was another layer of black modesty petticoat. The outer was as heavy as a tarpaulin – a protection against the ambushes of rude bad-mannered winds whose gusts revealed the forever to be concealed of a lady's decorum. This chaste clothing was not conducive to dexterity or goodness of temperament. She was pulling and tugging at her Rosary and tassled cincture that had become entangled. She was struggling with herself before she even started.

She was teaching us Irish. Beside the blackboard, a big cardboard chart on the wall showed a village in which a blacksmith, a carpenter, a cobbler and many other characters displayed all their tools and weapons of trade. White labels with Irish words written on them had been stuck on the chart and indicated what they were. I was good at Irish.

With the heat of the sun and the lack of a good night's sleep, my mind wandered to the toy aeroplane in my pocket. I felt it. I could turn the little propellers. Suddenly she shouted.

'Jack Leacy, stop fidgeting!'

My heart jumped and I blushed. In Irish, she told me to stand up and recite the words she would point to on the chart. Then she turned the chart to the wall and asked me to tell her the names of the instruments of the blacksmith. This was no problem to me since it was the one picture in the whole school that I loved. The blacksmith always welcomed me at the forge. When I recited the instruments perfectly, she seemed annoyed. She made me sit down. She instructed the class to get out our maths copies.

She announced, after the prayer to the Holy Ghost for enlightenment, that we were doing fractions. I groaned internally. This could be grief. Fractions were probably the most dreaded word in a schoolchild's vocabulary. Worse still, it was money fractions!

She spent about half-an-hour explaining them. I stole odd glimpses at the toy aeroplane in my pocket. When she was writing on the blackboard, her back to the class, I placed it on the ledge underneath the top of my desk. She detected something and swung around. 'What have you got there?'

I blushed and hung my head.

'Speak up,' she barked, this time in English. This was serious and no mistake.

I handed up my prized possession. She seized my toy aeroplane triumphantly.

'I'm confiscating this,' she said.

Anguish took me. But, there was more.

'Out to the top of the room'.

I obeyed.

'Hold out.'

I held out my hand.

The stick had once been a three-feet pointer in the style of a billiard cue. Due to exertions in its unorthodox use, it had broken, and there remained an eighteen-inch butt, or handle, which she used for punishment.

She struck me hard. Twice on each hand. My hands were very sore. Her face was flushed. Upper fourth class and sixth class, who shared the room with my class, were hushed. Sixth had been assigned poetry memorisation and the 'to and fro' rocking motion, which pupils employed to rhythm their brains to ensnare the quatrains, had stopped. Their heads were still and bent over their books. Upper fourth class sat there, just gaping.

'Back to your writing,' she snapped at them.

They immediately corrected their gaze to their blue-lined copybooks and inkwells.

'Up to the blackboard!' she ordered.

I picked up the chalk, refusing to cry. I held my gaze evenly at her but not defiantly. The last thing I wanted to do was challenge her.

'Write this sum down. One and sixpence ha'penny added to two and seven-pence three farthings and add them up'.

        s - d
        1 - 6½
        2 - 7¾

When I had the sum written, I drew a line underneath. A ha'penny plus three farthings was a penny-farthing. I knew that. There were three columns.

Shillings, pennies and farthings. I knew I could put down the farthings in the farthings' column but how did you write down a penny in the farthings' column. Due to my focus on my toy aeroplane, I had missed the instruction to carry the penny forward and add it up with the other pennies. There I stood, unable to start.

'Well?' she enquired.

I shifted uneasily. Would I ask, or should I not? If I asked, would she wallop me? Maybe I would get inspiration. I looked back at the black-board and tried to stare my concentration into inspiration. Nothing would come. I could sense panic. My stomach was turning around towards my back.

She swooped like a black-draped demon. She held me by my elbow and hit me three times with the stick on the back of my left arm.

'Now will you be so stubborn and not do your sums?'

She was clever. She pronounced my inability to proceed as wilful dis-obedience. Fear was in me now. I could not now ask her to solve my dilemma since it would seem as if I was contradicting her findings of dis-obedience, or else I was being doubly clever. My concentration had long since departed and I was enveloped in intellectual ignorance.

She roared,

'Answer, can't you?'

I thought her question on my stubbornness had been rhetorical. I moved immediately to defuse an explosion.

'No, Sister,' I answered. She immediately twisted it.

'So you are refusing to answer me, then.'

She moved and caught my left forearm once more. She started to wallop me with the stick on the arm once again.

'You are a brazen . . . (wallop) . . . impudent . . . (wallop) . . . child . . . (wallop) . . . and I'll not . . . (wallop)' – she moved to my left leg – 'have you . . . (wallop) . . . treat me . . . (wallop) . . . in this fashion.'

Her strokes were vicious. I was reacting to each clout with sobs and cries. The pain from the bruises was numbing and stinging at the same time. She was flushed red and panting.

'Were you at Communion this morning?'

'Yes Sister,' I higged.

She moved in again with her black mass. The demon was gone but now the vulture had arrived, intent on indulgence. She moved to my left, raised her eyes to heaven and said,

'Sacred Heart of Jesus help me with this child.'

She gave me somewhere between ten and twenty strokes as she decried the presence of the Blessed Sacrament in such an unworthy body.

By this time, I was hysterical. I was trapped in that most terrible of childhood experiences – the powerlessness to answer, the inability to resolve. My dignity left me and I disintegrated into a quivering jangle. Some of the girls in the class started to cry. She ignored it.

I was standing at the board shaking and shivering when my body came to my rescue. I wanted to go to the toilet. I turned to address her,

'Sister?'

She lifted her head from fixing her long rosary beads, which had become entangled in one of her strokes and had broken. In barely audible strains, I asked her in Irish, '*An bhfuil cead agam dul amach go dtí an leithreas?*', for permission to go out to the toilet.

'You most certainly will not leave here until you apologise to me and this class for your disgraceful conduct here today. First, you disrupt the Irish class. Secondly, you disrupt the maths class. Thirdly, you stubbornly refuse to do a perfectly simple addition sum. Then you impudently confirm this attitude. And now you have the effrontery to look for permission to go out.'

I was in great distress. I was in a black hole, a bottomless pit. Was there no escape from this torment? I cried uncontrollably and as I did, my dignity abandoned me entirely and flowed uncontrollably with my tears, down my bare legs, wetting my trousers, and then poured into a puddle on the black polished timber floor.

'Take him out! Take him out!' she yelled. Michael Larkin came over and gently put his arm under my armpit and led me out, tenderly.

It took me twenty minutes to stop higging. When I did, it was half-past twelve and time to go home for dinner. Michael kept saying,

'She's nothin' only a fuckin' bitch. She shouldn't be let teach.'

When I got home, my mother saw the state of me. She asked me about it and washed my arms and legs. I hated being a tittle-tattle and I was reluctant to not take my batin' like a man. She told me not to go back to school in the afternoon. No way. Back I was going. Ignatius tried to teach me fear. But I was learning fortitude.

That afternoon she ignored me. When we were going home at three o'clock, the other children inspected my bruises. I was like a celebrity.

'Did you see his arms?'

'There's a big black wan on his left leg,'

'Are the red wans worser?'

When my father came home from work, he put me out to play. Later he drove off in his Morris Minor motor car. At a quarter past nine, he came back. I was dressed for bed and I was sitting listening to the *Clitheroe Kid* on the wireless. My two younger brothers were in bed and my sister had been taken back to the Mercy Convent that morning.

He asked me to turn off the wireless and sit on a stool beside him. My mother stopped her knitting. As he spoke, he looked into the fire. He told how he had gone to Canon Harpur who was the School Manager who rang the convent and requested the Reverend Mother and Sister Ignatius to come over.

Sister Ignatius said she was not able to teach without using corporal punishment. My father told her if that were so, she had better give it up.

I was proud of my father and I felt so restored and valuable that I welled up inside. My mother started looking for a knitting needle behind her, but they were both in the cardigan sleeve she was making on her lap. I did not know how to say thanks. He just put his hand on my head and said,

'There now. Everything will be alright. Get a cup of milk and a cut of bread out in the back kitchen and go to bed now.'

As I was doing so, Father Williams came in as he usually did. When I finished I said goodnight to them all. Father Williams said I would need to be in good form for the County Final on Saturday.

When I closed the door behind me, I sat on the bottom step of the stairs to listen to them talk about my experience

Father Williams concurred with my father that the nuns were frustrated. He said they knew nothing about children and had forgotten what family life was like. He asked my mother if she had been very upset. He said he would have reacted in the very same way himself if it had been a child of his very own. I thought that was a very odd remark for a priest to make.

I stayed on the bottom step for a long time and only skedaddled to bed when my mother went to get the tea ready. The last I heard was my father saying:

'Well I'll tell you wan thing, she won't ever think of doing it again'.

As I lay in my snug bed, I imagined my father letting Ignatius have both barrels and fell asleep smiling.

Sister Ignatius never referred to the incident after that. However, my little toy aeroplane with the propellers was gone. It was a symbol of how matters would stand. She knew she had no right to it but would not offer it back. And she knew it would not be asked for. It was part of the land of nod and wink over-populated with blind horses.

I was not the only one to have suffered at her hands. Her reputation for temper explosions was infamous and her capacity for brutality never lost in the telling as the more merciful qualified their condemnation.

Months later she was transferred back to the mother house in Dublin, after a suitably appropriate passage of time that could not easily link the two events. But, years later, she returned to the convent near the little village. Her final weeks consisted of hysterical shrieks and shouts as she finally lost control and had to be held down by the other sisters until finally, fatigued, she slowly collapsed down into the waiting arms of her Eternal Master.

(Adapted and abridged from
The Year The Whales Came In by Simon W. Kennedy)

3.

The Elk

I didn't like the Elk at first. Although he was only fourteen going on fifteen years of age, he was as big as an eighteen-year-old with a shock of blonde red hair. He was tall and had a swagger. He was a bully, but boy, could he play the mouth organ. He wasn't bad at the guitar either.

I met him the first day I went to St. Patrick's College. He was loafing around with a couple of 'hard chaws'. I was thirteen and a gawk. I was a wimp by comparison.

On our first day in the secondary school, we were all assembled in the Pugin chapel which was laid out in monastic formal choral arrangement with pews facing across the aisle in rows of five, each row raised eight inches higher than the one in front.

The College was divided into a Major and Minor Seminary. The Minor Seminary was for second level lay students from thirteen to approximately eighteen years of age who were being prepared for Leaving Certificate. The Major Seminary was for preparation for the priesthood and provided a steady supply of curates for the Diocese. There was a total population of about three-hundred in this Gothic institution.

On the first evening, I accidentally crashed into the Elk. 'Watch the fuck where you're going,' he said. We were off to a bad start. I made my first mistake.

I said, 'Sorry.'

'You will be if you do it again.'

What was worse, I said it politely.

He was setting down his territorial boundaries. Many of the lads didn't like him because of this and some were more than a little resentful. Others cronied up to him. Whenever he poked fun at them, they joined in. They lacked gumption.

The Senior Dean of Discipline shepherded us into the chapel. The President of the College gave us a lecture in formal lofty tones in words we barely understood. We understood the tone though.

'Be ye therefore perfect as also your Heavenly Father is perfect,' he intoned. 'Your job here is to become perfect Christians. We are cast with that responsibility and you must now shake off the ways of the child and take on the ways of the man as St. Paul advises us.'

He spoke from the steps of the altar. All eyes were glued on him. This was our first introduction to secondary school.

'If any man comes to me and hates not his father or mother and wife and children and brother and sisters, yeah and his own life also, he cannot be my disciple. You are all Catholic young men and though the quotation I have just given might strike you as odd that Christ is calling you to hate your parents, what he is really saying is you must put Christ before your parents. In that sense, you must take your direction from those in authority. This is one of the normative means of spiritual progress. Clarity and reason based on experience demonstrate this.'

The stage was being set. Most of the professors in the college were priests. They were the representatives of Christ. 'You will be called upon in your five years here to obey them. Obedience is superlative.'

'What the fuck is superlative?' the Elk whispered hoarsely.

'I think it means top of the range,' said Paddy Prate.

'The only range I knows is the one that me mother boils the kettle on,' said the Elk.

Smothered sniggers all round.

The President continued:

'Obedience is a supernatural and moral virtue which inclines us to submit our will to that of our lawful superiors in so far as they are representatives of God.

'You will take note in your time here that various of your superiors have different authorities and functions additional to teaching.

'I will now introduce you to the Dean of Discipline who organised this meeting, who has my authority. I have the authority of the Bishop who has the authority of the Pope to run this ecclesiastical establishment in accordance with the norms of the Church. We will turn you into fine Christians and soldiers of Christ. See well to your task.'

He turned towards the tabernacle, genuflected and left the altar. Then for the second time we saw the Dean of Discipline: Sikey. He stood on the centre of the altar wearing a frock coat and scarf. He was balding and in his mid-thirties. He had an aura. I could tell I was not going to like him.

'That's the biggest fucker in this place,' said the Elk.

The Elk had an older brother who had spent four years in the college.

Sikey stood for a good ninety seconds or more until there was a complete silence among the sixty assembled first-year students.

'When you leave this place you will forget a lot of it – but you will always remember me!'

It sounded like a threat.

The silence turned into a deathly quiet.

'It is my job to train your will and I will do that through the virtue of obedience. Obedience is a supernatural moral virtue which inclines us to submit our will to that of our lawful superiors in so far as they are the representatives of God.' He paused. 'All of your priests are representatives of God but it is my job to enforce that obedience and make you subservient to it.'

He was standing on the top step of three at the altar. Then he descended them one after the other, slowly and deliberately for dramatic emphasis. At the bottom he evenly measured his stride to further maintain the drama as he advanced towards us like the demon in a pantomime might attempt to enthral his audience – except this was not funny.

'The will in man is a governing faculty. Being free, the will imparts its freedom not only to the acts it performs itself, but to the acts it bids the other faculties to perform. It gives them their merit or their demerit. The discipline of the will means the discipline of the entire person and a well-disciplined person is one that is strong enough to govern the baser faculties and docile enough to submit itself to God. Remember! I am a representative of God – and I am the representative of God whose well-disciplined will, you will cross at your peril!'

He paused at the lowest step and then stepped on to the carpeted apron inside the Communion rails and down inside the rails talking towards the wall he was facing as he paraded.

'You may not know this coming from the countryside. One of the virtues you will learn here is one of a filial and reverential fear, which causes us to dread every offence against God. Disobedience to your lawful superior is an offence against God. It is a sin displeasing to Him and one that is my job to root out. While you are here you will learn to be submissive, and willing, and you will joyfully accept all the crosses that Providence may see fit to send you. The Council of Trent teaches us that it is a great token of God's love for us that he deigns to accept as satisfaction for our sins patient endurance wherewith we suffer the temporal ills He visits upon us.' He paused and placed his hands on the two lapels of his black frock coat lined by his paisley scarf. He faced the student body.

'Remember the words of the Scriptures about Christ. He was made obedient unto death, even death on the cross.'

Then he continued his parade in front of the troops once more.

'We have devised a rule of life here. This rule is firm enough to sustain your will and yet will be elastic enough to be adaptable to the various circumstances arising in real life which you will frequently face when you leave here. My job is to see that you keep the rule. When there is silence – there is silence – no whispering. When there are lights out – the lights go out – no torches. There will be no laxity in silence when there is silence. In doing what you are told, you will do exactly as you are told and in this way, this well-defined rule of life will save a considerable amount of time. You will waste no time. There will be no hesitation. You will know exactly what to do and when to do it.

'Your duty is to become perfect and faithful and you will do this through authority and faith, from time to time when you fail in this respect I will call to aid what I refer to as my "civiliser".'

(Nervous sniggers)

For the first time Sikey produced a bamboo cane about three feet long shaped like a walking stick and smacked it off his coat. There were more sniggers. He reacted with a smirk. There was no smile on the face of the Elk. He knew the story.

'The fucker,' he muttered.

I went to bed that night feeling anxious and homesick. I looked up at the moon and stared at it for awhile. I missed my father and mother. Though I had an older brother as well with me, I still missed my younger brothers and sister and I had a sense of foreboding of what was to come. I imagined to myself if I could go to the moon I could look down on my home and see exactly what my father and mother were doing, how they would have said the Rosary, listened to the wireless, read the paper, my mother knitting, and my younger brothers doing their homework and getting ready to go to bed.

The bed in College in which I slept was hard. When my older brother came there first he was put sleeping in the tower. The tower was an imitation of the entranceway to Hampton Court Palace in London. It was built from Ballyhack stone; a stone quarried not three miles from my own home. The stone was a type of ermine colour, a product of volcanic rock. When my uncle, who had served jail in the Civil War, saw the quarters that my older brother was going into, he was horrified. He said he had been in prisons that were more comfortable. The exterior was pretentious and authoritative.

This was the time of change. John XXIII had become Pope, President Kennedy had become the US President. At last, a new and rejuvenated population, educated and equal to any British public boys' school, would shortly emerge. The Hampton Court façade said it all: If the Brits could do it, we could too.

The Battle of Waterloo was won on the playing fields of Eton, the British had proudly boasted. Our training fields would be hurling and football fields and lashings from Sikey to toughen us up and mould our subservience. We, like them, would obey our superiors, and if privileged, command also like them, in time in their case, in the name of King, Country, Kaiser, and Fatherland, where the generals either sat mounted on the top of hills far removed from the battle or sat in the recesses of Whitehall shifting toy soldiers around on large maps laid out on tables as if war was a game of chess and the life and death of unfortunates mere counters with which they kept the score. In our case in the name of God, the Pope, the Republic and its Catholic traditions offering the first morning prayer, the Morning Offering for the Pope's intentions and either by collecting with mite boxes for the Missions or, if God so ordained, those privileged would labour in the mission fields far from the Shamrock Shore.

Eton or St. Patrick's. It was all the same; subservience and loyalty to the rule were paramount.

As we were ordered, we left the chapel in silence. I awkwardly tripped into the Elk accidentally. Sikey called him: 'Have my words been lost on you?' he asked. He took out the cane. 'Hold out your hand.' He drew down on the Elk's hand with the cane. 'It's your first day,' he said. The swish from the cane choked everyone to silence. I shifted as far and as fast away as I could. I knew I was for it from the Elk. If I snivelled, I'd get hammered. If I excused, I'd get hammered. If I stood up to him, I'd get hammered.

Eventually I fell asleep. I awoke to the sound of the morning bell whose peal was a rapid succession of bangs and the sound it made was 'nag, nag, nag, nag.' It was like a hammer on a bucket but it could be heard throughout the entire grounds. It hadn't the slightest suggestion of a musical instrument. It was a metaphor of what was to come. We called it 'the tin can'.

'Ya little bollocks'. 'You got me first slog for me.' 'I'll break yer fuckin' neck.' He grabbed me. My friends deserted me just as Peter and the other apostles in the Garden of Gethsemane did when the Romans arrived. I was too frightened to say much. I looked at him in the eyes and said, 'I'm very sorry but it was an accident.' Then I scored. 'We may watch out for that fucker.' It was the first time I used bad language as my mother had continually corrected us against it. It worked in reverse on the Elk. I had transferred the blame to Sikey.

The Elk released his grip. 'One day I'll level that fucker,' he said. 'Don't be in a hurry,' I warned. 'We have a long way to go.'

'Be careful where you put your big splaw feet again,' he said.

We got talking about where he was from. He introduced me to a friend of his and suddenly, without knowing it, I was nearly in. I didn't regard myself as tough enough to survive in that clique. However,

I knew I had handled it the right way.

On our first day in class, we met all the professors. There was Rulo who, within the first three weeks, set us an exam. He earned the name Rulo. If we made a mistake, he got a metre stick, or ruler of more than a yard long and half-an-inch thick, and brought it down on the backs of the knuckles of his victim for any mistake that had been made in the exercise. It was the most stinging pain I ever felt. Within my recollection, he did it only twice when I was present.

There was Foher who was the Dean of Studies, tall, bald and harmless. His disposition was one of nonchalance. He loved music. He had a terrible voice. He was charged with making sure the professors maintained the syllabus. He was regarded as third in command.

The Vice-president taught on the Ecclesiastical side and we saw little of him. He looked ascetic. He didn't appear to be much fun. Then there was a raft of new priests that had come fresh from Maynooth. One of them was a little cynic. Little Plum we used to call him after the character in *The Beano* comic. You could fit him in the pocket of his soutane.

When Laurence Sinnott, who had a stammer and had recently arrived from the Christian Brothers, referred to him as 'S-S-S-Sir,' he turned on him. 'I was ordained a priest of God and you will call me Father.' He hit him with his right hand straight into his face. Blood squirted everywhere. Sinnott pulled out his handkerchief. 'May I go out to wash my face, S-S-S-Sir?' 'Get out,' Little Plum snarled. It recalled memories from my primary school when I had received a beating. Were they all the same? It seemed that the only method of education they could use was inculcation by fear and brutality.

In my second year, the Elk and myself ended up in different dormitories. I didn't see as much of him then but I bumped into him on the football pitch and the hurling pitch, where we played on the same team.

I settled down to the humdrum of College life and learned to get on with it. Beatings became part of everyday life. I don't remember any day that passed without getting a beating. Maybe it wasn't true, but that's how I remember it. We studied, ate, studied, slept, studied, hurled, studied, slept, day in, day out for five years.

The Elk maintained he was the only one that came close to having an academic understanding of Julius Caesar. 'That fucker had the right idea. Bate the shite out of all in front of ya. That's what gets respect.' There was a real good side to him. He shared whatever he had and he hated scroungers. If he got cake, everybody got cake. If everybody got cake, he got some too and if he didn't, the cute-arse who didn't share was ferreted out.

He was cute enough, too. He sidled up to those that were over the team – something I found repugnant. Maybe it was that I wasn't good enough. Maybe they were more interested in keeping him on board than they were in keeping me. Maybe I was simply jealous. And then there were other fellas who were befriended by others of the staff.

It appeared to me that apart from the few lads I hung around with, nobody was that interested in me and my results began to fall. Where I had started out as second in my class and was shoved up to the highest class where I came ninth, my progress descended steadily downwards over the next three years. Nevertheless, I got my Intermediate Cert with two honours, which was a big deal at the time. I was smart enough but my application was elsewhere. Little Plum told me, 'Your brain is all over the place.' He was probably right. I found it difficult to concentrate.

During the year of our Intermediate exam, we were taken to the beach for a swim. Slinky, who was one of the professors, remarked that I could not swim. I excused myself on the basis that 'my stomach muscles weren't strong enough.' Instead of telling the truth, I hid the fact that I was afraid of my daylights of the water. I had been born beside the beach but I had inherited my father's landlubber's instincts. 'I could give you exercises to remedy that. Call to my room at seven-thirty.'

When I arrived in Slinkey's room, he put me sitting on a bentwood armchair and sat on a wicker stool lower down beside it. He asked me to indicate where my stomach muscles were weak. I looked at him quizzically. I indicated and he asked me to undo the top two buttons of my trousers. At the time, we did not wear underpants, as they were expensive.

I undid the top two buttons. Then he pounced, 'Here, let me help you.' He moved both of his hands. My boundaries were well in place. I knew on the instant what he was at. I bolted to the corner of the room, buttoned up my trousers and looked at him, my eyes hunted. 'Oh don't be so stupid,' he said. 'There's nobody going to harm you.' He bade me sit down and moved back. His eyes became dull and glazed, expressing the lifelessness of a cheated shark. For half-an-hour, he gave me a lecture on purity, temptation and sexuality. He was going through the motions and attempting to exonerate himself. The anger was rising in me but I was powerless.

For half an hour, I listened to the diatribe. He then allowed me to leave the room. Having closed it behind me, I turned round to the door, clenched my fists, gritted my teeth and made faces at it and the priest behind it. I told no one. I kept my silence. I could see what the regime was doing. The culture was one of conquest by isolation. We were disempowered and vulnerable. We had no one to whom we could turn. And anyhow, no one would believe us against a priest.

The memories came flooding back of the first day in school. The power of the priest of God. The position of the priest. The authority of the priest. Who was I? I said nothing about it but in the following year, he approached me twice to do some handwriting of a manuscript which required transcription. This was, of course, all a ruse to ingratiate himself. He asked me to come to his room. I told him I would oblige him by doing the writing if he brought the material to the study hall. I was getting clever.

I would not be caught out so easily again. He left me alone after I demonstrated my ability to uncouple myself from his grip without confrontation. Unfortunately, it would be discovered very much later how he had moved onto other easier victims. I did not easily forgive myself for my silence then when I discovered this years later when the clerical abuse scandals broke. I was reminded of Edmund Burke, the eighteenth-century Irish political philosopher about this type of silence; a silence that imprisoned the spirit, that stifled speech and paralysed thought for eternity. He said: ' All that is necessry for evil to triumph is for good men to do nothing.'

The following year, which was my second last year, my younger brother joined me in college. The Elk and myself and others were getting on well.

I was still hurling, and playing football, though I had not advanced as well as the Elk who had grown to over six-feet tall although he was only seventeen years of age. He was as big as any man I had seen. He was tough as nails and had developed a reputation over the years for fighting – on the field and off the field. In many ways, I envied him. In other ways, I pitied him. When he felt down, we spoke a lot about what we would and wouldn't do when we were finished. He knew he could trust me because I never broke a confidence.

One afternoon in my last year, I asked for permission to go down town with my younger brother who had joined me in the college the previous year. I was told to be back at teatime. It was a Wednesday. Teatime on Wednesday was usually at four o'clock but on this occasion, unknown to me, the time had been changed to three because the junior hurling team was playing a match in the nearby park. When my brother and myself were strolling back at a quarter to four, for, as I thought, tea at four o'clock, Sikey met us. He challenged us why we were late for tea. I told him tea was at four to which he responded it had been at three o'clock. I told him I was unaware of the change in times. He said he would deal with me later.

That evening he came into the study hall and walked up and down in the eerie silence that descended on study halls when he entered. As he was passing my desk, he stopped. Then he walked on past. When he came back, he stopped again and then he passed on to the back of the study hall. He paused. He called my name and a shiver ran down my spine. I stood up. 'Why were you late back for tea today?' he barked. I muttered that I was sorry that I was unaware that teatime had changed. 'A likely story,' he said. Then he strolled up and cuffed me on the back of the head with the back of his hand.

'Hold out,' he commanded.

He took out the cane. He pulled on me with slicing strokes. They bit. They scalded. They hurt. I bit my lip. The pain was intense. He slogged me six times, three on each hand with his bamboo cane. I held my hands under my arms to soothe the pain after the administration of the punishment. Then with a sneer, he demanded, 'What class is your young brother in?' He was letting me know he was going to administer the same

41

punishment to him. I felt a pang. I summoned up my courage and said to him.

'If there is fault in this matter, Father – and I don't agree there is – then the fault is mine, not his.'

With a sneer he replied, 'The cow rushing to the defence of the calf.' He paused and broadened his sneer. 'Perhaps you would like to take his punishment for him.' I looked at him evenly and said 'Yes, I would.' I called his bluff. Then he called mine.

'Hold out your hand.' He gave me six more. I took some of the strokes on my wrist. I thought my hand had been broken but it was only badly bruised. He left the study hall to the awe, terror and rage of the entire body of students.

The Elk was raging. He fumed in his desk and when the bell went at the end of study, he came immediately over to me together with others and they swore revolution. The smartest boy in the class, Wallace, came first and said what we were all thinking, 'In years to come we will wonder to ourselves how there wasn't a revolution by us in this God-forsaken place.'

As it happened, the following day was a free day and by chance my father called to the College. He needed to buy some clothes for myself and my young brother for the winter. He had received permission from the College President for us to go down town. When we were going out to our parents, we met Sikey. He held his cane out like a barrier impeding our exit through the courtesy door to the foyer and the outside world. We halted.

'If you have permission to go down town I'm revoking it now,' he said. When I went to the car, my father said to me, 'Get your coat quickly. We're going down town. I have permission from the President.' I then told him what had happened the previous day, and what Sikey had said to me on the way out. 'I'll fix that lad,' said my father.

He had been a tough footballer in his day. He left the car, walked up the granite steps, and pressed the front door bell. He could see through the coloured plate glass in the oak-stained door to the end of the foyer. He could see Sikey reading the paper and ignoring the bell. Not to be intimidated easily, my father opened the door and beckoned Sikey who looked up from his reading in the nonchalant, indifferent, ignorant manner he could choose with ease.

'Yes?' he said.

My father said, 'I'd like to speak to you in the front room.'

My father went to the front room and told him that whereas I was thinking of becoming a priest, he couldn't understand how an example like he had set could influence me in such a direction and that certainly if he had anything to do with it, the last place I would end up would be in a seminary. He told him that he could embarrass him by calling on the College President to invoke his authority but that would cause a row.

'There's something perhaps you should know,' said Sikey, 'Inside these walls we have authority over your children which you gave us.'

He eyed my father.

'If you wish to take your children with you now, no one will stop you.'

My father stepped forward.

'In two seconds Father, I'd knock that smirk off your puss and stretch you on the floor and that collar you're wearing would count for nothing either.'

Sikey kept the curl on his lip.

'I've known priests all of my life and most of them have agreed with me that if anything should happen to the Church, it's not the people like me will be to blame. It's the priests like you.

'My sons don't have a choice about where they get their education. Perhaps you're more stupid than you look. Let me tell you this,' he said. 'Both of my chaps will be out of here next year. Should I ever come across you again in circumstances where they won't be capable of being victimised by you, we'll deal on leveller terms.' He was heading for the door of the large carpeted reception room. Like the sneak he was Sikey said after him:

'Your attitude doesn't surprise me.'

Challenged in this fixation the father turned and faced him square on.

'Well, Father, your attitude surprises me, though perhaps it oughtn't. Perhaps we have been too trusting over too many years and it has given you the arrogance to think you can do what you like. You treat us like dirt. Frankly, I feel like bringing the chaps now. If I were to do so I would gratify myself by stretching you on the floor for your impudence, your ignorance and your downright arrogance, not to mention the assault you made on both of those chaps without my permission. If you as much as lay a hand on either of them in the future I promise you it's Jervis Street Hospital you'll want because the equipment necessary to resuscitate you won't be available for you in the County Hospital. I hope I make myself clear.'

With that, he stormed out leaving Sikey in his wake.

My father recounted for us word for word what he had said. He wanted us to see that he knew what was going on but he wanted us to have the advantage of a secondary education no matter how difficult teachers were. It was a gateway to the better opportunities which he never had.

That evening I told the Elk. He was delighted. 'The only pity is that he didn't hit the fucker a skelp. Jesus, I'd love to have seen it happen.'

Rosary was said at eight o'clock in the evening and because we were so engrossed in the conversation in the field, we missed the nag of the bell when we were at the bottom of the field at the furthest extremity from the church. We had three minutes to get to the church. The bell and its rope were located under the gothic door in the cloistered squares fronting onto the buildings which shielded the field from which we ran. It was a minute past eight when we got there.

Sikey was standing under the belfry which was the entranceway to the church. I ran my best and as I was passing under the door, he gave me a knock with his knuckles on the back of the head. I thought it better to let him have his gratification rather than face a belting later in the evening. The Elk wasn't having any of it. When Sikey made a shot at him with his closed fist at the back of the head, the Elk ducked. When he did so, his rear end protruded. Sikey tried to kick him in the rear. Too quick from the fitness of his hurling training, the Elk straightened. Sikey missed the kick with his right foot, accidentally pulled his left leg from under himself and went flat on his backside on the ground.

We got into our seats in the church as the Rosary had just started. The Elk was shaking with the laugh at the notion of Sikey ending up on his arse. I was hoping that was going to be the end of it. And indeed, probably because of the embarrassment, Sikey didn't show his head that night. We dined out on the strength of it, and had cake feasts for weeks compliments of the frightened, the envious and the inquisitive. This was our Last Hurrah.

The Elk wasn't sorry to be leaving St. Patrick's and neither was I. Both of us took bitter memories from it.

Years afterwards, we met and we compared notes. Only one in our class had died and that was through an accident and this was some twenty-five years later. The professors didn't fare so well. The entire College was investigated for sexual abuse and prosecutions of the teaching staff made the expression of the name of the College synonymous internationally with corruption and sexual deviancy.

Sikey committed suicide.

'Were we stupid fools to put up with it?' I asked the Elk one day.

'I don't know,' he said, 'but we were sure as tough as nails.'

Well perhaps we were, perhaps we weren't. The reality lies in the fact that if we were to get an education we had to run this gauntlet. Those in charge could dictate our fate. The simplest thing we believed was to keep the head below the parapet. But my father taught me a different lesson.

The injustices wrought that I witnessed stirred my nobler instincts. It was these instincts he taught me to rely on. I could do something about it. I could do as I learned from my father and the Tans, and my grandfather with the British Empire.

I resolved to become a priest and use authority as it ought to be used. There had to be change. It was now in the air and it would not be denied. There was a new world order, a young new Irish US President and an Ecumenical Council of the Catholic Church.

There had to be a new structure. The Elk felt the same way. We would do this in the noblest calling of them all – the priesthood. We both went to seminaries. He would be at home in our native diocese and I, with the heathen in the Foreign Missions. We would hand our lives over to God and let Him use us in the way we would submit. He could work out his plan in us. The covenant was kept by Him and Us in the mysterious immutable way of the Divine.

God would work his will through us and correct these injustices in a new generation in a different way. Perhaps that's what happened. The Elk became a banker. I became a lawyer.

4.

The Sheep

The ecclesiastical students kneeling in their black soutanes in the Seminary Chapel teetered nervously on the brink. During the post-Communion reflection, someone farted.

The consternation of the students was obvious. It was told in the facial expressions etched on the canvas of the po-faced, the pained, the bewildered, the bemused, those at a loss to know what had happened and those who did.

The Reverend Dean Celebrant sat in his *cathedra* in front of the altar. He no longer faced away from the faithful since the recent changes wrought by the Vatican Council. The liturgy was still part Latin, part English as the Church made efforts to gradually incorporate the congregation into the liturgy. Nineteen of the forty-two realized this vocation was not theirs and they had left.

The Dean was concelebrating with the remaining twenty-three recently ordained Deacons. They were the 'Fourth Divines' as Divinity students in their last year were called and they were due to be ordained priests at Christmas. Rory O'Donnell, on the Dean's left, and Michael Barraclough on his right, headed the two concentric semi-circles of Deacons now ranged around the altar. When they had entered almost seven years earlier, there had been forty-two.

The Dean rose solemnly in order to enunciate the Communion

antiphon. He timed it in order to ease the irreverent giddiness and glided to the centre of the altar. He genuflected with a reflected semi-pause for effect, the better to emphasise and acknowledge the Real Presence, and remind his congregation of where they were and who they were.

He turned to face the congregation with hands joined, his holy fingertips pointed at right angles to his breast. A short nod of the head, curt but dignified, acted as a signal for Donaghy.

It was part of Donaghy's duty that week to represent the congregation on the altar for specific prayers and rubric. He came from the pews exuding perspiration from the strain of the last few minutes and the dread anticipation of being next on stage. Like a beast from the swamp, laden with sweat, he made his way to the lectern. He felt the pressure. He intoned.

'Brethren, be sober, be watchful, for your adversary, the lion, as a roaring devil goes about seeking whom he may devour.'

The congregation collapsed in a spontaneous uncontrolled cacophanous laughter for a full five seconds. The stern rebuking slicing glare of the Dean killed the laughter – dead. Donaghy had confused his 'lions' with his 'devils' and inadvertently mixed them up. Profusely blushing, he retreated to the safety of the 'jungle' and awkwardly banged his foot on the pew as he got in past two students to his own place.

When the reverberation of the awkward noise died, the Celebrant stayed in pause mode and then, painfully, he raised his arms in epiclesis style and intoned, in Latin this time, the prayer.

'*Oremus!*'

He bowed his head before moving on in the liturgy. Everyone was more settled. He had 'out-rubriced' the vulgar with fastidious observation to rite – a discipline of quiet determination acquired during his years of spiritual formation and the three he had spent since his ordination as a priest. Discipline through practice. Discipline through mortification. Discipline through prayer and grace and commitment.

Though lankier and taller than all of his classmates, Kelly failed to get Donaghy's attention as the students walked down the cloister to breakfast in pairs. There would be '*craic*' about this after 'works' had been performed, but not until major night silence was over. Major night silence prohibited conversation under the seminary's ascetic regime, which followed the rule of Saint Ignatius. Discipline was paramount.

Seven classes, totalling some one-hundred-and-eighty black-soutaned future missionaries, filed into the Refectory Hall of the most modern seminary in the country whose mission was the Pacific region.

They went to their chairs and tables. Spiritual reading took place during silent breakfast. The Dean arrived and stood at the end of the Refectory beneath a five-foot crucifix.

At five-and-a-half-feet tall the Dean looked limp, drained and anaemic as he received a queue of students lined up to whisper their transgressions. This was not confession. It was a self-reporting honour system for breach of regulation, equivalent to admission of imperfection in duty, but nothing to do with the Sacrament.

'I spoke during major silence, Father.'

'I took time from study to go to the TV lounge and failed to make up the time later, Father.'

'I went to the Priests' front corridor (which was off limits) without permission, Father.'

Nobody was expected to say, 'I broke wind in the chapel this morning, Father,' but it was expected that if you laughed at Mass you reported yourself. Missionaries were expected to be candid. It was a code of honour. One day they might be called on to stand for their word, at the risk of death. Moreover, they had to mean it. In the 'fifties, some of their members had been martyred.

The Fourth Divines sat at the top of the Refectory. They were the 'cool' guys. About to be ordained, they had, in the eyes of their juniors, the aura of the matador. The men about to combat the beast. None was more admired than Rory O'Donnell.

Though diminutive in stature, he had the determination of a lion in his chosen sport of racquetball. He had a kindly demeanour and gentle expression. He was brilliant at his studies and yet, he was understated. His popularity was immense. Discernment and discretion were his middle names, yet he was truly candid

'There is a big difference between chastity and celibacy,' he once said. 'God knows what that difference is, yet we have to not just learn it, we must know what it is and then we must live it. But who will teach us?' He had a knack of 'hitting the nail on the head'.

Nobody taught us. True, there were theological and spiritual observations about the efficacy of prayer, which were taken personally and accepted. However, they were equally understood as being remote to those who could only aspire to asceticism. All aspired, but what of those who would not achieve? We were told we would be given a special grace from God.

Then there was Barraclough. Barraclough had been an English solicitor. He was plummy in tone. Barraclough never spoke, talked or conversed. He pronounced.

At the other end of the Refectory, there was Kelly and the young bloods. Thirty-three of them arrived one September a little over twenty-four months ago. They included Doyle, Doran and Donaghy. 'Poor ould Donaghy' who was always unlucky.

A standing house joke was that there were three Ds in Kelly – Doyle, Doran and Donaghy. They regarded themselves as the 'hard' men. Kelly and Doran played on the college hurling team with three of the Fourth Divines. Here they established friendships that lasted and in the odd way that sport allows, gathered respect. They were the liberals who detested the civil service mentality of the Church as advanced by the conservatives in the Roman Curia, and in particular their nemesis, Cardinal Ottaviani, the secretary of the Sacred Congregation for the Propagation of the Doctrine of the Faith, who had taken a bit of a hammering at the Vatican Council.

Ottaviani did not favour *aggiornamento* (bringing matters into the present time). He had a lot of support in the Council and indeed outside of it. He had a passionate mistrust of the young liberation theologian, Hans Kung.

Doyle was at the breakfast table.

'Who farted?' he whispered to Kelly.

'Donaghy,' he hand-shielded his reply.

A voice came out of the blue.

'Flog off, you flogger,' said the voice.

Donaghy had overheard the conversation and had used the mild epithet which was a psychological replacement for the traditional more prolific 'Fuck' so regularly used by the population at large, and frowned on as being too sexually explicit and vulgar for seminarians.

'You did,' said Doran.

'I did in me arse,' answered Donaghy, verging towards the vulgar.

'My, but I do declare,' quipped Kelly, as he mimicked gentility.

Doran sniggered. Involuntarily, he snorted tea out of his nose. The giddiness that had been quelled in the chapel was beginning to emerge once more. It broke the concentration of the spiritual reader. He stopped and started. The flock of students in the queue to the Dean blocked out detection of the culprits, but not from everyone. The spiritual reader redroned. He stopped at the signal from the Dean. Brief communal thought of confrontation was submerged in 'Grace after meals'.

As Kelly and his comrades tidied the table preparatory to performing their assigned works for the morning, and before Kelly made his way to the Fourth Divines' corridor to commence his duty of dusting and sweeping, he was ambushed by Barraclough.

'Mr. Kelly!' pronounced Barraclough. 'If there is a rule of silence it ought to be obeyed.'

The impudent young Kelly replied, 'Since when did you become the Dean, Mick?' The disarming reply left a floundering Barraclough purple with rage, as the arrogant young blackguard went about his business with a smirk on his puss.

'I gave that shagger his answer anyway,' Kelly bragged later between drags of a cigarette.

'Getting too big for his boots,' said Doyle.

'Needs to be taught a lesson,' said Doran.

'Kick in the arse,' said Donaghy.

'Jays, you have nothing else on your mind except yer arse,' said Kelly.

More belly laughs and then the bell went for class.

While daydreaming during class, a mischievous thought came into Kelly's mind right in the middle of Dr. Frankie Litton's lecture on Dogmatic Theology entitled ' The Sacraments and Sacerdotal Office'.

The curved window was lazily dragging the low slung November sun to Kelly's biro as it meandered across the page. 'Shepherds!' said Litton.

'Thematic for the role of the Priest in Tradition'. He bored everyone.

Kelly was musing about revenge on Barraclough. Then suddenly the bright Martin Scanlon asked, 'What about *Optatam Totius*?' a reference to the Council Decree on the training of priests. Litton shot him a glance. Challenges were not appreciated. 'Not in my class,' he retorted. No more discussion. The classic reaction of the lackey. React by retreat and then stonewall. Allow no discussion – ridicule if necessary – but no discussion. We are the authority, and obedience and loyalty to God's word and God's law were fundamental prerequisites.

Kelly went back to his biro. 'Shepherds indeed,' he had been thinking ruefully to himself. 'More like we're being trained to be sheep'. Then inspiration struck him. The college had a farm and as the song said, 'And on that farm he had some sheep'.

At tea and biscuits, Kelly revealed his brainwave.

'Sheep!' he said excitedly, 'We'll put a sheep in Barraclough's bed!'

'What? said Doyle.

'We'll what?' said Doran.

'Sheep?' said Donaghy.

'Perfect,' said Kelly. 'What a dirty big sheep he is'.

They wondered.

'For the craic, boys, for the craic,' pleaded Kelly.

They hovered.

'Done?' asked Kelly.

'Done!' they all laughed together.

The laughter had barely died down when out of the blue a bombshell landed. Somebody said that Rory O'Donnell was leaving the seminary. The hero to the anti-hero Barraclough was leaving. Their champion was leaving the fold.

'Rory?'

'I don't believe it.'

'Rory?'

'One of the soundest.'

Worse was yet to come. He had been asked to leave by the Regional Director.

The regional office had no input into College affairs. How was this happening?

He was asked to not take ordination. He had not been expelled. Typical of Rory, he replied that he would accept not being ordained a priest – but after the ordinations at Christmas, he would be back at the start of the new term. He had been ordained a Deacon already, after all.

This was unprecedented.

Everything was now in a state of wobble.

Apparently the Regional Director did not like Rory's attitude to authority because he had spoken candidly. He believed in the implementation of Vatican II, and his support of Hans Kung's liberation theology was apparent.

'Hans Kung!' said Doc Flynn of Moral Theology. 'That bastard, Kung!'

Liberation Theology and Doc Flynn did not go well together. It was a question of authority and the attitude to it. It was obedience or rebellion. No 'ifs', 'buts' or 'ands', the Doc had said.

Barraclough proclaimed, '*Mens rea* is what is required to commit an act wilfully. Without the act, there is simply wilfulness. You cannot have an offence without an act, yet you cannot have a priest who wilfully proposes to be disobedient to established traditions.'

The pompous lawyer had it all rationalized and defined. He was clearly not on Rory's side whose ordination was now postponed indefinitely.

'Defined?' said Kelly when he heard.

'Redefined!' said Doyle.

'Diluted,' said Doran.

'Indefinitely postponed,' said Donaghy 'Flog it anyway.'

'Pain in the hole that fella,' said Kelly. 'Let's give him his lesson.'

When they caught the sheep, they hid it in the basement while the student body was at Benediction. When Barraclough later left for the local convent, they took the sheep from its dungeon and tied it down on his bed.

'A sheep on its back won't go far,' said Donaghy.

'What about a sheep on its arse?' said Kelly.

'Flog off, you clown,' said Donaghy.

They reconnoitred in the TV lounge after the deed was done.

'Do you know what?' said Kelly.

They looked at him.

'We might as well be hung for a sheep as a lamb!'

'Oh you're such a howl,' said Dongahy with mock sincerity.

The adrenalin pumped bursts of suppressed hilarity, which they tried to mute. In turn, it gave rise to an even more clandestine feeling. They were almost high.

'I mean it,' said Kelly. 'Let's put one in the Dean's room.'

They stopped in their tracks.

'He means it,' said Doyle.

'What?' said Doran.

'Shite,' said Donaghy.

'More sheep shite Donaghy,' said Kelly as he rallied the troops. 'C'mon'.

The four 'cowboys' went back once more 'on the range' and rounded up another 'steer'.

The negotiation of the Dean's room was a more delicate operation as it was off limits on the Priests' corridor. It was also more serious.

One of the older priests was walking up and down the corridor reading his breviary. When he turned his back, they swiftly conveyed the 'livestock' into the room.

'Washed, bathed and ready for bed,' panted Kelly in puffed, muffled and giddy whispers as he secured the sheep with ropes on the mattress.

'I'm flogged out,' said Doyle.

'Same here,' said Doran.

'Let's get out of here,' said Donaghy.

Mission accomplished, it only remained 'for the fuse to burn'.

Donaghy and Doyle went to their rooms. Kelly and Doran went to the TV lounge. The adrenalin was pumping too hard to do anything else.

At 10 p.m. one of the Deacons walked in to the TV lounge and said:

'The Rector wants to see the two of you in Barraclough's room.' He left as suddenly as he had arrived leaving both of them looking at each other.

Barraclough's room was located on the corridor where Kelly did his 'morning works duties'. When they sauntered into the bedroom, there was no Rector. Instead, there ranged around the four walls were as many Fourth Divines as could be squeezed in. Their faces were composed, serious and solemn. There was no sheep. Cool as a breeze, Kelly saluted them.

'Good Evening Boys,' he said. He eyed one of his teammates from the hurling team with a mischievous glint and that undid him and the contrived solemnity of the proceedings.

He snorted out at Kelly's brass neck, and collected himself immediately again. But too late. The contrived stern atmosphere was shattered. Without a falter, Kelly twirled on his heel, did a one hundred and eighty degree u-turn, smiled broadly and chirped, 'See you around guys' and marched out of the room back down to the television lounge.

Poor Doran blushed to the roots. He was paralysed by his being discovered. Such was his shock that he stayed.

'You big shit. You lobbed me in it,' he said to Kelly. 'Ya know, ya bollix, twenty minutes later and the sheep was dead'.

The blood drained from Kelly's face. He got up quickly. Barraclough's sheep was nearly dead. So what about the sheep in the Dean's room? It must be in distress at least.

The scene of the second crime was surreal. The sheep looked like a reclining harlot streeled across the bed. Its head was lying over the side in the manner of a Jack the Ripper 'Penny Dreadful' illustration, except, instead of having its throat cut, it was gurgling the ominous 'death rattle' from the recesses of its larynx.

When they got the sheep off the bed, its feet splayed under it on the polished floorboards. It wouldn't stand. It couldn't stand. They pushed it and shoved it, and eventually it began to slide and slithered on the highly polished slippery surface. They opened the door gingerly to check if the coast was clear. Perspiration began to appear. They, hauled and mauled the animal to the lift, and from there to the basement, to be eventually released out into the night air on the front lawn and 'let it find its own way back to the farm, be fecked'.

There was one big problem. The sheep still couldn't stand. Donaghy tried, Doran tried and Doyle tried. However, the poor animal's debilitation was considerable.

'Stand back!' said Kelly. He 'stood back about ten yards and literally and actually gave the sheep a running kick up in the arse,' as Donaghy relayed later. 'I never saw anything come back to life so quickly in me life. He went in buck jumps down the lawn,' he chortled, 'Kelly must've nearly broken his foot. Imagine how the poor sheep felt'.

The story spread like wildfire. It was heavy-duty, light relief in the middle of all the tension in the seminary. Some saw it as a prank. Some saw it as a step too far. Others saw potential for a wing-clipping exercise. Still others saw expulsion looming for the culprits given the current climate.

Next morning at Mass, Donaghy came forward to say the bidding prayers. These prayers were new to the liturgy and designed to elicit from the congregation an invocation, which was spontaneous. Inevitably, the 'spontaneity' was generally 'prepared spontaneity' and organised in accordance with Roman rule and culture but this time, the preparation was different, and was bold.

'Let us pray for the Fourth Divines who are soon to become shepherds of sheep that they may tend to their flocks faithfully. Lord hear us,' he antiphoned outrageously.

'Lord , graciously hear us.'

The response was barely audible. Doyle nearly died. Doran blushed to his usual crimson. And Kelly kept his head down. Only the concealed faces and shoulders of the concelebrating Fourth Divines higging up and down with suppressed mirth were visible. The smothered sniggers normally revealed on their faces were hidden in their hands.

After breakfast, Kelly began sweeping and dusting the Fourth Divines' corridor. There was the occasional 'maaaaa' and 'baaaaa' as the Fourth Divines passed him on the corridor. Then Barraclough, on whom the 'crime' of 'forcible sheep entry' had been perpetrated on his august legal personage and sleeping quarters, pounced. With great, rolling, fat-hipped strides, having espied his nemesis with no escape route at the other end of the corridor, he advanced.

There is no more reprehensible sight than the self-appointed guardian of morality cornering his quarry. He paced himself for effect, letting his unflinching, determined demeanour and deliberate stride act as a portent of impending doom in order to intimidate. He brought himself to a halt in front of his prey.

'Mr. Kelly!' he pronounced.

Kelly stopped sweeping and casually put both hands on the top of his brush in the manner that charge hands and labourers do when 'taking a spell' while their overseers are absent.

'I heard what happened in my room last night,' he paused.

Then, as if the rest need not be said and for better effect, he raised his voice, like bullies who believe in their own authority generally do.

'But get this straight. If the like of this should happen again, I'll go straight to the Rector!'

Kelly straightened. He eyeballed him with defiance, and with cheek and cleverness delivered his devastating riposte.

'Why, Michael,' he said, 'If there is a rule of silence, ought it not be obeyed?'

He stared unflinchingly into the eyes of his adversary, which began to dull and water. The message got home alright. If you seek refuge in the monolith be prepared for the ambush of the rapparee when you're on your own.

Thunderstruck, Barraclough's jowels wobbled with paleness and he exited with much less finesse and fuss than he had entered. The rest of the Fourth Divines had pressured him not to report the matter to the authorities.

The practical joke was told and re-told throughout the day and the boys basked in the glory of legend. It acted as a type of conductor in releasing the pressures of recent events but it did not solve the problem.

The tension resumed when Rory declared his intention to return after the Christmas Ordinations. Outmaneouvred, the Regional Director decided to interview all of the Fourth Divines.

Having interviewed the entire class, he pulled a stroke of masterful political genius – he postponed all ordinations indefinitely. Nobody would be ordained. In this fashion, he took away Rory's grip over the house and over the Regional Director himself.

After Christmas, twenty-three came back, including Rory. Rory stayed for eight weeks and then left.

Barraclough went on to lecture in Canon Law.

Doran left and later became a lay missionary in Africa. He got married. He died a middle-aged man.

Donaghy got ordained and later left the priesthood. He married and separated.

Doyle rose through the ranks in the Missionary Society and became a bishop.

Kelly left and became a writer.

The following Easter, the twenty-two of the original Fourth Divine class of forty-two that were left after Rory departed, were ordained. One of those that was ordained and later left the priesthood wrote a letter to one of his friends back home at that time. Thirty-seven years later, Kelly came across that letter.

This is an extract:

'When I was in the seminary, I was young and idealistic and perhaps a little naive and I took on board everything I was told. It is evident now with plenty of proof that priests are no different from ordinary people.

'As a priest I became disillusioned with the priestly life and my own life as a priest. I was expected and I expected of myself to lead a full priestly life including celibacy. I felt I could not do this. I did not want to live a lie.

'For me, it was a more mature decision to have left than to have entered the priesthood in the first place. The perception of the 'special grace' factor however for the priest is still around. Personally, I as a priest, never witnessed any of it.'

As for the sheep, its fame spread far and wide with the missionaries across the globe. It must have been the most famous sheep that ever lived.

It was after all the first sheep to silence a sacred cow.

5.

The Will

Mr. Colfer, solicitor, sedately and carefully negotiated his sleek, green and gleaming MG motorcar with its canvas top, down the rocky, pot-holed lane to the farm of John Comyn (locally Cowman) of the parish of Aclammon. His apprentice, Seamus, bounced beside him in the well-sprung, leather passenger seat.

It was seven o'clock on a Monday evening in mid-September. The piercing blue of the fading evening sky after rain had the early chill and resignation of autumn.

Colfer was from the old school. His father wore a bowler hat and a butterfly collar daily. The notions that went with it lingered with his son.

He had gone to Terry Conron's funeral, another solicitor, wearing a bowler hat and sporting a bone-handled walking stick. At that time he asked Seamus if he would wear a bowler. Seamus replied he would not though he did not give the reason. He believed his Republican ancestors, who had rejected such false formal fashion, would turn in their graves. Looking away from Colfer then he said, 'I think I'm too young'. Colfer looked at him for about ten seconds and then let it go.

As they got into the car Colfer placed on the back seat a briefcase full of sheets of judicature paper for the making of the will of John Comyn. John Comyn had a son, Patrick Comyn, and Patrick Comyn had a wife. Patrick had a drink problem, everyone knew. His middle-aged wife looked after their seven cows and calves with the help of Big Mary Kate, her big-breasted daughter. Making a will was serious business. Going out to make a will required a serious frame of mind.

Seamus asked his master to open the car boot in order that he might put in his football boots and hurl. He had left his boots in the office after a district match a few nights before. They made strange bedfellows in the boot beside his master's croquet sticks.

'When you are going to make a will,' gravely intoned the master as they meandered down the lane, 'you need God going with you in one hand and luck in the other'.

They discussed briefly John Comyn's situation. He had one son, Patrick, and Patrick had a wife, Mary. And then there was Mary Kate. Patrick Comyn was not particularly good-looking but it was believed in time he would fall in for his father's thirty acres and land was more endearing than looks or charm. He did not always drink. Some said she drove him to it. She was a grafter and too sweet to be wholesome – but she worked hard between cows, pigs and hens. Their holding was little less than thirty acres. They were entitled to the farmers' dole which he drank. She managed the farm and the money made from the farm.

'It's a pity the daughter wasn't a son,' said Colfer. Seamus looked up from his book on the Succession Act. 'Oh you needn't look at me like that,' said the older solicitor. 'Look in your text book and see what the Minister for Justice had to say on this when the Succession Act was passing through the Dáil nearly ten years ago.'

Seamus dutifully opened his book to where the Dáil record was quoted by the author.

'Read it aloud,' urged his mentor.

Seamus reverted to his red book entitled *The Succession Act 1965*.

'Later in his speech the Minister used an incident in the Old Testament as an illustration of the sanctity of inheritance as a great safeguard for the family. He said: ' It is recorded in the Old Testament in the Book of Numbers that the daughters of Salphaad came to Moses and claimed a right of succession to their father who had left no son. They pleaded so movingly that Moses brought their cause to the Lord and Judgement in their favour was pronounced as follows: 'The daughters of

Salphaad demand a just thing, give them a basis among their father's kindred, and let them succeed him in his inheritance.

'The point is, Seamus, there is nothing more powerful or more capable of causing enormous problems than land, sex and religion. When you come to the inheritance by a farmer's girl – that's if she is his daughter – you have the potential for a disaster for a solicitor and, worse still, a granddaughter. His daughter-in-law, Mary Comyn, said to me this morning on the telephone that her father-in-law, John, wished to give it to their only child, her daughter, Mary Kate. The daughter of herself and John's son, her husband, Patrick.'

'I don't see the problem,' said Seamus somewhat bewildered.

'You are assuming, young man, that Mary Kate is the progeny of the union of John Comyn's son and heir, Patrick, and his wife, Mary. This is the exact equivalent of what you just read in a modern context. One of the 'daughters of Salphaad is demanding a just thing' that her daughter succeed her grandfather and bypass his own son, her supposed father '.

'You mean there is a question of her legitimacy,' said the apprentice.

'There is always a question of legitimacy. Who is to say what side of the blanket she was born on? For God's sake, Patrick Comyn is not exactly an oil painting; he is a drinker and his wife had a flighty reputation. And isn't it strange that they performed so well together that they had a child very soon after they got married – had one child – and that was that and then he took to the drink'. Colfer's suspicious mind took off.

'Supposing she is not Patrick Comyn's daughter and we make a will leaving her the beneficiary, bypassing her father, the natural heir, who will be blamed? The solicitors who made the will, of course, will be blamed. And if he makes a will leaving it to Patrick, his son and Patrick later finds out that another man is the father of his daughter. Or if his wife dies before him and he doesn't make a will and it is then discovered that Mary Kate is not his daughter, what then?'

'But that seems rather unlikely...' Seamus began.

'Young man learn this. what seems likely and unlikely are dangerous propositions for any lawyer to proceed on. You must be certain. If you are not certain, you are leaving yourself at risk. If you are leaving yourself at risk, you don't deserve to be a solicitor. You cannot assume. And when circumstances are unclear, your professional duty obliges you to be suspicious,' admonished the Master. The apprentice was quiet and chastened.

At last Mr. Colfer had arrived. He parked his MG well in on the cement apron in front of the Comyns' house. The thatched roof on the white-washed house had been replaced ten years ago with a corrugated iron roof, the most that twenty-nine acres and the 'farmers' dole' could afford. Seamus, the apprentice, had previously brought pig meal and coal and cylinders of Kosangas down this same lane when he was helping his father in his grocery business before going to Law School. He knew the Comyns as Cowmans then. But that had been ten years ago and he was now a solicitor's apprentice.

Immediately the car pulled up, the kitchen door opened and out beamed one very enthusiastic sixty-year-old Mrs. Comyn, in a blue polka dot crossover apron followed by her equally beaming, enthusiastically buxom, heavyweight daughter, Mary Kate, in a pink chiffon dress. Both had smiles, more like grins, which were accompanied by monosyllabic grunts of approval, in the form of – 'Yeh, Yeh, Yeh' and an occasional 'Heh, Heh, Heh'. There would be nothing but co-operation, assistance, appreciation and approval. Any social awkwardness would be taken care of by undisguised grovelling and overindulgent flattery. Yet, there was a strange sincerity in these false smiles. The forced nature of the sincerity was from anxiety that the farm might yet be drank out if the wrong party got his hands on it.

'Hello, Mr. Colfer. Hello Seamus,' said Mrs. Comyn.

'Hello, Mr. Colfer. Hello Seamus.' said Mary Kate. 'Yeh, Yeh, Yeh'.

'Good evening Mrs. Comyn,' correctly enunciated Mr. Colfer completely ignoring the daughter's heifer-like presence and her 'Yeh, Yeh, Yeh'.

'Come in, come in,' said Mrs. Comyn.

'Come in, come in,' said Mary Kate.

A naked bulb hung from the rafter of the big kitchen. A cast iron range with a shiny grey kettle, steaming like a train, was on the left-hand side of the front door. On the other side was a door into bedchambers, and at the opposite end of the kitchen, suspended from wall to wall, was a large, full-length gingham curtain. There was a big table made from deal in the centre of the kitchen.

'I've come to make the will,' said Mr. Colfer.

'Yeh, Yeh, Yeh.' said Mrs. Comyn subserviently.

'Yeh, Yeh, Yeh,' parroted Mary Kate.

'I need to take some formal instructions from the family before I speak to Mr. Comyn,' he said solemnly.

'Yeh, Yeh, Yeh. Yeh, Yeh, Yeh,' the chorus of two responded.

'How many times was Mr. Comyn married?'

'Only the wanst.'

'How many children did Mr. John Comyn Senior have?'

'Only the one,' said Mrs. Comyn sharply.

'Only the one,' her daughter said.

'Patrick,' said Mrs. Comyn, indicating that her husband was sole progeny of her father-in-law John, owner of the farm.

'Daddy,' said Mary Kate copper-fastening her connection, and adding the habitual and unsolicited hallmark of approval, 'Yeh, Yeh, Yeh.'

When did Mrs. John Comyn Snr. die?

'Granny. She died in 1956 after the All-Ireland – we were in Dublin at the match.'

'Granny,' said Mary Kate, 'Heh, Heh, Heh'.

'When were you married to Mr. Comyn junior?' asked the solicitor, as Seamus took notes.

'Patrick?' she said, 'Sure that was 1945, just after the war, twenty nine years ago, God Bless us,' said Mrs. Comyn.

Mary Kate beamed confirmation and nodded effusively, 'Yeh, Yeh, Yeh'.

Then Mrs. Comyn steadied herself and with great deliberation said: 'He wants to "lave" it to Mary Kate.'

She eyed Colfer. Seamus looked up from his notes. He caught Colfer's eye looking away. It was pretty clear that Mary Kate was a good bit with thirty.

There was a pause. Seamus had stopped writing. There was tension. Seamus wiggled his pen. Now there was the problem of Mary Kate's ill-timed birth. Seamus calculated the gestation period as the time ticked in the empty silence. He nearly burst out laughing when it occurred to him this really was a pregnant pause.

He too steadied himself, this was no time for giddiness.

'He wants to "lave" it to Mary Kate,' reassured Mrs. Comyn, which only succeeded in making Colfer cringe further. Was Mary Kate John Comyn's grandchild? Was she pregnant when she took up with Patrick, the proposed testator's son? The questions he had been reciting for Seamus were coming to life like a nightmare in front of him. Had she been legitimised by the subsequent apparent marriage of her parents? But the pre-marital pregnancy raised the possibility that Mary Kate had been 'fathered' by other than Patrick Comyn before the marriage.

'We shall see what the man himself wants,' properly replied the middle-aged lawyer, with reference to his client, her father-in-law. No need to cross the bridge until it's come to. Seamus gathered his papers and notebook as his boss stood up.

'He wants to "lave" it to Mary Kate, anyways,' said Mrs.Comyn somewhat disconsolately. She led them, past the kitchen table, down to the curtain which she pulled back in order to let them through with herself and Mary Kate following. Her father-in-law lay on a black iron-framed straw mattress bed behind it.

'You will have to remain out here,' said Mr. Colfer, 'while we take instructions.'

Colfer halted for emphasis. There would no allegation of duress or undue influence permitted to be suggested against Mr. Colfer. He stopped them both in their tracks and, comically, they almost bumped into each other.

Mr. Colfer entered. There before him, like a beached whale, lay the heap of corpulence that passed for John Comyn, patriarch, widower and farmer. The pillow was small relative to his big head, his huge rotund belly, and his toothless moustached gob, all of which accounted for ninety per cent of his charisma. A knobbly nose with small purple veins betrayed the residual effects of Powers Whiskey. The nose was otherwise a chalky white. His eyes were closed.

'Good evening, Mr. Comyn,' announced Mr. Colfer grandly and importantly.

Comyn's eyes flickered, closed, flickered and closed once more. A slight pause followed, and then Colfer, once more with feeling:

'Good evening Mr. Comyn,' repeated he, but louder this time.

The eyes locked open immediately and stayed fixed on nothing. The inner giant deep within was rousing.

Mistaking this for attention, Colfer kept his tone even, 'I am here to make your will.'

The pronouncement was taking its time to permeate the numbed skull of its addressee. No flicker. Colfer positioned himself deliberately over the bed, 'Your daughter-in-law asked us to come out to make your will,' he repeated distinctly, deliberately and slowly, once more.

There was another flicker, a head movement, some type of awareness. Before he would lose him once more, Colfer pounced.

'Who would you like to leave the place to?' There was a pause, another movement of the head and a gnarled sound emanated from the bed, 'MMMmmmFFFfff!' the lips had pursed and gathered all of his intense effort to co-ordinate in order to vocalise and then collapsed into this mumbled muffed snort.

Colfer looked at Seamus and Seamus looked back. Colfer looked at his quarry to see if he could possibly elicit a more coherent response. Adhering to legal rubric he intensified and more in hope than anticipation he repeated his question.

'To whom do you wish to leave the place?'

There was a swish of the curtain and Mrs. Comyn stuck in her head and beamed, 'He wants to "lave" it to Mary Kate.'

Seamus almost burst out laughing.

Colfer turned red with rage. 'Get out! Get out! You are violating my instructions,' Seamus reddened. The curtain closed. Colfer seethed.

Duly chastened, she retreated as rapidly as she had poked her nose into her father-in-law's business.

After a shocked pause, Colfer sighed with exasperation. 'We'll have to leave it,' he said simply. 'The man doesn't know what's going on.'

A sinking disappointment realised itself on Mrs. Comyn's face when Colfer came out and packed away his Parker biro and refill pad into his leather briefcase.

Seamus packed away his fresh BIC dispensable biro thanking God they were getting out of there before the sun set and maybe he would be able to get some hurling in 'before the light was gone'.

'It's no good,' Colfer declared as he passed into the kitchen. Mrs. Comyn backed away behind the table with a look of perplexed consternation on her face. Seamus followed his master out of the penumbra into the dazzling light of the bulb.

'What'll we do?' entreated Mrs. Comyn.

'We will have to see how he gets on,' replied the serious solicitor in wilful fashion.

'Oh dear, oh dear,' said Mrs. Comyn.

'Oh dear, oh dear,' said Mary Kate.

There was an awkward pause until eventually Mr. Colfer said, 'Right then,' and made for the door. As the pair of lawyers departed out into the night, Mrs. Comyn and Mary Kate took up the role of withering silhouettes in the framed door-light.

As they departed down the muddy lane, there was an equally awkward silence in the MG motor car. Seamus felt uncomfortable both with the cruelty of their disappointment and the severity of the heavy hand of the law and his almost burst of laughter. Still, he knew what was done was right.

'We had a close one there,' said Colfer. Seamus was not sure what he meant, but felt he had to approve, but was not yet hypocrite enough to simply assent.

'I suppose,' he said.

'No supposing,' Colfer said, 'it was quite plain that, that lady, (reference to Mary Kate) was not a 'Comyn'. 'Or a 'Cowman' for that matter,' he added with vengeance at his discomfiture at being placed so unfairly, in his view, in such an awkward predicament. After a reflective pause, he declared scathingly on the difficult question that had been raised but not answered.

'It's pretty clear too that she was born on the 'other side of the blanket'. I'm too long on the road to fall for one like that,' Colfer complimented himself.

Seamus knew enough to know this was a good time to say nothing.

And that was the end of that, for the time being.

A year or so later Seamus qualified as a solicitor and the lure of his native heath brought him back from the city. Shortly after he had started practising with Colfer, one drizzly morning he got a phone call from Mrs. Comyn and Mary Kate to know if they could come in to see him.

'To be sure, to be sure,' he almost emphatically lapsed into Comyn mode with the end of sentence echo. The moment he realised his lapse into colloquial familiarity, he corrected himself instantly.

'Of course you can. Come in, at half-two – after lunch-time,' he invited.

But could they come in tomorrow when her husband would be going to the Mart and they had a few springers for sale.

Why not? But of course they could.

At half past two the next afternoon they arrived at Colfer's office. Seamus conscientiously asked whether they would not prefer to see 'the boss'.

'I seen ye at Mass a' Sunday,' she camouflaged. 'So I sez to meself – there's the man for me, the man that'll see Mary Kate right – see her fixed in the place – no better man.'

'No better man,' said Mary Kate, 'Heh, Heh, Heh. No better man.'

'How's the old man? How is John?' asked Seamus, hesitantly, of her father-in-law.

'He's grand altogether – absolutely grand. He could bury us all, Heh, Heh, Heh.'

'He could bury us all,' chirped Mary Kate, 'Heh, Heh, Heh.'

Out of the blue, much to the relief of Seamus and the disappointment of his clients, divine providence struck. There was a knock on the door of his room and Colfer walked in.

'Pardon me, Seamus. Oh hello Mrs. Comyn! Miss Comyn.'

They blushed. 'Oh hello Mr. Colfer'. '...Mr. Colfer,' said Mary Kate, faintly, after her mother's gritty salutation.

'They called in about the will. Mr. Comyn is better,' explained Seamus.

'Indeed.' Colfer barely hid his sarcasm. He kept his gaze steady.

'We thought he could make the place over now and not wait till he was dead. I mean couldn't he do it now? We have the money, we're after selling some springers today.'

Mr. Colfer looked as if a fog had lifted.

Then Seamus said slowly,

'You mean a Deed.'

'The very thing,' said Mrs. Comyn – detecting a chink of light. 'A Deed.'

'The very thing,' said Mary Kate. 'Heh, Heh, Heh'.

'He'd have to pay stamp duty,' said Colfer.

'Oh 'tis we'll have to pay,' said Mrs. Comyn, determined to make sure everyone knew what was where.

Without anyone noticing, Colfer's small black pupil went to the corner of the pince-nez glasses he was wearing, towards Seamus, and an extra crease came into his squint, as he considered the solution his protégé had proposed. No will, No litigation. Where a will could be challenged later because the testator had not mental capacity at the time of making it, the immediate effect of a deed meant he who made it was still alive and well able to meet any challenge. The question of Mary Kate's legitimacy could not arise.

'A Deed of course is different – its effect, immediate, definite and certain,' loftily Colfer opined.

There was silence for a full minute. The experienced Colfer knew it would take three weeks not to mention a minute, for the effect of what his apprentice had said, to sink in with the two ladies. He waited patiently and lit his pipe. Seamus looked at the flame and then back at his clients.

The Comyns never noticed the flame, the pipe or the pince-nez. Their eyes were focused on Seamus.

Mrs. Comyn leaned forward.

'Seamus, m'lana, would you explain that to me the way you and your father used ta talk when yiz brought down the pigmeal to the house?'

They were now on a level footing and Colfer was up in the 'crow's nest' admiring the view.

'What it comes down to Mrs Comyn is that Mary Kate will get the place, and there won't be any tax to be paid once your husband signs it and it becomes hers,' explained Seamus.

Lending his approval, Colfer philosophically ignored Mrs. Comyn's implicit rebuff in bypassing him, but was unable to let the matters pass without sarcastic observation above the comprehension of its target.

'Remarkable the strides modern legal education has taken nowadays. Never was such intricacy explained with such simple alacrity,' and then he repeated what he had himself stated not three minutes before.

'A Deed of course is different – its effect is immediate, definite, and certain.'

Seamus nodded knowingly.

Mrs. Comyn was not quite sure but was aware enough to know that Mr. Colfer believed his genius was going unrecognised. And then with devastating understatement she remarked:

'I suppose when you solve a hard case like ours it makes the next wan aisier.' Colfer swallowed his breath and stared at the notes on Seamus's desk for a minute. He was smarting from the remark.

'Seamus will have to draft the Deed,' he said in mid-swallow.

'No better man,' said Mrs. Comyn with welcome relief. 'No better man.'

'No better man,' said Mary Kate sensing success. 'No better man. Heh, Heh, Heh'.

'Very well then,' said Mr. Colfer.

'I'll leave you to it. I can't remember why I came in. Must be old age,' he joked about his supposedly failing memory.

'Oh yer still a young man,' said a sweetening Mrs. Comyn as he rummaged for the doorknob.

'Heh, Heh, Heh,' said a spontaneous Mary Kate equally glad she would soon see the back of him as he stopped in the open doorway.

Seamus looked back at the now fortified Mrs.Comyn and looked back at his notes previously taken on the file. The notes reminded him of the detail he had been careful to write down meticulously and in keeping with his training. The visit to the house – the questions asked of John Comyn – which reminded him of the swish of the curtain and Mrs. Comyn telling Colfer:

'He wants to lave it to Mary Kate.'

'When I have it drafted I'll leave it down in your room for your approval,' said Seamus to his master.

The trace of a flicker of concern passed over Mrs. Comyn as if she feared her plans might yet come to nought and be vetoed by Colfer.

'Can you bring it out Seamus to have him sign it when it's finished – he doesn't lave the fire you know,' she bravely ventured.

Seamus looked at his boss.

'Only one witness is required but because of what happened it were better a doctor were present to ensure that he is up to it,' said Colfer.

A look of disappointment came over the poor woman at the prospect of more waiting.

'I could have Doctor Kehoe call over tonight?' she offered.

'It won't take long to have it typed,' volunteered Seamus, eager to undertake the responsibility and establish himself as the organising solicitor.

'I'll have Miss Keane, my book-keeper prepare the bill,' said Colfer.

'That'll be grand,' said Mrs. Comyn, 'Heh, Heh, Heh'.

'That'll be grand,' said Mary Kate, 'Heh, Heh, Heh'

John Comyn signed the Transfer that night much to the delight of his daughter-in-law Mrs. Patrick Comyn. Mary Kate glowed in her now new found status and eligibility.

Doctor Kehoe drank their good health having certified that John Comyn was compos mentis (mentally sound) and all present joined in that toast including Seamus.

'A bird never flew on one wing,' said the much older doctor to Seamus as they walked to their cars.

'Let's call in to Hallahans for a night cap,' he suggested.

Standing at the counter when they walked in was a rather unsteady Patrick Comyn who was buying for all and sundry after 'a good day at the mart'. She must have given him something to let him off to the pub and out of harm's way while the serious business of the transfer was being transacted at home.

'A drink for the gentlemen,' called Patrick Comyn.

To avoid controversy both men had a whiskey.

'Your good health,' said Doctor Kehoe.

'And your own,' he responded.

'And your family's,' joined Seamus.

'And me own,' he slurred as he awkwardly, but not yet fully drunk, added. Whiskey made him maudlin.

'To me very own,' he toasted. ... 'of whom I have none. None of them wants me. None of them wants me, not him, nor her. Not him nor her'.

He was indulging his well-nursed resentments.

'Left me with nothing.'

Seamus looked at the doctor and finished his drink.

'Left me with nothing. No farm. No mother. No wife. Nothing.'

He slumped over the counter and started to cry. Hallahan came to him and brought him into the snug to quiet him. Someone started to sing 'I'm Nobody's Child'. The two professionals left.

Before they drove off Seamus remarked confidentially to the doctor on how badly Patrick was taking the transfer to Mary Kate.

'Oh, that's nothing to do with the transfer,' said the doctor. 'This happens all the time when he gets drunk, not just tonight'.

'What do you mean? asked Seamus.

'Patrick had to be married,' said the lubricated doctor.

'Thank Christ for that,' said an unrestrained Seamus.

'Why do you say that?' It was now the doctor's turn.

'It proves Patrick was Mary Kate's father – not that it affects the deed – that's solid now. But it could cause unease in the family if it was discovered someone else was the father,' Seamus replied.

The doctor looked at Seamus and said,

'Patrick is not Mary Kate's father'.

Seamus stiffened and froze.

'Patrick's father, John Comyn is Mary Kate's father. Patrick is her brother. I think I am the only one around who knows – they had to tell me – they were afraid not to because I treat them and I would have to know. Mrs Comyn Snr. was still alive when the present Mrs. Comyn became pregnant'.

'But it could still be that Patrick was responsible.'

'It couldn't. You see he got a kick from a horse when he was a child

71

and I'm the only one who knew the real damage it caused. He couldn't have children.'

Slowly the picture began to emerge.

Seamus said slowly and haltingly,

'You mean Mary Kate is the child of Patrick's wife and Patrick's father, John Comyn'.

'That's exactly what I mean,' said the doctor.

'That would make Patrick and Mary Kate half-brother and half-sister'.

'It certainly would,' said the doctor again.

'And each would have an equal claim to the farm,' he reasoned out.

He paused in order to allow his racing brain slow down.

No wonder, he thought, no wonder.

A scandal had been avoided by Patrick marrying Mary Kate's mother and nobody would be any the wiser of Patrick's embarrassing disability – a source of obvious distress for him. His attempts to hide it bore in on him particularly the implied taunt by his wife about his disability. And she would now be secure once Mary Kate had the place which was obviously promised by the old man but never written down. And here he was nearly dead and unable to tell his solicitors what to do when Mrs. Comyn pulled back the curtain to speak his mind for him to a tetchy solicitor and his 'God-between-us-and-all-harm' apprentice. Seamus smiled to himself and then broke out into a series of heart-breaking guffaws as he shouted aloud,

'Never was such intricacy explained with such simple alacrity'.

6.

The Principle of the Thing

I.

Somebody from the home crowd fired the butt of an apple at the Manager of the visiting U-21 Gaelic Football team. His team of tanned, lean athletes, resplendent in their start-of-the-season crisp, green and white cotton jerseys, were getting a raw deal from the match referee. Then somebody roared at the referee.

'You stupid blind bastard.' And then the row 'ris' and all hell broke loose. The supporters of the hardy and awkward sons of the soil with their blue and yellow serge jerseys were throwing their weight around intent on not yielding their advantage on their home turf. Somebody shouted, 'Fuck the Blueshirts.'

The crowd invaded the pitch. Fists flew. Then you could hear shouts, screeches, yelps, curses, hisses, and jeers flung with the venom and passion of insult fury and rage. His family and supporters spirited the Manager out of the melee. His father, aged sixty or more, a small empty lemonade bottle in his fist, had come running like a greyhound released from a trap across the field in the direction of the crowd at the start of the invasion.

Onlookers from the crowd stood gaping, goading, and guffawing. Some were smug, self-satisfied grinners. Some women gawked in shock, disbelief and awe with hands over their mouths while trying to keep an eye on the little ones who clung to the bottoms of their mothers' coats. The more responsible tried to stop the fighting and calm matters down shouting, 'For Jaysus sake lads, it's only a game!' The clichéd plea for calm and rationality, forever used in such situations, reflected the not unusual overflow of temper in football matches. Pitch invasions were now less common than twenty years previously. Civilisation was evolving, but slowly.

One of the main reasons that the Gaelic Athletic Association was founded in 1884 was to toll the death knell of the faction fights so prolific at fairs and markets in Ireland. The GAA had coaxed tribal conflict into a sporting agenda the better to mellow the people and civilise manners and tempers. And thus it arrived into the mid-20th century. The football Manager played with the adult club team but his job on that day was to manage the under-21 team in order to perpetuate the tradition of evolved sport in the name of culture. This generation would set the standard of behaviour for the next generation.

The Manager's younger brother was playing on the team. Conscious of the predicament of his older brother, he grabbed him and helped in his removal from the melee just as quickly as it had started. It wouldn't do to have the *New Ross Standard* carry the headline story of an assault involving a solicitor at a football match. Because he had been whisked away, the Manager didn't see how the row finished. But he knew he would be blamed for starting it.

He was glad his mother wasn't there. Like all women, she hated roughness and the uncouth. Women never admitted to being cowed by male strength. It encouraged the show off. In an age before feminism, in a time when girls had to leave the Civil Service when they married, when women wore mantillas going to Mass, his mother, like all women of the time, knew her place. Nonetheless, like all those who are subjugated, she developed her own means and method of manipulating power in a much more effective fashion: the maternal glare. The glare could paralyse.

Her husband, John Lacey, had led the charge across the field with a bottle of 'Little Sister' orange in his hand. When he saw his progeny threatened, he charged from the top sideline with the conviction and passion of the warrior into battle. A shopkeeper, he had stayed fit all his life dragging bags of coal and pig meal from the store to the waiting vehicles of his customers. His passion was sport and his belief was in God. He had a direct relationship with both.

It was Easter Sunday afternoon. The early warm spring sun brought out plenty of women, decent women, respectable girls, sporting a modest sparkle of modern fashion. Easter, and Easter Sunday and this display of the seductive in such a mild surreptitious fashion, was a custom as old as Bealtaine and the Pagan god Baal himself. It was as old as Saint Patrick entering into grips with King Laoighre when he lit his Paschal fire on the Hill of Slane, the celebration of light and life in the early budding of pastoral seasonal spring in the agricultural heartland.

This was the season after Imbolc, the Celtic time that marked the global phenomenon of milk filling and welling up in the udder in the all embracing way of nature.

Whether it was early garlands, gambolling lambs, sporting heroes, druidic ceremonies, clerically-latined incense or the more exotic form of Easter Parade on Fifth Avenue, New York, displayed in the cinemas, the expression of the exuberance of the joys of spring all merged in confluence in whatever fashion was appropriate to the times. It was place and providence expressing itself in full-blown enthusiasm and sincerity, summer was just around the corner. Its anticipation provoked energies, which had hibernated over the winter, blew the dust off themselves and 'the twinkle in the eye' drew out the spirit innate in all, in a fashion expressive of the embrace of life, demurely at first, until the first opportunity of extravagant expression presented itself.

Perhaps that is what really caused the row: a raw display of male prowess in front of a captive female gallery. It was the 'remote' cause as they used to call it in history. It was not the immediate cause.

His fiancée was not there to see the fracas. She was a teacher and had gone home for the Easter Holidays. 'How grown men could behave like that,' his mother would empathise with her later. 'Maybe they should give them all a ball each!'

In typical frustration, his father would say, 'Will you stop woman. We've been taking it from that crowd for long enough. Year in, year out, we've been too quiet for too long.' He expressed justification by exasperation. These discussions took place when the television was turned down after The News and the nightly cup of tea was presented to whichever of the relations might happen to call in to discuss the match. It was, in other words, 'the post-mortem'.

'Football!' she declaimed. 'Hmmf. More like tribal warfare. What grown men see in chasing a leather bag of wind around a six-acre field is beyond me.' The father looked at her with concealed mirth at her inability to understand the necessity to vent passion in masculine expression; the need to express prowess; the need to express supremacy, to achieve what was believed to be beyond grasp – the need to win. 'Maybe they should give them all a ball and let them parade around the pitch with leather handbags,' he sniggered in mock imitation.

'You know well what I mean,' she rebuked him.

It was the difference in the genders. If you want to tune women out of a conversation, talk about football. However, if you want to tune them back in, notwithstanding their disdain, talk about a row, preferably a row over some woman. A row over a leather bag of wind was a waste of romantic excess.

'Wasn't it the athletic virtuosity of my father that attracted you in the first place?' intoned the row-causing son mischievously. She flashed a heart-stopping glare. 'And you a solicitor – hmmf!' The withering weapon of the mother – the glare – much more effective than the weapon of a bottle of lemonade his father had in his hand going into battle that afternoon. Regardless of criticisms, they returned to their discussions on the football match.

'Nineteen points to a point we beat them back in '33 when they opened their pitch and they had all the county stars and they still haven't got over it,' said the father.

Whenever the teams met following that encounter, the father would bring out his story which echoed and re-echoed in the ears of his sons down over the years embedding itself in their memories. Whilst it produced a bemused reaction from them, it nevertheless seeped into their psyche unknown even to themselves.

'When we came in off the pitch having beaten them nineteen points to one point, Phil Flaherty took off his cap threw it down in the grass and said, 'God blast it lads, who let 'em get the feckin' point?'

And then for effect and putting it up to his sons he added, 'I never remember them beatin' us.' Whether it was true or false, the sons never found out.

Equally, the case showed the sons what they had to live up to. It confirmed the father as a parish patriarch who had upheld the honour of his native parish in his day. Shake their heads, and smile though they might, the sons were caught up in the tradition. And here, this Easter Sunday, it was again being lived out by them – fresh buds from deep, deep roots.

'Never could depend on that crowd,' said the father.

'Same thing in the 'Troubles'. Isn't that why Larry Murray had to go to the States when the money went missing?'

There was silence at the mention of the more sinister and macabre times, the blacker times, when, after the 'Tan War, brother had fought brother, when the monies amassed by the Old IRA were not fully accounted for and Murray left the neighbouring parish for America in the dead of night. Passions ran deep and ran sore.

'They couldn't wait for the truce to be called before they started feckin' stuff. Patriots me arse. It couldn't be over half quick enough for them – took what they could and lived off the people.'

There was bitterness there. It was a deep-seated bitterness. Though it was hard for the sons to understand it, it rattled around in their father's memory like a steel ball in a tin can. Sacred ground was being ploughed up once more. The sod had not been well turned before it was being harrowed. Then he might soften alright.

'Except for maybe Francie Doyle and a few more lads. Few enough of them ever had any gumption when it was put up to them.'

The mother got up from the chair and put the teacups back on the tray. 'I'm taking the vessels out,' she glared. The conversation was killed dead. Full stop and a comma. By this deft action, she terminated any possibility of allowing the conversation degenerate to the bitter times all wanted to forget. It only required a little spark to have it all flare up again.

It was amazing the way passion, sport and tribalism had merged and continued the expression of struggle for survival by cloaking itself in virtue and morality by way of justification for the expression of the raw, and more basic, and still more primeval, instincts. Yet, the father would not let it go without some reference. 'And then they surrounded the house at home, nineteen of them, to take poor Pat to jail and he only nineteen years of age at the time. Nineteen of them ya know. Nineteen.' The mother knew. That was why she had left and gone to the back kitchen. He would no longer have the audience of someone who knew what had happened. Left with only his two sons, the harm would go out of the conversation and they would go back to talking about football.

Yet, equally she knew, this game of football was a lightning rod for the silenced frustrations and the bitter anguish that had been so much part of the early history of the young State.

They smoked, and chatted and plotted. The football Manager dragged on the reddening long ash of one Afton Major cigarette after another. The mother still smoked but the father had given them up some years ago. The cigarette had a spearheaded point as a result of the football Manager's animated inhalations, dragging the nicotine into his system and savouring it in his attempts to quieten his mood.

'Bloody feckers.'

He dropped his head trying to hide his rage.

'If we had only got fair play. That last feckin' free. That's all ye'd ask, a little fair play.'

The younger brother wanted to know what had started the row. The older brother recounted the rule that all mentors were required to stay on the sideline during the course of play. There was a minute left in the match and their team was a point behind. They had been attacking the enemy's goal and one of the defenders put the ball out of play over the endline and the referee awarded a 'fifty' yards free. In undisciplined fashion, all of his attacking forwards congregated on the square around the goal, packing it too tightly so that if the ball broke loose there would be a difficulty for any player kicking for a score if they got the ball.

He ran up the endline to get them to spread out. As he was doing so, a well-known supporter of the others, the Welder Whelan, had been basking with his girlfriend in the scutch grass at the back of the goal. Because of the animated nature of the concluding stages of the match, the Welder had by now risen from his nest with mischievous glee and stood in the way of the Manager on his way up the endline. He stood in front of him with a big grin and said, 'Away they go, lawman.' The Manager walked around him and said nothing.

The Manager got his troops to disperse and he went right back down to the sideline. When the free was taken, the ball was again put out by a defender. The referee awarded another 'fifty' but not before one of the Manager's own team had received a bloodied nose. To his frustration, as the ball was being taken out to the 'fifty' spot, players began to bunch once more in the square. Again, the Manager walked up the endline and again the Welder Whelan stood in front of him and again the Welder Whelan jeered, 'Away they go, lawman'. He walked around the Welder for a second time, roared at his forwards to get out of the square and went back down to his spot on the sideline once more. He could hardly believe it after the free had been taken, it again went out for another 'fifty'.

Such was the intensity of battle at this stage, that his immature charges again lost their concentration and started to move back in on top of the square again. To his utter frustration, he again had to go up the endline to get them to spread. For the third time, the Welder stood out in front of him. This time he jeered.

'Away they go, fucking lawman. Away they go.'

Too much for the Manager, he stopped and looked him evenly in the eye and said, 'Look here now, Willie. I walked around you twice already, now get the fuck out of my way.'

The leering oaf grinned at him, taunting him, inviting him with both hands to 'Come on – Come on,' luring him into a fight.

'I took a swing at him with me closed fist and missed him by about two inches – if I'd connected they wouldn't have found his head this side of Carrickbyrne.'

'I saw that,' said the younger brother.

'So, it seems, did everyone else,' the Manager replied. They both laughed because at that stage of the match the father had started running. The next minute he was whisked away. The crowd were in. Fists flew in all directions. The referee blew the long whistle to end the match because of the invasion and before the 'fifty' could be taken. And that was the end of the account of the match.

The father got up to go to the toilet . . .

The mother came back in having overheard the last of the story.

'I hope you're both very proud of yourselves. You could have got your father killed and he sixty years of age.'

The brothers both looked at each other and grinned. The younger said, 'I'd say he'd have taken a few with him the way he was swinging that bottle of 'Little Sister orange.' The mother's countenance started arranging itself for the glare.

'Will you shut up, for Jaysus sake?' said the older brother.

'Grown men fightin', she glowered as she closed the door and went to bed.

'What are you goin' to do?' asked the younger brother.

'I'm going to sleep on it,' he said and they both went to bed.

II.

On the following evening, the team were called together in The Haven public house in the middle of the parish. The calling of the meeting was, as they said themselves, 'of a hurry'. A team member had discovered grounds for objection to the enemy's victory. Their full forward was over-age. By a full year. 'Should we object?' It was up to the team. It was also a foregone conclusion.

'Of course we should object.'

'They'd say we couldn't take our b'atin.'

'B'atin? B'atin?'

'Winnin' isn't everything, you know.'

'Winnin'! Winnin'! What about cheatin'? Were they ever different? If it wasn't over-age players, it was other club's players. Those fellows couldn't lie straight in the bed.'

'Didn't they leave you on the Cross of Sheilbaggan when they were supposed to bring you for the county trials so their lads could be on the county team and keep you off?'

'Not just me – there was Doran before me and Kelly before that.'

'They'll stop at nothing. They're at it all their lives. We're takin' it all our lives. We're not takin' it any more though. We're fed up with it.'

'Settled then. We'll object.'

The secretary filed the objection that week in accordance with the rules of the GAA.

The illegal constitution of a team by including an over-age player in an under-age grade carried a number of penalties. Firstly, they'd lose the match. In addition, the chairman and secretary of their club would be suspended for two years. (It so happened that the chairman and secretary were two card-carrying members of Fine Gael. Membership of that political party converted the prejudices of their opponents into valid opinions.) The moral indignation was justified with philosophical quips, 'Sure what could you expect?'

This time they would make sure it would come out. The club would be acknowledged at last and all the generations of the deprived and deceived (and deceased members) of the club would be appreciated and be defended by at least one man who was not afraid to stand up to them. He would show them where to get off. For far too long now the lads had been unable to match their wiles but he would employ the skill he had and show them up for what they were. It was a matter of principle now. They might have deprived him of his chance to play for his county but he would show them. By the rules, mark you, by the rules. Revenge is sweet and particularly so when the chance to get even falls into your lap.

All week his court cases took second place in his mind. Though his work was tough and difficult, he was thorough and diligent and his humour was equal to it. Couldn't he just see their faces when they got the objection? The secretary opening the letter, his jaw dropping, his face reddening with rage, probably with embarrassment at being caught out, his phoning the chairman, their calling a meeting in the Parish Hall. He paused. Would they really follow correct club protocol? No be Jaysus – there'd be no meetin' over there. Oh, they'd meet alright at one another's houses and even then know what they were going to say and do before they'd meet. No such thing as getting a democratic representative view. They were riddled with cronyism. Nothing only gossip, rumour and plots and plans. Treacherous blackguards and cunning schemers. Masters of guile and deception. Theirs wasn't a club at all. It was a full-time conspiracy.

The telephone wires over there would be meltin' with them 'phoning each other and plottin' and plannin' and schemin'. They could scheme all they liked. The game was up and he would haul them before the committee and the court of public opinion. Wouldn't it be a grand day entirely? Justice would be done. There was a God in the heavens after all. And mother would have to acknowledge we were right. As the guardian of the family conscience, particularly when passion came into play, she, too, would have to acknowledge the truth of the situation. The father had been right all along and the son felt the rising compulsion to justify his parent that the traditions of striving for supremacy inculcated. Presented with the facts, the devious and evil manner with which they once more tried to cod everyone would be obvious to mother. What sort of example was this to be setting for young under-age players? It was a full ten days before the County Secretary acknowledged the objection but when he did, the first bombshell dropped. A sub-committee of the county board – the football board – would hear the case against them. But, who do you think was the chairman of that sub-committee? It was Mylett, the enemy's representative on the County Board.

The Manager consulted with his more experienced father.

'He'll have to vacate the chair in favour of someone else.' And drawing on his legal expertise the Manager proclaimed, 'A person cannot be a judge in his own cause.'

'Me poor man,' said his father, 'You've a lot to learn. Do you think that fella will budge out of the chair and let someone else throw their team out of the championship, along with their chairman and secretary. For two years?'

Duly chastened, the son retreated into himself gloomily. As he undressed for bed he fumbled in his mind for clarity. What would they do?

What would we do?

It was like table tennis in his mind. Over and back. Back and over. He fell asleep.

Next morning the postman brought the answers.

Unable to contain himself he went straight to the father. Not only did the enemy deny their player was over age, they cross-objected on the basis that one member of our team was also illegal because he had been born in their parish and had attended their school in their parish when he was a youngster. The father was stony-faced. The Manager continued. 'He,' they say, 'played his first match with them and was never lawfully transferred to our club when he changed schools and went to live with his grandparents in our parish.'

'Though he feckin' lived here with them all his life. For Jaysus sake.'

It was a technicality. Nevertheless, it could disqualify the team even if they won the objection. It did not, however, carry the sanction of the suspension of the chairman and secretary.

'You may call a meeting,' said the father stoically.

The meeting was called.

'I never seen such hick-a-prits,' the secretary dyslexically blurted. They laughed at his enthusiasm. The treasurer compounded it. 'You mean you never seen such pricks?' More laughter. 'Yiz never seen a friggin' objection before, ya pair of gobshites,' said the chairman at the meeting, which, as they said, 'put the tin hat on it.'

Another voice said, 'We'll be the laughing stock of the county. It's all very well to laugh. We may withdraw the objection.'

'And let them get away with it,' said the secretary.

'What else are we going to do?'

'Let's talk to the players,' said the Manager.

'The neck of them,' he said. 'The bare-faced neck of them.'

'What did I tell you?' said the father later. 'A leopard never changes his spots,' he said sardonically. 'Did you think they were going to turn over and lie down? Not on your life. There's only one language those hoors understand on the pitch or off the pitch: Give them the dart, full belt, but make sure you give it to them first.'

When they came home after the meeting, the analysis continued.

The mother was quiet at first. The younger brother was quiet for a different reason. He was learning from his father and his older brother about past injustices. The current injustice gathered the bile in them. And now in him.

'They definitely won't give up the chair now,' said the father. 'This won't be let go to a vote. There's no uncertainty here. He'll rule the entire matter out of order.'

'They have no grounds for having their chairman stay in the chair,' said the son.

'But stay there he will, even though they have no defence to the case against them and they'll get away with it. Wait and you'll see,' said the father.

'He can't do that,' said the son.

'They have no grounds for a counter-objection either, but they're makin' one,' said the father. 'And they'll get away with that too.'

'Over my dead body,' said the son.

'And mine too,' said the youngest son who was birthed into reality on the playing pitch and who was now attending baptism at the hands of his father and younger brother.

The mother interjected: 'Don't you think there's been enough trouble without causing more of it?' Before the son could answer, 'That's not the point, woman,' the father said. 'Winning isn't everything. It's how you refuse to let them treat you like dirt and take you for a fool. It's about getting up after you've been knocked down and particularly when you've been knocked down in the dirty fashion we were.'

'It seems to me like you're all fools the way you're carrying on,' she said.

'Can't you simply take your beating and prepare better the next time you meet them?' she asked.

The football Manager's son looked at her in disbelief.

'You mean give in to them?'

'Will we let the chaps be cheated and then lie down and do nothing?'

She felt the sting of the accusation of betrayal in his rhetorical question.

'I'm only saying there's a lot of trouble over what's supposed to be a sporting game.'

Her statement left them hanging in mid-air. And hang there they did, leaving each with their separate thoughts: she with thoughts of concern for her family and in particular the indoctrination and proselytisation that her youngest son was going through; the Manager anxious to demonstrate his team was better and, given a fair chance, he would prove it.

The father believed he knew what sport was about and it was how you dealt with defeat and victory. You couldn't let yourself be humiliated. There was honour in defeat when it was fair. When it wasn't, you fought for what was fair. The Manager believed that too, but in a way, that you would turn a philosophical disposition into a strategy and be successful. He would have to draw on all his lawyerly skills, and well he knew it.

III.

The County Football Board met in the Talbot Hotel. The meeting was billed for eight o'clock on a Monday evening. As predicted by the father the chairman refused to vacate the chair notwithstanding his club was involved. His committee prevailed upon him for over an hour to do so but to no avail. He called in the parties and, without stating a reason, said he was holding that the objection was out of order and that consequently the counter objection was irrelevant. He declared his club were the winners of the match and closed the meeting almost before it had started. The Manager just sat there with the secretary and said nothing.

'Say something,' said the secretary.

'Hould your whisht and say nothing,' said the Manager.

'For Jaysus sake say something,' repeated the secretary to the Manager.

The Manager maintained his resolve and said nothing.

He knew what he was doing. The public mightn't understand the niceties of legal argument. But they would all understand that they hadn't been given a chance to say anything. They would understand that it had been ruled out of order before anyone could open their mouths, that the others had been declared the winners at the very outset of the meeting and that meant the result was decided before the meeting started. Fair play how are ye?

When they got out of the meeting, the distraught secretary said to him, 'They'll Jaysus kill us when we get home for saying nothin'. Why didn't you say somethin' – anythin' Jaysus-to say nothing – nothing at all. Were you afraid or what?'

The Manager looked at him and quietly said, 'Are you a jackass or what?'

'What do ya mean?' challenged the secretary.

'We're goin' to appeal to the County Board, the next highest body.'

The secretary kept silent.

When the appeal was put in, it appeared in the *New Ross Standard* and *The Echo*. The chairman of the County Board was no fool. He allowed the appeal and ruled the objection was in order. He directed that the football board could now hear the case as the objection was in order and referred it back to them.

A Hearing. That was what the Manager wanted. He was used to Hearings. The sawdust dryness of rules and regulations was not unlike the hard grind of legal argument in Court Hearings. It was the same challenge that was contained in sport. Strange, he thought, the way you can get caught up in the game when pursuing victory. The club would bounce from this if they won. It would inject them with a new confidence. If they won, it would give the club a huge boost.

They were back before the football board. The most uncomfortable chairman could not now rule the objection out of order. He had to listen to it.

'The chairman being an interested party should leave the chair,' submitted the Manager.

'This chairman will not leave the chair under any circumstance!' declared the chair.

'Under any circumstance?'

'Under no circumstance whatever!'

'Even if it threatens the reputation, impartiality and independence that proper procedures require? Even if it damages the reputation of the Association into the bargain?'

'There will be no impropriety.'

'That is exactly what is alleged against your club,' replied the Manager.

'And yours,' replied the chairman.

'I'm not in the chair,' parried the Manager.

'You'd do well to remember that,' said the chairman disarming him.

There were guffaws of laughter from the others. The Manager was stung and was unable to resist a 'cut' at his adversaries.

'Nor did I bring along a company of chimpanzees to act as a Greek chorus.'

Shouts of 'Shame! Shame!'

'Withdraw that remark.'

'Order! Order!' said the chairman. 'Get on with matters but no more personal insults please,' he said pointedly to the Manager.

The case against the others was put by the Manager but before they responded, the chairman looked the Manager in the eye and asked,

'Is there no way this can be resolved without the objection proceeding?'

He was hinting at a replay but there had been too much talk, too much hurt, too many issues. Now that they were caught in a corner, they wanted to play fair. The tradition of hatred had gone back too far and too deep. This was too little, too late. They were caught and they would pay the price. An eye for an eye. A tooth for a tooth.

'None,' responded the Manager spontaneously without the slightest hint of demur or hesitation.

'That's too bad,' said the chairman.

'I thought it could be settled like sportsmen do.'

This was political. If the objection had to be conceded by the chair, the objectors would be left with little honour.

'Sportsmen don't cheat,' replied the Manager.

'Mistakes can be made,' said the chairman.

'Or it might not have been a mistake at all,' replied the Manager.

'Take that back,' shouted a member of the Greek chorus.

'We have presented our case,' said the Manager coolly. 'If you have a defence then let's hear it.'

Then Father McCarthy got up. 'If this man is going to use his profession in this matter then maybe we should get professional advice, too.'

There was silence. Such was the tension you could hear the hotel carpet sweat.

'I didn't bring my profession into this,' came the reply. 'And if it is relevant, then maybe the Reverend Father might look to his own profession and examine his conscience and that of his cohort and whether he wants to be associated with lies or truth.'

The priest had been challenged on the truth. The room was stunned. The imagined sweat from the carpet rose like imagined steam. The chorus recovered and came back. 'We all know where the lawyer and the liar are,' replied the Reverend. The room resounded with laughter.

The Manager looked at the chairman, 'I believe you said there were to be no more personal insults. May I ask if you are going to chair the meeting objectively and fairly and enforce the rule you indicated at the outset?'

This had never happened before. A clerical confrontation and challenge to integrity. The priest's word was supreme always.

The chairman was caught. But the priest eased the grip, 'Perhaps I ought to withdraw my remark but I cannot do so without honestly stating he started it.'

'No, Father. Your crowd started it when they lied about your full forward's age. Now you're looking to justify it.'

'That's no way to speak to a Priest of God,' whined their secretary.

'Order! Order!' said the chairman asserting his authority.

'What answer have you to the claim that one of your players was born in our – uh – their parish?' the chairman asked.

'He was born in the County Hospital in Wexford according to his Birth Cert,' came the smart semantic reply from the Manager.

'Don't get legalistic with me,' said the chairman. 'Most of the locals were born in the County Hospital but the mother's residence at the time of confinement for delivery is regarded as the place of birth for all other purposes as well you know.'

The chairman was forcing the Manager into a corner in which the lawyer in him knew he could not get out. The emotional yeast in him was rising and the obligations to his heroes and the memories of their determination to stand against adversity welled up in him as he threw decorum flagrantly to one side, the better to indulge himself rhetorically and 'cut the stuffin' out of that shower of gombeens.'

The Manager lost the run of himself.

'I know if the child had anything to do with it, it wouldn't be born in the middle of your crowd.'

'Withdraw that remark.'

'He's makin' a mockery of the whole thing.'

'Order! Order!' said the chairman.

'He obviously preferred to be born in ours,' came the riposte.

'When he came to the use of reason, he preferred to play for ours,' retorted the Manager.

'Admission! Admission!' cried the Priest.

'Order!' said the chairman. 'Order!'

The chairman knew the objection had succeeded, but so had the counter-objection. He disqualified his own team from the championship and noted that as an automatic consequence, the chairman and secretary of the club would be disqualified for two years. He also ruled the counter objection be upheld and the Manager's team was suspended. Hostility between both parties sank to new depths. The meeting broke up amid scowls and dirty looks.

Outside, the supporters of the other club asked what happened. He promptly told them that both teams had been thrown out of the championship.

'I suppose you're happy now,' one of the onlookers challenged the Manager.

Still angry from the boardroom battle, he stopped for effect and with memories of the Welder Whelan burning in his brain, he glared at his challenger and said,

'I'm really fucking delighted.'

'You bloody bollix,' said the other and struck him with a fist on the chest.

The Manager looked down on the much older man who had just struck him and glared, 'Let that be a lesson for ya – and your chairman – and your secretary.'

'C'mon,' said his secretary. 'D'you want to start another row?'

'Wasn't that the way he started the whole thing anyhow?' asked the older man.

IV

Two years later the two clubs met in a match at the Strawberry Fair Tournament in Enniscorthy. This time the Manager played in the full forward line. There was nothing at stake except pride. It was just an opening round. The others had five from the county team on the panel.

The Manager's team won that evening and his younger brother played with him that night and they both played a stormer. They won. As they were coming from the field, they exchanged witticisms.

'They had a full muster tonight,' said the young brother as they traipsed to the dressing room. 'Indeed,' said his brother, 'all the stars were out tonight,' he quipped. The young brother entered into it. 'Just so. But there mustn't have been any moon. It was a fairly dark night for them.'

'They had two from outer space as well,' said the older brother. 'Look over there.'

There on the embankment were the recently reinstated chairman and secretary who had been suspended two years before. He grinned mischievously at the younger brother. 'Watch this.' He walked past the embankment and looked up at the two 'aliens'. 'Good night, Pat! Good night, Pat!' he said to the two Pats.

They were unable to reply. He might as well have hit them a slap in the puss, as he said later, 'The offence offered by such a trouncing could not have been more severe.'

He could hardly contain himself until he and his younger sibling got home to tell the father.

'How did you get on?' he asked.

'They scored five points and we scored six,' said the son.

'You beat them by a point?' he queried.

'Hold on,' he said. 'I've been listening to you a quare long time talking about beatin' those hoors by nineteen points to a point over the years. Well we scored eleven goals as well and they scored none!'

The father looked at them disbelievingly. The son repeated, 'That's right. Eleven goals and six points to five points. Thirty-nine points to five. We beat them by thirty-four points. I scored six goals meself.' The father laughed and laughed and laughed. Belly laugh followed belly laugh.

Five or six weeks later, the clubs met again in another seven-a-side tournament in Stoinin in the final. Cute enough, the others sent down a bad team for fear of having their good team beaten a second time and establishing a trend. Just when you think God is smiling on you, when you think you have Him in your pocket, He gives you an unmerciful boot in the arse. The others won by six points.

Having scored six goals against their 'star' team at the Strawberry Fair, this evening in Stoinin the Manager of the U-21 football team, playing full forward, had been handed five balls on the edge of the square in the course of the game and kicked the five of them wide. Had he scored two they would have won. He could not bring himself to tell his father when he got home. The other crowd never forgot it. Neither did he. Nobody laughed and laughed and laughed. Pride comes before a fall and the seat of wisdom is humility. That seat – in the physical sense – is located more or less convenient to the seat of the pants. In short, it sometimes takes a severe kick in the backside to infuse wisdom.

Years later he still pondered on it when he became an old man. How easily our traditions become our tyrant, when the need to win becomes tied up in putting the other down. They had done it to us by cheating and we would do it to them – if we could, without cheating. And wouldn't we be the smart fellows except we were only fooling ourselves. It was all about winning – and that is where everyone loses.

'How grown men could behave like that!' Maybe the mother was right.

'Maybe they should give them all a ball each'.

7.

The Ring of Truth

Steam rose from the wet overcoats, and the rubber wellington boots which squelched on the cement floor were smothered by nervous guffaws as a crowd of elbows and fivers fought for the attention of the barman in Power's Public House in Ballycullane on Court Day, the third Thursday in April.

Criminals, ne'er-do-wells, farmers and poachers fortified themselves with half-ones and doubles to meet the weather and what decisions they might have to deal with at the whim of the District Justice.

Laying claim to the centre stage, where the drama of dispensation of Justice would be carried out, were the Guardians of the Peace – the Gardaí. Like Conquistadores laying claim to the terrified, the conquered and the owned, they strutted up and down the floor of the body of the courtroom with an ease and arrogance intended to intimidate and dismay the most hardened criminal their task had to endure.

Solicitors used their own private cars as consultation rooms unless they were early enough to avail of the one room the courthouse traditionally used for that purpose – the toilet.

Removed from the vulgarity and rudeness of this motley gathering, the host for the occasion, the District Justice, was now comfortably ensconced in the snug adjacent to the lounge, which could only be accessed through the portcullis and moat of the private dwelling of Mr.

Power, publican. His hors d'oeuvres would be consumed before court and afterwards he would regale his patrons with embellished accounts of theatrics and characters whose fortune or misfortune it was to appear in front of him that day.

District Justice, Arthur Lannigan O'Keefe B.L., had a no-nonsense disposition when it came to dispensing justice in the time-honoured custom of hearing complainants in public in the community from which they arose.

'It's an awful pity we can't start at two o'clock,' said the Court Clerk.

'Regulations are regulations, you know I can't start before three.'

The Garda Superintendent was there too.

'Still t'would be a lovely day for the beach or a round of golf.'

'Regulations are regulations,' was the reply.

Suddenly there was a downpour of hailstones.

The Hall at Ballycullane, across the road from Power's public house, served as replacement for the old Assizes Court in Arthurstown five miles distant across the brown furrowed fields. It was now known officially as Ballycullane Courthouse and the place in which the District Justice, reigned colourfully. To the locals, it was still known as The Ploughing Hall.

The Ploughing Hall had been rebuilt only a few years earlier in 1971. In his enthusiasm, and without consultation, Canon Murphy had the headstones in the churchyard moved to the surrounding walls and, to the consternation of his congregation, the graves were covered with tarmacadam. The dead ought not to have been disturbed. The controversy threatened to explode, but it spluttered and bubbled before fizzling out in a string of malediction and bad humour. Canon Murphy stood his ground but approximately two years later, the black dog of Doorty had been seen again. It was reported satirically in the *New Ross Standard* that the local sergeant had stayed up to keep watch. It was generally regarded as 'baloney', but the more superstitious in the population regarded it as an eerie omen.

It was functional and spartan in its furniture. There was a wooden desk for the judge, a table for the clerk, and a trestle table for the solicitors, all raised at the same level, two feet from the ground, just sufficient to demonstrate the boundary between the officious and formal and the accountable and common.

There were three steps up to the witness box to which the ordinary ascended to have their testimony examined by the learned, and tested by the clever from whom would be elicited a wise and discerning judgement pronounced in sombre tones, duly resourced and dutifully observed. Recognizances would be fixed to remand those on bail who would appeal for a re-trial on disputed facts, or clemency from the severity of summary justice, to the Circuit Court in Wexford.

At three o'clock the drill of the hailstones on the galvanised roof of Ballycullane Courthouse had stopped the proceedings just as they started. Now, at three o'clock and ten minutes exactly, the District Justice emerged from his chambers for a second attempt and sat on the bench. He was barely warm in the seat when the hailstones started again. They belted as loud as they could down on the galvanized roof. As the locals said, 'You couldn't hear your ears.' The Judge threw his eyes to heaven. 'Common sense how are ye,' he said. 'We could have had half the work finished.'

He rose and waited for nature to have its way and wait until the daffodil sunshine streamed through the window of the ramshackle courthouse once more.

On his way back up the steps from his 'chamber', he turned to the Court Clerk and said, 'I still don't see why we can't start the court immediately after we're finished in New Ross. New Ross is held at 11 a.m. – Ballycullane at 3 p.m.' The Court Clerk, who had a good relationship with the Judge smiled and said, quoting from Seán O'Faoláin: 'Rules is rules, Joxer.' 'Regulations from the Department,' said the District Justice. 'Everything has to be done in triplicate. It has to be sent to four departments, efficiencies must be improved if we are to join the EEC,' he said sourly.

'God be with the days when a Guard could give a fella a kick in the arse and we'd only have about half a dozen cases to see in Balllycullane Court. Now we have two dozen.'

When the hailstones eased, the Judge returned. From the Judge's chambers emerged the ageing Mr. Fintan O'Connor, solicitor, the only connection with the ancient assizes and the heretofore doyen of the local bar. He had a reputation for mischief and cleverness.

'Superintendent, where were we?' addressed the Judge to the Garda Síochána.

'The complainant had given his evidence of the car accident and Mr. Leacy, for the defendant, was about to cross-examine the complainant's witness, Mr. Sands, before the hailstones came,' said Leacy who was the newest product from Law School.

'Oh yes, Mr. Leacy, you raised an issue in relation to time.'

'Yes, Justice. The complainant admitted under cross-examination that he did not remember the date the accident occurred and this is an essential proof if the case against my client is to be admitted,' said Leacy eagerly.

Sands went to the witness stand and took the Bible to swear the oath. Though a smallish man, he towered over the Court Clerk who was standing a full foot below him. The witness box had a false bottom, as it required reinforced flooring to support the chair and the witness. The witness box was of local manufacture and was a cross between a dock and a pulpit. Everyone who saw it knew it was a serious place to be.

The witness gave evidence of the date crucial for the prosecution case.

Young Leacy started his cross-examination.

'You heard the complainant's evidence?'

'I did.'

'He got an awful fright . . . '

'He did.'

' . . . and he was hurt.'

'He was.'

'He broke his leg.'

'He did.'

'He had to go to hospital.'

'He did.'

'And he was there for a week.'

'He was.'

'He probably had to fill out a lot of forms.'

'I suppose.'

'For doctors and nurses...'

'I suppose, I don't know, I...'

The Judge interrupted.

'This witness cannot give evidence which the complainant knows from his own knowledge only on these matters.'

'Very well, Justice,' resumed Leacy, 'I'll move on.'

'That's a good idea,' said the Justice sardonically.

'Silence,' said the Court Clerk to quell the vulgar laughter.

Leacy resumed.

'So you remember the date, Mr. Sands?'

'I do.'

'You weren't injured?'

'I wasn't, thank God.'

'In fact, you went straight to one of the local pubs.'

'To steady me nerves.'

Judge, (to one side), 'Sensible man.' More laughter.

'Silence.'

'You stayed there a while.'

'For a little while.'

'How long?'

'I can't remember.'

'What time did the accident happen?'

'I'm not sure, I think 'twas about half-past six or seven.'

'It happened at half-five.'

'Maybe.'

'So the Garda report says.'

'The Guards would know.'

Smothered sniggers. The Court Clerk looked up sternly.

'What time did you go home?'

'Closing time.'

'You were there five or six hours?'

'I s'pose.'

'How much did you have to drink?'

'A few half ones and a few pints.'

'How many?'

'I can't remember.'

'You can't remember? You can't remember! You can't remember how long you were in the licensed premises and you can't remember how much you drank and yet you clearly remember the date?'

'I do.'

'This is very extraordinary. You can't remember how long you were there, what time it was or how much you had to drink, but you have it clearly and indelibly marked on your brain, what the date was.'

'I do.'

Leacy, sarcastically again,

'Perhaps you would like to share with the court how you remember this so well.'

Sands smiled at him.

'I put a ring around the date on the calendar next morning when I got up.' Leacy looked at him with 'a-likely-story-indeed' look.

Muffled sniggers from the assembly angered Leacy. The Judge was stoic.

'You put a ring around the date on the calendar,' said Leacy with mock belief and for effect.

'I did,' replied a nonplussed Sands.

'Have you ever done this before?'

'What?'

Impatiently, Leacy repeated, 'Put a ring around a date on a calendar to remind yourself of the date?'

'No. Never.'

Leacy went for the kill.

'So tell me, Mr Sands. Why did you put a ring around the date on the calendar on this particular occasion?'

'So's I wouldn't forget it.'

There was an uncontrolled explosion of laughter, which drew the Court Clerk's admonishment.

The Judge looked at Leacy bemusedly. Leacy had walked into it. He was flattened.

'Any more questions?'

'None,' said Leacy and sat down. Better to take your beating he felt.

'Any witnesses, Mr. Leacy?'

'No, Justice.'

It was clear the case was over. His client was fined and convicted. The business of the court moved on. Next case.

'Garda Moore versus John Miskella,' announced the Court Clerk.

Mr. Fintan O'Connor, solicitor, stood up and so, too, did a big countryman with a collarless stud shirt and a brown overcoat with a belt.

The hailstones started their din again. No more business until the shower stopped. The Judge would have to retreat to his chambers once more.

'I'll rise,' said the Judge as much over the din as he could raise his voice.

The April chill was clearly etched in John Miskella's well-weathered features. A fresh redness had massaged the purple veins in his big nose. He was the butt end of nudges and winks, to which he was oblivious. He sat on the seat beside Ned Murphy. They could have passed for brothers, each minding his own business. This was not theatre. This was as serious as Mass. They were of the indigenous population; the faithful, the salt of the earth, the plain, or, as they used to say around the place, 'the dacent', the unnoticed, the unimportant, the men of no status but without whom there would be no men of importance or status.

Over a cup of tea in his chambers, the Justice observed to the Court Clerk: 'The more the regulations come in, the less decency there is. The more you make rules, the more rules there are to be broken. A bit of common sense would go a long way.' The Court Clerk and the Judge sat inside by the fire. 'Tell us this,' said the Court Clerk, 'and I hope you don't mind me asking, but I often wondered...'

'Go on.'

'Would you ever know when a fellow would be lying?'

Too cute by half, the District Justice looked him back in the eye and said, 'Now if I told you I would, do you think I'd be telling you the truth or a lie?'

The Court Clerk laughed.

'The ould dog for the long road'.

'And the pup for the bohreen – though I think you're a bit long in the tooth for a pup,' laughed the District Justice.

'To be honest though, the more you go into the country, the less they observe regulations and the poorer people are, the less they have to lose by telling the truth.'

They paused for a moment looking at the fire.

'I suppose that's about as far as you could go,' said the Court Clerk.

The hailstones stopped.

'That's as far as I'm going to go anyway!' laughed the District Justice as he sprang from the chair to make his way to the bench.

The cement floor was damp in spots. There was an oil-fired paraffin fire beside the judge's desk. Two 100 watt bulbs hung from the ceiling. Bare and naked they failed in their task. The shadow prevailed. The gloom remained. The crowd who fumbled and mumbled through the proceedings, looked for this, that and the other, shopping lists, cigarette boxes, matches and newspapers. The floor was grimy. Here and there was a bottle of lemonade, an ice pop wrapper, and the grottiness was compounded by stubbed cigarette butts, spent matches and toffee papers.

A man with balding red hair approaches Mr. Fintan O'Connor, solicitor. He looks intense. O'Connor gets up and goes with him into the consultation room – the toilet. They were there for a while. Leacy goes and speaks to Ned Murphy.

'You still want to go on with it?' Leacy asks.

'The sow is mine and that's that,' Murphy says.

'You know we have no one to back you up?' Leacy says.

'I'll back meself up,' says Murphy.

'We'll be on after this,' says Leacy and goes back to the long seat on the podium behind the trestle table.

Moving towards half-past four, O'Connor addresses the Judge about John Miskella's unlicensed dogs.

'Mr. O'Connor,' says the Judge, 'one unlicensed dog I can understand or maybe two. But six! He'll have to get into the witness box and explain that to me!'

John Miskella's brogues take up most of the witness box and he looks awkward as his big plough hands smother the Bible from view as he solemnly swears by Almighty God.

His ungainly lean muscular shirt is now revealed through his rumpled open overcoat, through which protrude a pair of enormous knees on which he plants each hand. He shifts uneasily on the hard seat and commences his evidence. He looks at the Judge who eyes him evenly.

'Well now judge, boy,' says Miskella. The inappropriateness of his address is lost on him until the sniggering starts.

'I had wan dog and a bitch came and had four pups.'

Tittering.

'You'll have to exercise some control over...'

The crowd snorts. The Judge goes pale as the clerk calls for order.

'One more outburst of this nature and I'll clear the court and imprison those responsible for contempt,' says the Judge with a frosty stare.

The fun, now gone, he turns on Miskella.

'My title is Justice,' he glares.

'I'm sure he meant no disrespect, Your Worship,' says O'Connor hearkening back to the demeanour he adopted for assizes.

Mollified, the Justice munificently accepts the apology.

'I'm sure, Mr. O'Connor,' he replies. 'But his dogs will cost him two pounds a head. Twelve pounds fine,' he declares. Manners descend on the assembly. Twelve pounds is a week's wages for a labouring man. Thus ended John Miskella's adventure that day in Ballycullane Court. That was how it was reported contemporaneously in the *New Ross Standard* in order to void accusations of inaccuracy or possible suit for libel. For the same reason, the next case was not reported.

When the hailstones descended for the third time to the Judge's increasing frustration, he declared he would rise for five minutes and if the shower was not finished by then, he would adjourn the court. He would have adjourned it there and then but for the fact the next case was the last case.

Ned Murphy's sow was worth twenty-five pounds, and it had ended up in the Boss Hanrahan's piggery.

Ned was one of the last to hold on to the pigsty at the rear of the cottage and keep it in use. These pigsties had been part of the cottage plot given to those in need of social housing. The government had been promoting a policy of self-sufficiency long before Sean Lemass introduced 'The First Programme for Economic Expansion' in the early sixties. The introduction of agricultural economic development through the European Economic Community farm-modernisation scheme rendered these policies and their markets redundant. But Ned was good with pigs, and with assistance, he was able to cure the meat. He fattened for his own table what bonhams he didn't rear for breeding and because he knew his craft and loved it, his Landrace pigs were renowned.

'The closest to the human,' he would say of this remarkable animal. But pigs were delicate and prone to the dangerous and often fatal condition of oedema.

Mr. Fintan O'Connor approached Leacy.

'Can we speak, off the record and without prejudice?'

'Of course,' he replied.

'We won't look for costs and we won't sue for defamation if he withdraws the case.'

'There's not a hope,' he replied.

'Take instructions anyhow,' said O'Connor.

The young solicitor approached his client once more.

'The sow's mine and that's that,' said Ned.

Leacy was still smarting from the 'put down' by the witness in the last case. He had breached a cardinal rule of cross-examination: 'Never ask an opposing witness a question, the answer to which you do not already know.' He did and he had paid the price. It would have been easy to stop. Too easy in fact. His pride drove him to go for the kill and he ended up impaled on his own stake.

Now he would have to fight for a stubborn Ned Murphy with only his own assertion of fact as evidence against the slippery Hanrahan and the even more cunning, and much more experienced, O'Connor.

As quickly as they started, the hailstones stopped. The sun streamed across the field outside the courtroom window, revealing two unruffled if bedraggled goats, and stole in transforming the dusty sunbeams of the courthouse.

District Justice, Arthur Lannigan O'Keefe flashed out of his room once more.

The Clerk announced,

'Edward Murphy versus Thomas Hanrahan.'

Leacy stood up.

'I'm for the Plaintiff. A case of wrongful conversion of property. A sow, my client's property, by the defendant,' he nodded.

'Alleged,' said the Judge.

'As alleged,' said Leacy.

'And denied,' quipped O'Connor.

'I gather,' said the Judge.

'Before we start...'

O'Connor was making his pre-emptive strike. Confuse, disarm and upset. It was a ploy as old as Methuselah.

'There is a concern about my client's character being detracted by these proceedings and it would be fundamentally unjust if they were allowed to tarnish my client in circumstances where the privilege of the court might be abused in such a fashion as to do him irreparable harm and damage. These proceedings are without foundation in fact, and defy credulity in their inception by the absence of the slightest element of objective empirical forensic evidence. Accordingly I must protest the litigation at the outset.'

The Judge looked sceptically at O'Connor but turned a nervous eye to the young Leacy.

'I take it Mr. Leacy you have sufficient evidence to advance your case beyond a direction. For if you cannot discharge the burden you bear to prove your case exists on the balance of probability, there is no need for the defendant to give evidence. And were this to prove to be the case, not alone would your client be at risk for costs, but might well be in contempt of court for bringing vexatious and frivolous proceedings. Indeed you would do well to reassure yourself on this matter, Mr. Leacy,' said the Judge fairly.

'My client is adamant, Justice, but I will convey the court's view if I can be given a moment to explain.'

O'Connor examined his notes. Hanrahan was examining his shoes in an unfocussed fashion. There was a brief 'hugger-mugger' between Leacy and his client that looked deliberate but not animated.

'My client is clear and wishes to proceed,' said Leacy.

When he was sworn, Ned Murphy sat down. He knew in the witness box he was in a strange place. He looked nervous.

He said he had missed the sow when he went out to feed the pigs on a Sunday morning last September. He knew the date because it was the morning of the football All-Ireland and he had enquired in the pub in Ramsgrange when he went up to watch the match that afternoon on the television set and no one had seen the sow anywhere. He knew Tom Hanrahan had a piggery with several pigs and he called up to see him but he said he had no pigs but his own in the piggery.

'It was when I was going back down the lane on the bike, I seen the sow and with that I turned me bike around on de lane and went straight back to him.'

The memory of it excited him. The adrenalin started to flow.

'"Me sow's in the field," sez I'

'"Faith'n it's not," sez he.'

'"C'mon I'll show ya," sez I.'

'"No need to," sez he. "I know mine and mine know me."'

'And that was it?' said Leacy, questioningly.

'S'true as God. Dat he may strike me dead.'

The sun was out now and cut a blinding shaft of light through the dust particles with which it toyed. The spectators for this local derby stayed to see the outcome. They listened to Murphy state the value of the sow and that it was one of two he had.

There were more sniggers when he described bringing her to the boar in an embarrassed but matter of fact tone.

'She was a good sow. Gave me turteen to the litter and never killed wan of 'em,' he said.

'She was a great sucker,' he lamented.

Leacy sat down. The Judge looked at his wristwatch. Ned looked at him. O'Connor stood up.

'Did you go into the field to see the sow?'

'I wasn't let.'

'Just answer "yes" or "no", and then if you want to qualify your answer, do so,' said O'Connor.

'Did you go into the field after the sow?'

'No, sir.'

'Weren't you at least forty yards from it?'

'Yes, sir.'

'Did the sow have a tag on it?'

'No, sir.'

'What breed of sow was it?'

'Landrace, sir.'

'They're the ones with their ears down over their eyes?'

'Yes, sir.'

'And Mr. Hanrahan's pigs are Landrace too, are they not?'

'Yes, sir.'

'Did your pig have a limp?'

'A sow, sir. No, sir.'

'Sorry, your sow.'

'No, sir.'

'Mr. Hanrahan had about forty sows he says, would you disagree with that?'

'No, sir. Not if dat's what he says, sir.'

'You'd take his word for it?'

'Yes, sir.'

'He's an honest man in your view?'

Murphy paused as the crowd went quiet.

'I'd take his word on the amount of pigs he had. I couldn't contradict it,' said Ned.

'I told you before. You can qualify your answer whatever way you like, but you must give me a 'yes' or 'no' answer.'

Ned was not going to be so lightly let off the hook that had been so cleverly fashioned.

'Yes. I'd believe him.'

'Thank you, Mr. Murphy.' He cut him off.

'Did your sow have any tags on it?'

'No, sir.'

'Did it have any brand marks on it?'

'No, sir.'

'Did it have any identifying marks on it?'

'No, sir.'

'Any marks whatsoever on it?'

'No, sir.'

'Wouldn't it be impossible to identify the sow as yours in those circumstances, fifty yards away?'

'No, sir. De sow is mine an' dat's dat.'

'Oh I know you're convinced the sow is yours but you cannot identify it, sure you can't?'

'De sow is mine an' dat's dat.'

'Must I remind you again? I'm entitled to a "yes" or a "no" answer.'

'Yes! De sow is mine an' dat's dat.'

O'Connor quipped, 'I know mine and mine know me.'

Laughter rose from the audience to the stage.

Emphatically, Ned declared: 'De sow is mine an' dat's dat.'

'No more questions, your Worship.'

'You may step down,' said the Judge.

'I'm applying for a direction,' said O'Connor, and grandly offered his legal reason. 'The plaintiff hasn't proved his case sufficient to require the defence call evidence to meet a case that has not been established to the appropriate standard of acceptable verifiable evidence.'

'Mr. Leacy?' said the Judge.

'I disagree with my learned friend,' said the youngster solicitor reflecting an attitude to cliché to which his elders were prone but which fell about him awkwardly. Leacy lapsed back to himself once this salute was over.

'Mr. Murphy has employed the same method of identification of this sow as his adversary, and, as this is so, his adversary cannot complain.'

'No method of identification has been advanced by me on behalf of Mr. Hanrahan,' said O'Connor.

'Indeed,' said the Judge. 'Well, Mr. Leacy?'

'Mr. Hanrahan used the method of 'I know mine and mine know me'. Mutuality of recognition of *mansuetae naturae* of domestic animal. Familiarity with his stock is implicit and an acceptable method of identification. This has been advanced by both parties. Both say they identify and recognise through familiarity.'

The Judge looked at O'Connor. A dropped pin would have made a clatter. Of dropped jaws, there were plenty.

O'Connor rose to his feet.

'Seems to me Mr. Leacy has a point,' said the Judge.

The wily O'Connor was too shrewd to disagree with the Judge at the first hurdle.

'Very well, your Worship. Mr. Hanrahan please.'

He called Hanrahan to the box.

The remains of yellowy reddish tight curls trimmed Hanrahan's bald pate like the hedgerows around a wrinkled, furrowed lea. He raised his eyebrows in tune with the cadence of his vocal exertions. He had a tetch in his speech. Before each sentence, he would kill a starting stutter with 'Eh!' His 'Eh!' more or less immobilised the stammer and gave him a grip before he lost it.

'Eh, I swear by Almighty God. Eh, that the evidence I shall give. Eh, will be the truth...'

He sat.

'I believe you breed pigs,' said O'Connor.

'Eh, I do, yeah,' said Hanrahan.

He went on to describe his enterprise, how he was in the Farm Modernisation Scheme and had to have 'a modernisation plan.' He had erected a piggery with slatted units. He had fifty sows. The breed was Landrace and the animals were reared for breeding and production on an economic basis. The old ways of pig farming were disappearing. These animals would be fed indoors unlike previously when they would be let loose in the fields. His sows were kept inside all of the time.

The court continued:

O'Connor: 'Mr. Murphy says he saw his sow in your field.'

Hanrahan: 'Eh, he didn't see any sow of his in my field.'

O'Connor: 'He says he went back and told you.'

Hanrahan: 'Eh, what would I be doing with an ould sow of his with a ring in its nose eh, an' 'atin all sorts in the fields.'

O'Connor: 'What do you feed yours on?'

Hanrahan: 'Eh, special diet meal. It gives greater and sustained growth.'

O'Connor: 'Would a sow like Mr. Murphy's take to feeding of this type?'

Hanrahan: 'Eh, maybe with time. Eh, but I don't think so.'

O'Connor: 'You know your pigs, don't you?'

Hanrahan: 'Eh, 'deed an' I do.'

O'Connor: 'And are you swearing under oath that all of the pigs on your farm are yours?'

Hanrahan: 'Eh, 'deed an' I am.'

O'Connor: 'And that you don't have Mr. Murphy's sow?'

Hanrahan: 'Eh, 'deed an' what would I want with an ould sow of his?'

O'Connor: 'Answer any questions Mr. Leacy may have.'

Now, it was Leacy's turn. Leacy took his time and looked at his notes carefully. An opening was difficult to see.

Leacy: 'Do you feed your pigs daily yourself?'

Hanrahan: 'Eh, well if I'm not dere, de lads do it and vicey versey.'

Leacy: 'You've got quite a few pigs.'

Hanrahan: 'Eh, fifty sows an' the rest.'

Leacy: 'Do you know all your sows individually?'

Hanrahan: 'Eh, maybe not be name like Mr. Murphy.'

(Laughter)

Leacy: 'How would you know them then?'

Hanrahan: 'Eh, sure dere never out exceptin' dere goin to the factry. Eh, dere always in.'

Leacy: 'And the ones that are inside are yours.'

Hanrahan: 'Eh, dass right.'

Leacy: 'What about ones that are outside?'

Hanrahan: 'Eh, my pigs are never out. Eh, it's part of me farm plan wit de piggery an 'aul.'

Leacy: 'So if a pig were out on your farm, it wouldn't be yours?'

Silence collected all pins once more.

'Eh – Yer tryin to trick me,' he grinned.

'Please explain,' said Leacy, flatly.

'Eh, for if I say yeah, you'll say de wan Ned Murphy saw was his den.'

'So Ned Murphy did see a sow?'

'Didn't say dat. Eh – he said dat.'

'But he told you that night didn't he?'

'What would I want wid his oul' sow?'

'Answer the question "Yes" or "No".'

'Wid a ring in her nose an' 'atin' all sorts.'

'Answer the question "yes" or "no".'

'Eh, Yes or No wha?'

'Dear me, I've nearly forgotten the question myself,' said Leacy.

'I think you were putting it to Mr. Hanrahan what Mr. Murphy had told him that night that he had seen the sow in Mr. Hanrahan's field,' said the Judge.

'Thank you, Justice. Well, Mr. Hanrahan?'

'Eh, well what?'

The young solicitor raised his eyes in exasperation.

Judge impatiently: 'Did Mr. Murphy tell you the night he called to your home, he had seen his sow in your field?'

Hanrahan: 'Eh, yeah, he did. Eh, but sure he'd say an'thin'.'

Leacy: 'Then why didn't you tell him to take it with him that it wasn't yours anyway because yours are never outside?'

Hanrahan: 'Eh, but sure maybe one coulda broke out.'

Leacy: 'Did that ever happen before?'

Hanrahan: 'Eh what?'

Judge: 'That one broke out.'

Hanrahan: 'I can't remember.'

Leacy: 'You can't remember. You can't remember.'

The remark Leacy made was the same he had made to Sands in the earlier case, just before he pounced when he told him he had put a ring around the date on the calendar. He steadied himself.

'Did you check after he had gone?'

'Eh, no.'

'Why not?'

'Eh, I didn't have his oul' free-range sow.'

'How would you know it was free-range?'

'Eh, t'would have a pig ring in its nose.'

'And yours don't?'

'No.'

Judge: 'None of them?'

'Eh, none of them? Eh, dey only ring dem to stop them rootin' in de fields and mine are always kept inside.'

Leacy felt he was close. He was also afraid he might make a mess of it again and let him off the hook.

'May I consult with my client for a moment, Justice?'

The hailstones came down in sheets again.

'You can consult with him over the next three weeks, Mr. Leacy. I'm adjourning for the day.'

The Judge picked his notes from the bench, packed his briefcase, walked down through the courtroom and ran, ducking the hailstones, to his parked Jaguar motor car. O'Connor ran to his new Toyota. Leacy walked to his Ford Cortina and gave Ned a lift home.

About a fortnight later, Ned called to Leacy's office.

'I want to call off the case,' said Ned.

Leacy was baffled. 'Why?' he asked, stunned.

'The sow showed up.'

'The sow showed up?' repeated Leacy.

'That's right,' said Ned.

'I woke up in the mornin' yesterday and 'dere she was rootin around in de field, de rogue.'

Leacy looked bewildered.

'He had it alright,' said Ned referring to Hanrahan.

'How do you know?' asked Leacy.

'Cause she's in young again,' said Ned.

Leacy paused for a moment. For a moment he doubted his client. He wondered whether the bould Ned had been looking for a free service from Hanrahan's boar for his son after all. Then to test him he said to Ned, by way of no harm, 'Maybe she eloped to get married.'

Ned looked up with a face full of grinning teeth. 'Faith'n if she did,' says he, 'she came back without the ring. The whole of the half-acre is all rooted up!'

8.

The Faiths of the Father

The barrel of the gun was pointed straight at his forehead. He had told the fourteen-year-old to go down to Cummins's to tell them the soldiers were coming and he had replied that he wouldn't.

'If you won't go I'll shoot you,' said the young English soldier to the fourteen-year-old Irish rebel.

'I won't go,' the rebel replied.

'You go,' said the soldier to Patsy Walsh who was also fourteen years of age.

'I won't if Leacy won't,' said an equally defiant Walsh.

A Cockney accent from the first of two Crossley tenders that had passed the two boys coming from Sunday Mass in Ramsgrange shouted to the Black and Tan soldier threatening the two boys.

'Leave them alone. Come on. They're only kids'.

In that fashion another atrocity by the Black and Tans in the War of Independence in South Wexford diminished. John Leacy senior, the fourteen-year-old rebel at the time, was telling his son, the lawyer, the story of how he was nearly shot when he was coming from Mass in the parish church one morning in 1921. When the two boys were coming out from Mass a member of the IRA had approached them to bring a despatch to Cummins's, a safe house, where some rebels were lying low. The little gate outside the church door where suspected informers were handcuffed as a warning to others, was where the subversive document was handed. When the first of the two tenders had passed the boys on the road, they stopped as regulation demanded. Before the second arrived to conduct the interview in accordance with procedure, Leacy handed the despatch to Walsh and Walsh stuck it in the hedge out of sight. It was right on the bend of the road. The Tans wanted the two boys to raise the alarm in Cummins's safe house such that when the rebels within would break for the fields they would reveal themselves.

'That's the very spot there,' said Leacy senior, the rebel, to his lawyer son that date in 1990 as they were coming home from the hospital. Leacy the lawyer knew the spot well and knew the story better. His father had been nine weeks in the hospital and was now coming home. The son knew he was dying but said nothing. The father knew he was dying. He said nothing either. The reality of the circumstance went unspoken like other things too numerous to mention and too painful to recall.

The father, the rebel, had been in perfect health up to the previous November. He had placed his foot on a chair in the kitchen to tie his shoelace when he lost his balance and fell over. His leg was caught between the chair and the table and his eighty-one-year-old tibia snapped. In hospital he contracted pneumonia, recovered, relapsed, beat it a second time, and later a third time. But the bone wouldn't bond. After fourteen months of solid determination to live, he finally allowed himself die in peace.

At the start of his attempted convalescence, the father didn't think he was dying. He certainly didn't show it. He maintained his lively spirit by regaling his visitors at his hospital bed with his endless supply of stories. He was a great raconteur. But his stories revealed a pattern of thought of more subconscious goings on.

His experience at this place during the Tan war was something he wanted his son to remember. It was as if he were saying, 'This was a terrible moment for me and a terrible place but I withstood the threat because of what my father had taught me and now I am telling you'. His father was a Fenian and a sailor. He was present in Boston at a meeting where John Devoy, the Fenian, had given a speech. A culture that went with Fenianism translated itself into Republicanism at the start of the twentieth century and Leacy, the Fenian, through a process of story-telling, transmitted the tradition to his progeny. In their turn they became known as 'the rebel Leacys'. Leacy, the rebel, was continuing the process with Leacy the lawyer, the new generation. He was passing the mantle. But it wasn't just politics that was being transmitted. There was a more haunting aspect to it. A matter that went close to the soul, an affinity between native place and freedom. Of connection with place through experience with it. The Fenian Leacy had reared his family here. The rebel Leacy had taken a stand here, and the lawyer Leacy would live here and rear his family here as well.

The lore of place names goes back to the Dinnseanchas before the Red Branch Knights and even before Christ. It lives deep in the Irish psyche.

'I never saw such tall nettles in a field,' the father remarked. The awareness of that awful place hung like cobwebs from an ancient mausoleum on the dewy skeagh thorn bushes that arched against the moon in a spooky horror film.

When the history was explained the father was thrilled not alone with the explanation but with the son's interest. The lawyer was acknowledging and empathizing with the rebel who had, in turn, passed it on from the Fenian. What John Devoy had preached to the American emigrant was winding its way back home and realizing itself in the father's own lifetime when his son started to practise at the Bar.

But in the manner in which time passes, when big events are immortalized as watersheds and points of reference, it is in the small things, and their recollection and observance, that the truth and reality of what is sovereign is revealed, for that which lasts is what is true.

The need to observe and the need to proclaim loyalty to tradition became extreme on occasions. In the distilling process of the Irish story the ridiculous was lampooned in reminiscences laced with burning sarcasm. People were kept in their place in this fashion.

On another occasion when returning from hospital, having had his leg X-rayed, the father recalled being 'sent for' by Mrs. Doyle of Taulaght to bring Annie to the Mental Asylum after 'she took sick in the head.'

'There we were, her mother, herself and meself,' he said, 'driving along the New Line Road when up she springs in the back of the car, like a bird on a bush. Says she to me, 'I seen the Blessed Virgin'. Before I could mutter, her mother sliced her in two. 'Faith 'n if you did, you were the first of the Doyles of Taulaght who seen her'. 'I damn near crashed the car', he laughed.

And so father and son fell into discussing imagination, damnation, the next world and its influence through religion on this one. Neuroses provoked by extremes of piety were still not uncommon in the 1980s. The recent phenomenon of the moving statues as an example was given and theories were offered on its cause. The people, caught up as they were in the drudgery of day-to-day living, and coping in the depths of a financial quagmire of spiralling interest rates, rampant inflation and industrial unrest required some exotic spiritual spectacular to extract them from the suffocating bog in which they were sinking, the remedy to ills so often invoked in the past and still only barely subliminal.

Newspaper stories of spinning icons and apparitions in grottoes appeared. It became even tackier with the re-emergence of green-canvased mission stalls from their musty hibernation of the fifties and sixties. Back then the missioners knocked sparks out of the pulpit, suffusing the congregation with clouds of smoke and sulphur – all the better to engage them with their imminent prospect of eternal and infernal damnation. The stalls belonged to pedlars. The canvas stalls took up about the same amount of space as the modern roadside vendor of potato chips or strawberry sellers except the canvas invariably was carried on old-fashioned Ford vans in the nature of the Model T variety and their reappearance in the 1980s appeared more like an exhumation than a resurrection. The rubric with which they were associated was long gone and betrayed an incongruity in its attempted revival. These stalls were now getting a fresh lease of life.

Internationally, our embarrassment was barely checked when in the following year, a BBC interviewer taunted an established novelist from Ireland. He enquired of her,

'Where have all the moving statues gone, dawling?'

She levelled him with her reply: 'Why, they all emigrated and joined the English soccer team!' came the smack in the puss.

'They always loved making little of us,' the father said, 'but we've only ourselves to blame.'

Indeed it was so.

The son reminded him of the time a woman had come to help him at home. She was from the only house down a little country lane. This place was called Toberboy. There was a pagan well there which gave the place its name. One morning as the son was going to work, she called him. She was ashen-faced,

'There's a problem in the house over at home.'

'What's the matter?'

'I hears voices and when I'm upstairs, the furniture moves about downstairs.'

'And then there's a sound at night like stones on the roof. I'm wondering what I should do?'

The son was sceptical and more than a little cynical. He gathered as much diplomacy as he was able.

'Well maybe the Guards should be told about the stone throwing . . . '

Instantly she knew she was being fobbed off. She was talking about ghosts as easily as she might speak of Mass and the Sacraments. He had, he believed, more of an intellectual approach.

'The other business would be more in the Canon's department,' said he, avoiding entanglement.

He left herself and her voices, her stones and her moving furniture, to the tender mercies of an anticipated indifferent police, and a perhaps more sympathetic, but not so foolish, Canon, who would attempt to excoriate superstitious errors in the imaginations of his vulnerable flock, where heretofore his predecessors had attempted exorcism, but, with probably, equally ambiguous results.

The father took it all in.

'People are slow to change,' said the son.

He recalled an incident relayed by a member of the Folklore Commission who had been seeking out stories of manifestations of fairies back in the thirties. When queried as to whether she believed in them, one woman remarked, 'deed and I don't. But sure they're there anyway.' The father laughed as they drove home. Conversations of this nature intrigued him and he enjoyed their common-sense nature especially. They settled with a routine. Each day his wife called with their youngest daughter to see the grandparents. They had a ceremony each day when the five-year-old helped make the Bovril for grandad to keep him strong and warm and well. Each day he gloried in his grandchild and remarked that it was what made his life worthwhile. 'We live for them so that they can live for us,' he used to say but the son was never quite sure what he meant.

A short time later, perhaps a week or two, he engaged the son with great earnestness. He was reflective now. The son was becoming aware of the looming abyss ahead into which his father would fall and they both would separate, one, into the past with the ancients, the other into the future, with no one to look to for approval.

He was on his way to work when the car phone, which was as big as a shoebox, rang. The mother told him to come back immediately, the father had said he was dying. When he got back the father had rallied a bit, but he'd had a fright. Earnestly he said to his son, 'Tell the priest I don't want any bullshit over me when I'm gone. I can't stand that stuff. If I thought there was going to be nothing in Heaven except popes, cardinals, bishops and priests, I think I'd just as soon be in the other place.'

Though the son laughed, he felt a pang of guilt and wondered if maybe he had been too dogmatic in their conversations about religion and beliefs. Had he stripped his father of his mixture of Christian and pagan comforts which were the make-up of the old-fashioned Irish Catholic? Was he now discarding them all, dumping them as if they were junk, just as he arrived in front of the Avenue of Light? The son alerted the family of his descent to this landing stage on his outward journey. He was still very alert. He was rummaging amongst his collection of stories for something transcendent, something insightful and eternal, some silver thread of connection which would make sure that connection would remain, after he had crossed over and that all would not be undone.

Around this time, the son came across a handwritten original anecdotal history of the parish. It had been signed by the author some fifty-four years ago. What he read, however, he hadn't bargained for. He wondered how he would tell the father and decided to let the writing do the talking so to speak.

The manuscript had a description of the first local parish church and its first pastor during Penal times. Though physically fading, his eyes had that searing brightness of alertness as the son read aloud to him.

'The first sermon he preached in the chapel was often conned over by the old people in the early days. This sermon was relative to a woman who lived in Toberboy . . . She was one of those who kept a school of witchcraft. . .'

The father was very focused.

'She pretended that she was able to divine future events and by her enchantments she used to set about curing diseases in cattle...'

'But when he got the people in front of him in that dear old thatched chapel, he, from the altar steps, set about dispelling their superstitious errors. He denounced the Witch of Toberboy, in all the moods and tenses . . .'

The words rang in their ears, 'The Witch of Toberboy', 'The Witch of Toberboy' . . . 'The Witch of Toberboy' . . .

They simply could not believe it.

Here it was, written down fifty years before the son's home-help had told him of the enchantments she had witnessed in that very spot – her place. They still couldn't believe it. The father's gaze was altogether taken by the son's reaction.

'What do you think?' he asked his father.

The wonder of it took them.

'Gor,' said the father, breaking the silence. 'It's all very strange'.

They read a bit more about how the Priest brought her nefarious career to an end but not before she'd had her revenge.

''Tis said the mare fell dead under him as he was passing on a sick call, at the quarry hole, at the end of the lane going over to Toberboy and for this the old woman chuckled at her power of revenge.'

Not unlike the Druids and St. Patrick.

'I remember a woman being killed down there by a butt from a ram in the field opposite,' the father said in a matter-of-fact fashion.

It didn't take a shake out of him. Not alone that – he seemed very comfortable with it, it almost seemed to steady him, to reinforce him emotionally in his own story.

How hard it must have been for the father looking at the son as he was slowly dying. He must have been wondering whether he had told him all he wanted to tell him or maybe he couldn't, because he thought he might frighten him, or simply he wouldn't believe him because of his education, perhaps so much at variance with the father's acquired wisdom.

Shortly before he died, the son called in home one evening to see him. He had fought off the last bout of pneumonia but it had taken its toll. When he walked in, the son looked at him and instantly knew something was amiss. 'Did Kent come with the horses yet?' he said.

He was doting. He was back in his youth. And then, the heartbreak, 'Come on,' he said to the son longingly, 'we'll go home.' Over the next two days, the family started to gather around him as he slipped in and out of a deep slumber. He waited there at that spot until a brother came home from England next morning.

In mid-afternoon on the second day, in the middle of the third decade of the rosary, he unmoored his boat. He filled his lungs like a sail that billowed lightly from a phantom breeze for the last time. He exhaled, gently pushing forward the last few inches on the silent pool of life. In the presence of all his family, he nailed his becalmed sheet to the mast. The son went quiet as the father glided over the precipice, leaving his corpse and family behind.

His was a princely departure for a new home and though the tears coursed down the son's face, the silver trace they left was the real silver thread – the vacuum left behind would be filled by the son's opportunities inherited from him and the memory of him and his ways and demeanour would inspire the son to emulate all that he had seen in him that was good.

At Mass the following morning he brought all of his young family to say goodbye to their grandfather one by one in their own little way. Leacy's five-year-old daughter looked at her grandfather's coffin taking it all in and then asked her mother, 'Did they put the Bovril in with Grandad?'

His words came back, 'We live for them so that they can live for us'.

9.

The Whole Truth

It was a simple enough case. The Hi-ace van that had been sold as new had clearly been fundamentally damaged when Paddy Cash bought it. He sold carpets for a living, typical of many in the Travelling community. His living was now threatened because of the poor performance of 'the vehicle' as the proceedings described his van.

'When you buy a vehicle new and you're not in the trade then you buy as a consumer. When you buy a vehicle as a consumer, there is a presumption that a later discovered defect in the goods purchased was there at the time of purchase and entitles the consumer to full satisfaction.' That was Leacy's initial letter to the Motor Company, for his client Paddy, and that had been four years ago.

'It won't be on for at least an hour Paddy, so go and get yourself a cup "a tae"', said Leacy.

He hung around to leave himself available to the approach of a calculated conversation by his opponents of mohair-suited sales directors with attendant secondary 'wigs', keeping an eye on the developments.

He returned and watched with contrived nonchalance to see if the motor company might make an approach. Paddy went for the 'tae'. When he was gone, Leacy sat there musing to himself at the brass neck and barefaced cheek of the motor company in the manner they falsely played the system out to the last. Well, they would not get away lightly today, he would see to that. Every last shilling, penny, farthing, brass nail and washer that could be exacted from them, would be, or else, they would face the wrath of the Right Honourable Judge Sean P. McDonagh S.C.

They had their own out-of-town solicitor with them. 'A rale cute arse Cork hoor,' Leacy thought to himself. Thought the poor auld Traveller couldn't afford the four-year delay. Thought he'd crumble because he wouldn't have the money. 'We have become so powerful and mighty in our ways. We learned well from our former "masters"', Leacy thought to himself. He thought maybe he'd have time for a cup of coffee himself but as the thought was forming in his head, Paddy was back almost as soon as he had left. He looked annoyed.

'They wouldn't give me a cup a' tae.'

Leacy looked at him with surprise. 'What do you mean?'

'I means they wouldn't give me a cup a' tae because I'm a Traveller.'

The veins in Leacy's neck became bulbous. 'We'll see about that,' he said, the anger rising in him. 'Come on with me.' They headed down the road the one hundred and fifty yards to The Wig and Gown Tavern. Leacy confronted the proprietor: 'Why won't you give this decent man, a client of mine, a cup of tea?'

'We don't serve Travellers. If you are having a cup of tea with him I'll serve him.'

'That's completely beside the point. You can't discriminate on that basis. He's entitled to a cup of tea. This is a licensed premises open to the public. You can't have discrimination on the grounds of his ethnic class.'

'Well I'm not serving him.'

'In that case I'll have to call the Guards.'

As he was about to storm out from the public house, behind a screen in a snug in the corner of the pub, a tall gentleman stood up. He had a head of hair, greased backwards, as if railway tracks were forming the texture of his hair. He grinned at Leacy. 'He has the right to refuse, you know.'

Leacy was stopped in his tracks at the surprise intervention.

'He doesn't, you know,' Leacy involuntarily answered.

'Oh yes, he does,' came the reply.

'Oh Mr. Hanrahan,' said the lawyer stung by the intrusion, but now recognising the grease ball.

'Yes, indeed, Mr. Leacy, and I'm a proprietor myself and I make it my business to know the law.'

'Well you have it wrong this time,' retorted Leacy as he turned with a vengeance to exit the establishment.

He went back up to the court determined not to be distracted from business by the incident that had occurred. Leacy was still fuming and Paddy was saying, 'Oh sure what matter? Oh sure what matter? That's what happens all the time.'

Leacy well knew the social prejudice and how deep-seated it was against the Travellers, particularly when it came to licensed premises. He argued many times with licensees and publicans about it, and indeed many others. Travellers were easily recognised by several mannerisms, often and not least, their accent and demeanour. And the prejudices would be lumped together: 'They smell.' 'They're a shower of knackers.' 'They'd lift anything. Take the sight out of your eye.'

Leacy had one argument for them all. 'You know they said the same about the Irish in both America and England: 'No Blacks, no dogs, no Irish'. The notices were put up outside of boarding houses.'

He cooled down little by little. Suddenly he was approached by his cute arse Cork colleague to know if they were interested in discussions. Leacy was in the humour to deal with him now. 'Give us what we're looking for, the amount is stated in black and white. If you've got something to say, say it, or else face the wrath of the court.'

'Loss of earnings was never claimed,' said the Corkman ignoring the curt remark.

'Have the argument in front of the Judge. You have your option, take it or leave it.'

He went back to the motor company for instructions. Leacy waited.

All of this was taking place out of earshot of Paddy. Eventually Leacy was approached and offered the full value of the vehicle and costs.

Paddy's foxy head of curls beamed into a broad smile.

'What about your expenses?' he asked Leacy.

'Oh they'll pay me as well.'

Case done and dusted. The case settled and Paddy walked out of the court one happy man. They went their separate ways and Leacy went to the Garda station to complain about the way Paddy had been treated in the public house. The Garda sergeant was unsympathetic. 'No complaint,' said the Sergeant. 'I can't do anything without a formal complaint.'

'Very well then, I'll get my client. But I believe you have a public duty to prevent the incitement to hatred to which my client was publicly subjected.'

'Nobody knows the law better than you Mr. Leacy. Take that argument to court if you like – but the Guards don't have to.'

As the client was not present, Leacy was unable to pursue the matter there and then and he left the town with a bad taste in his mouth notwithstanding his success in court. He'd work out his frustrations on the hurling field that evening.

As luck would have it, there was a league match on. It was not too keenly contested. These were bouts and encounters early in the year before the championship started. Coming off the pitch, a 'settled Traveller', Miley Doran, called him. 'Heard you had a great win in Wexford today against the motor company?' In the Traveller grapevine word travelled fast. 'Paddy'd be a first cousin of mine.' 'Faith sure he would,' thought Leacy to himself. They discussed the case and in the nature of idle conversation drifted into the refusal by The Wig and Gown tavern to serve Paddy a cup of tea.

'Happens all the time,' said Miley. 'It happened to two cousins of mine last week in the Ritz Ballroom in town. No reason at all only because they were Travellers they were refused. Two of the grandest girls, Lord Jaysus. 'Twould make your blood boil at times, but you put up with it. There's nothing we can do about it.'

'Oh bedad there is,' said Leacy. 'The law that's there now is not the same as the old law.' The conversation deepened. The cleverness of the travelling man who survives on his wits and who has the ability to listen with intensity became manifest. He sat there in the seat of his car, asking question after question.

'Send them down to me,' said Leacy. 'We'll see what we can do.'

Leacy's vision of the world was that of an idealist.

Kathleen and Bridget Doran kept their appointment with Leacy.

They were what were known as 'stunners'. Elegant, graceful, beautiful.

Leacy could hardly believe his luck. Perfect, for the presentation of a socially unjust case that middle-class judges might comprehend. Nothing brattish here. Nothing common. These two girls were 'head turners' wherever they might go. Decent, polite, mannerly. Leacy had known their families from previous football and hurling encounters and knew this to be the case in any event.

The girls relayed their tale of how they had gone to the Ritz and had been refused not once but several times. On one occasion, one of the girls' boyfriends had been admitted – she was excluded. Her embarrassment was great. One could only imagine the shame she felt. She and a boy whom she was hoping to date were rudely, uncaringly and ignorantly separated. On another occasion, they were let in, and friends of theirs were not allowed in. The thing that grabbed Leacy's interest was that the proprietor was none other than Hanrahan who had stuck his nose in, uninvited, on the morning of Paddy Cash's case with the motor company, claiming the Licensee had the right to refuse whomever he wished. Now he would be put to the test.

Leacy told the girls they could object to the renewal of his licence on the grounds that he wasn't a fit person to hold one because his actions could be considered as an incitement to hatred, a fairly recent law that had been enacted which had come from Europe. It hadn't been tested, but a couple of lawyers had been discussing the possibility. Here was a perfect opportunity to strike a blow for the right of a person to be considered on their own merits and own behaviour, otherwise the bad behaviour of a few would allow the rest to be judged as people of bad faith when they might well be acting in good faith. Everyone is entitled to their opportunity to believe as they think. It's only their behaviour should be judged.

The objection was filed and the case appeared in the District Court in front of Judge Wesley Cooper. Leacy groaned to himself. They couldn't have got a worse possible draw. Pompous, arrogant, self-conceited, right-wing – an uppercrust snob.

The case was opened to him by Leacy. He informed the Judge how the girls had presented themselves at the ballroom separately and together notwithstanding they had been refused several times previously.

'Do I detect a campaign Mr. Murphy?' said the Judge to the ballroom proprietor's solicitor, ignoring Leacy completely.

'I beg your pardon,' said Murphy.

'This seems to me like felon-setting,' said the Judge.

Pat Murphy, the solicitor for Hanrahan's dance hall, beamed. He could see he was home and dry before the evidence was even given. Leacy steadied himself. He was going to have to be brave.

He folded his arms and he said directly and evenly to the Judge, 'I hesitate to interrupt your flow, Judge – but do I detect an attitude?'

There was an audible gasp in court at the challenge that was put out. Leacy was directly challenging the Judge's behaviour. A judge is not entitled to come to a view until the evidence is heard. It reveals prejudice. Everybody is entitled to a fair trial.

Startled for a moment, the Judge recovered himself and stared down at the impudent lawyer and said, 'This is an outrage.' He paused for a moment then he went on with greater conviction, 'This is a contempt of court.' He looked away from Leacy who was still holding the line, and then with a flourish of his pen across his judge's book, and with a reddening face he barked, 'I know what I'm going to do. I know what I'm going to do. I'm going to disbar myself from hearing this case.' Murphy was crestfallen.

Leprechauns were jumping with glee inside of Leacy; he made a rather stiff bow to the court and solemnly responded, 'I respectfully agree.' The Judge was furious. His eyes revealed it as he declared, 'Adjourned for mention to the next court.'

When they came outside, the girls were in a whirl. The experience of going into court had been a daunting one for them. Now they didn't know what had happened. 'You're going to get a fair crack of the whip before another judge. If the case had gone ahead in front of that clown, you would have lost,' Leacy rather intemperately told them. They still would have their day in court. Now there was some chance they might get a fair hearing.

It was the month of December before the case was heard. The case was in front of Cody, a man noted for his deference, politeness, his compassion and sense of fair play. Pat Murphy, solicitor for Hanrahan, approached Leacy before the case, to see whether the girls would withdraw their objection if they were allowed into future dances.

'So, instead of doing it to my two clients, he can do it to others as he's been doing?' said Leacy. 'Oh if that's the way let's get on with it,' sulked Murphy.

Kathleen was nervous taking the oath but she quickly settled down when asked what her experience at the nightclub had been. Apparently, in the previous year an undertaking had been given by Hanrahan to the court, that the premises would be open to members of the Travelling community. Kathleen had attended and discovered that a security man had taken photographs of her and her friends. Then some weeks later a doorman challenged her that she wasn't a regular. Given no reason for the refusal, she went straight to the Guards. On her return with the Guards, she was let in, but a relative with her was denied entry. The security man had said, 'You're lucky to get in. It's a pity the law doesn't change the other way.' She had been refused again later in the summer. Bridget told of similar tales.

They were stopped again during the Christmas period. They asked why they were being refused and were informed that they did not have to give a reason for the exclusion. This rang a bell. It was the same opinion voiced by Hanrahan at The Wig and Gown Tavern when Paddy Cash was refused the tea. Hanrahan had volunteered that the proprietor had the right to refuse entry or service by a licensee. Kathleen continued that her boyfriend, whom she was to meet at the disco, had been allowed in but that she couldn't get in to see him. She was turned away, she said, and felt very ashamed and embarrassed.

Murphy cleverly got from both of them that members of the Travelling community had been allowed in on that night. He then suggested to them that they had been barred because they had been spilling drinks previously, which they both denied. Immediately, Leacy leaped to his feet and objected at the line of cross-examination. This had never once been put to either of his clients ever before. The wrangle between the lawyers that took place tried the patience of the decent Judge who overruled Leacy, and said the girls should be allowed to answer the question. With triumphant glee, having won his point, the conceited Murphy moved to press home his advantage. 'Isn't it true you were barred for spilling your drinks?' he impatiently demanded.

The court held its breath. Bridget moved uncomfortably in the witness box. She looked away from Murphy. She turned her attention directly to the District Judge and said,

'But none of us drink.'

The courtroom spontaneously sniggered at the devastating reply Bridget had delivered to Murphy with such innocent candour. The District Judge betrayed a hint of bemused reaction and was unable to resist inquiring, 'Well, Mr. Murphy?' A stunned Murphy retrieved his composure by shuffling his papers with a, 'Yes indeed, Judge'. Shuffled his papers again and then rather sheepishly, 'They may not necessarily have been your drinks.'

To which Bridget calmly replied,

'We spilled nobody's drink.'

Leacy had to cool himself down. Hanrahan was the next witness.

Hanrahan gave such a sweet performance in the witness box. Yes, he had indeed barred the girls for spilling drinks. He had spoken to them personally, referring to the copious notes on observations he had made about the event. Leacy wanted to know why these allegations of misbehaviour were being raised that day in court for the first time. The witness glibly replied:

'I probably had not mentioned it to Mr. Murphy, my solicitor.'

The case was going to drag. The Judge looked at both lawyers and said:

'Perhaps the parties might like to take a break, whilst we get on with the rest of the court's business in order to see if they can reach an accommodation.'

After an-hour-and-a-half, Hanrahan was back in the box. No resolution. He indicated to the Judge that he was prepared to admit the objectors to the dance hall provided they did not seek to have anyone else who was barred, admitted. He also wanted an undertaking from them that they would behave.

Then they were back to the spilling of drinks business again. One saying it happened. The others saying it didn't. Then Hanrahan realised he was not doing badly at all. He got cocky. He gave a glowing account of the professional manner in which his establishment was run. Matters of this nature would have been discussed at a weekly meeting of the nightclub staff and would have been recorded in his notes. Records were kept, one detailing accidents and other notes were kept in a diary. Leacy then asked him:

'What sort of a diary?'

'An ordinary type of diary.'

'What size was it?'

'An ordinary type – the type you'd buy in a shop.'

'You can buy several types in the shops, big ones for desks, day-by-day diaries, small diaries, some embossed with say for instance 'cats'; what sort of diary was this?'

'One that you could put in your pocket.'

'What colour was it?'

'Black.'

'Where is this diary kept?'

'It's kept on the premises at all times?'

'How far are the premises from this court?'

Hanrahan now saw where he was being led. It was too late for him to pull back.

The Judge interrupted,

'Mr. Hanrahan,' he said, 'I want to make something perfectly plain to you. If it is discovered by this court that you have unfairly excluded these girls from the public dance hall of which you are the licensee, without good reason, by good reason I mean they were drunk, disorderly, or misbehaving or some such, if such is the case and it is found that you discriminated against them because of their being Travellers, this would suggest unfair discrimination and not reflect well of you. Now I want that diary retrieved and brought here, and in order to preserve you from the slightest hint of suspicion, I am ordering you to stay in court and have the diary retrieved and brought here, since the premises is only three hundred yards from this court. Do you understand me?'

An ashen-faced Hanrahan replied, 'Yes, your Honour.' He had been watching too many American courtroom movies where they called the judge 'Your Honour.'

'You may call me Judge,' said the Judge.

'Yes, Judge.' said Hanrahan.

'I will allow a half-hour for the retrieval of the diary. When it is brought back into court I want to be informed immediately, Mr. Leacy.'

'Yes, Judge,' said Leacy, coming back to life a bit.

Leacy's gaze briefly met Hanrahan's as he came around the corner of the witness box. Hanrahan reacted as if he had just accidentally swallowed vinegar. Hanrahan, Murphy and Cogley, the manager of the Ritz, went into a hunched consultation at the back of the courtroom. A local solicitor, Mernagh, gave Leacy a puck, 'Jaysus, this is better than television.'

'Have you got another case coming up today?' Leacy asked Mernagh.

'No fucking way am I leavin' here 'til I see what happens to Hanrahan,' sniggered Mernagh.

Leacy got up, went over to the two girls, and brought them outside.

Immediately, the fresh air was polluted with nervous gusts of exhaled and un-inhaled cigarette smoke billowing in clouds and giggles, 'What did he say? What did he say?' the two girls asked nervously.

Though they knew well what was happening, they wanted the matter confirmed, underlined, chopped up, cut up and sliced so that they could believe, savour and relish what was happening. They wanted every morsel squeezed, sucked, drooled over, belched over and then another morsel would receive the same treatment. 'Don't count your chickens before they're hatched!' cautioned Leacy.

'Why, d'you not think we'll win?' asked a shocked Bridget.

'That's a slippery hoor, that fella,' said Leacy 'You'd never know what he'd try but he'll try something.'

Cogley, the manager of the Ritz, walked towards the courthouse. The girls 'topped' their cigarettes, and quickly, scurried back inside the courthouse away from the December cold.

The other cases were proceeding in front of the Judge when the door opened to allow in Mr. Cogley.

'Mr. Murphy,' asked the Judge, interrupting the case he was hearing,

'Is that the manager of the licensed premises I see?'

'It is, Judge,' said Murphy.

'Has he got the diary?'

'He has, Judge'

'Hand it in to the Registrar, please.'

Solicitor Murphy immediately handed the diary to the Court Registrar.

The Judge continued with the case in hand and Leacy eyed Hanrahan and company. Their backs were bent and their three heads were down like three hens with their tails cocked up as if their heads were pecking into a small tin can of feed. Occasionally one would come up for air, and the other two would draw back, then one would lean forward to say something, and the other two, because they were whispering, would draw hens' heads back in, like broilers coming back to the feeder for the meal. The case at hearing finished.

The Registrar called Hanrahan's application for a dance licence once more and he returned to the witness box. The Judge instructed the registrar to hand the diary to Hanrahan.

'Your witness, Mr. Leacy,' said the Judge.

'Is that the diary to which you referred?'

Hanrahan looked at it.

'Yes,' he said, parsimoniously.

'Can you hand it into the Judge, please?'

Hanrahan handed the diary into the Judge. While the Judge was flicking through it, Leacy noticed that it was a small pocket diary, hardly one which would contain copious notes. He felt his temper rise at the stunt Hanrahan was trying to pull.

The Judge looked down at him and said, 'Have you seen this Mr. Leacy – there appear to be very few entries in it.'

'No Judge, I have not,' he replied.

The diary was handed down to Leacy.

There were a couple of nondescript entries in the diary for the rest of the year, which were of no relevance. They certainly didn't refer to ballroom management. However, there was an entry for January 16th, which read 'Two Travellers barred'. Leacy thought to himself, 'The utter gobshites.' It was obvious the entry had been made within the last hour. In their hurry to mend their hand, they proved the case against themselves. They had barred two Travellers! They were so arrogant they forgot that it was precisely because they had barred two people because they were Travellers that they were in trouble. This entry, entered in the fashion it was, proved the discrimination, by their own hand. The girls had been barred because they were Travellers.

Leacy handed the diary to Hanrahan.

'It seems you were right, Mr. Hanrahan,' said Leacy.

Everybody looked up in surprise, and most of all Hanrahan.

'You did have an entry in the diary which indicated that you barred two Travellers, after all.'

'I did. I did,' said Hanrahan, 'I told you I did.'

'No,' said Leacy 'I told you that. You barred two people because they were Travellers and it appears that's what the diary reveals. You said you stopped two girls because they were drunk and knocking over drinks.'

Before Hanrahan could reply, the Judge intervened, 'Whose handwriting is this in the diary?'

Hanrahan hung his head. 'The manager's,' replied Hanrahan.

'You mean the man who got the diary for you to-day?'

'Yes, Judge,' said Hanrahan.

'I want to see him in the witness box,' said the Judge.

Murphy called the manager of the Ritz, Mr. Cogley, who informed the court that on the night in question the two girls wanted to know why their companion was barred from coming in. He said they followed him around demanding to know this. He told them it was his recollection that they wanted him to let in a man who had kicked one of the bouncers in the leg the previous week. Murphy sat down. Maybe he was regaining a bit of lost ground. Leacy stood up.

'Do you find this case a little confusing?' asked Leacy.

'What do you mean?' asked Cogley.

'Do you find it difficult to remember all of the facts? I'm asking you if perhaps you're not confused about some of your recollections. Perhaps you made the entry in the diary so that you would not forget. Maybe it was written in much later, like – maybe today when you were sent to fetch it?'

The manager rounded on Leacy, 'I most certainly did not. It was written in on the night in question. I do accept it's written in my handwriting but it was made on the night probably after Hanrahan shouted in to me through the office window that he had barred the Travellers.'

'And you instantly wrote it down in the diary?' said Leacy.

There was a snigger in court.

Cogley's reply of 'Yes' was barely audible.

'And why did you not put down their names?'

'They weren't asked for their names'.

'But you wrote down "Two Travellers barred". Why didn't you write down "Two Traveller girls barred"?'

'Because the person they were trying to bring in was a man,' replied the Manager, 'and I wasn't sure if all three were being barred'.

'In fact,' said Leacy, 'if you had been listening to the evidence, you would have discovered that the person they wanted to bring in was a lady!'

The manager of the Ritz was stuck, he moved his lips like goldfish do when staring out of a bowl. He was unable to unstick himself.

'I've heard enough,' said the Judge.

The Judge remarked that he would need to be greatly persuaded that the licence should be renewed. He adjourned the matter to New Ross District Court on December 15th. In the meantime, he said that he expected the proprietor, Mr. Hanrahan to make a substantial gesture to an appropriate cause that Mr. Leacy's client would find acceptable. He also advised him to pay the legal costs of the two girls. It was a condition of the adjournment that the sisters would not be refused entry into the nightclub.

'Bejaysus Leacy, yer a hoor,' whispered Mernagh, covering his mouth with the back of his hand. The Judge was finished for the day and left the bench. Leacy and his clients were gone in a flash. The joy of the girls was beyond control. They smoked their lungs out. 'Let's go down to Rackard's,' they said. And down they went and giggled their way through bottles of Orange and Seven-up.

Over the following weeks, the solicitors entered into correspondence and an agreement was arrived at. A sum of £5,000 would be paid to the Travellers' Resource Centre, a sum of £2,500 would be paid to each of the girls and a sum of £2,000 would be paid to Leacy.

Anyone could have been forgiven for thinking that was where it would stop. The girls had won a major victory for themselves and their people. One of them, Sally Flynn, said, 'There's nobody knows how to travel like a Traveller does and nobody knows how to celebrate like a Tinker does.' They invited Leacy and the clergyman who had helped them though thick and thin and a local lady called Anne who backed their every cause and had helped them with their Resource Centre. Anne was over the moon with what the £5,000 'would do for them'.

The girls and their friends met Leacy, the Priest and Anne and went 'on the town' in Wexford. The first pub they went to was the one from which they had previously been barred. Then they went to an Italian restaurant where they had a superb meal. Then they went down the main street and into one of the celebrated pubs, where they had never before been allowed in. As they approached the steps, the Priest could hear one of the bouncers saying to the other, 'They're Travellers.' And the other one saying, 'They've a priest with them. That's a fucking solicitor as well.' The girls breezed by as the nicotine and smoke from the winter nightclub rushed out to meet them. They swanned in and up to the counter to buy more soft drinks for themselves and hard liquor and beer for the solicitor and priest.

By the time they got to the other end of the town, Leacy was in flying form. The Priest was singing, and Anne was in the best of good humour. They went up the steps into another nightclub from which they had previously been barred. The bouncer with the blonde head came forward to bar them once more, and then saw the Priest with Anne and Leacy coming behind. He recoiled. He knew Leacy. Stung by his disempowerment, the blonde bouncer waited until they had gone past. As Leacy was leaving the door he came up to him and tapped him on the shoulder and said, 'You're getting a bit hardy for this type of thing aren't you Leacy?'

Leacy turned around and through a half-drunken smile said, 'Ah Billy didn't you know – you're never too old to learn?' The girls nearly broke their hearts with the laughing. They knew Billy was being taught a lesson.

They danced until two o'clock. The proceedings were adjourned, with the remains of a bottle of whiskey and some lively rebel songs, to the flat of one of their friends. At half past five in the morning the Priest dragged Leacy in the back door of the local presbytery where he crashed out on a bed and didn't surface until half past twelve that day.

In the following week, Anne, the Priest and Leacy met. One of the girls had been unable to come out for the victory celebration and they wanted to have her included. The three would be available for some night next week to go to the local hotel and have a proper meal with her, just to let her feel included. The thoughtfulness was so great it could not be ignored. The three read the paper where the banner headline had been carried:

'Judge raps nightclub boss for turning away Travellers.'

Underneath the headline was a line which read: NIGHT CLUB COULD BE CLOSED DOWN OVER ALLEGED DISCRIMINATION.

The girls posted it up in the Resource Centre, Anne told Leacy.

'This will make some difference,' said the Priest. 'Maybe the message will get through.' Shrewdly, Leacy observed, 'It may get through to some, but there's nothing as deep-seated as bigotry.'

In the following week, they sat in the lounge of the hotel where they had just enjoyed a sumptuous meal. The proprietor, who lived in the establishment, was wandering through and looked to be a little the worse for wear. He invited himself into Leacy's company and started flattering him about the great solicitor he was. Leacy introduced him to everyone at the table, none of whom he knew, apart from Leacy.

'A great man entirely,' enthused the proprietor of the hotel where they had just dined.

Leacy could see he was going to become gushing and flattering.

'Not your ordinary solicitor you know,' he said ingratiatingly. 'Took them all on and won.'

'Not all of them,' interjected Leacy helplessly.

'Oh a great man. A great man entirely,' said the proprietor with inebriate emphasis.

And then came the clanger. 'Still there's one case I might be a hundred per cent against ye – a hundred per cent. D'ya remember that case ya had before Christmas with the two knackers up in Enniscorthy?'

Leacy froze. The girls looked ashen. Anne was aghast and the Priest low-ered his eyes. The two girls just stood up. Leacy stood up. 'Stay where you are, Jack,' said the two girls to Leacy, and then directly to the proprietor.

'Well mister, we left the best part of five hundred quid with you tonight. I don't suppose the rest of the pound notes in your till will have any trouble gettin' on with ours.' As well on as he was, the proprietor knew he'd put his foot in it, but he was unable to retrieve himself. The two girls walked out followed by Leacy, Anne and the Priest. Everything had been ruined. The girls started to shiver in the cold and were again smoking like chimneys. 'You had better go home girls, you'll get your death,' said Leacy. 'We'll talk tomorrow.'

The following day at half past eleven, Leacy received a phone call. It was from the proprietor of the hotel.

'Oh Jaysus, Jack. Oh Jaysus, Jack. What can I ever do to make it up to those two girls? What can I do?' Leacy smiled to himself. Let the hoor sweat. Maybe, 'twould get through. Leacy said he would enquire.

He spoke to the girls, Anne and the Priest. 'I don't want any of his ould money,' said Kathleen. 'Neither do I, 'said Bridget.

'Tell me,' said Leacy, 'where would you hit the begrudgers if you wanted to hurt them the most?'

The two girls laughed at him and almost in unison said, 'In the pocket.'

'Exactly,' said Leacy.

'We still don't want any of his ould money,' said the two girls.

'Well I think he should make a donation of £5,000 to the Travellers' Resource Centre, just to show how remorseful he is,' said Leacy. They all thought it was a great idea.

And pay it he did.

'Maybe the message is gettin' through,' said the Priest.

'I don't know about the message,' said Leacy. 'But I do know when something starts to cost money it doesn't take too long before you start to look to see what's causing it.'

The girls were never barred anywhere after that.

10.

The Utmost Good Faith

He shuffled along the beach towards the village embracing the sea breeze of May, picking up a stone here and there, lobbing it into the water to hear it splash and perhaps rise the seagulls. It was too early yet for any day-trippers or tourists. When he was young, the villagers used to call them 'bathers'. But that was a long time ago now.

He was still shaking from the experience, his first one, of life on the dole. He had drawn his Social Welfare cheque a month prior. He waited until all the queue had departed from the Garda station before he called, in the afternoon, on his own.

He felt embarrassed in front of the Guards. As a lawyer, he had cross-examined them in court on many previous occasions when he had been practising.

Bank interest was at 25 percent. Telephone bills were a fifth of his expenses. A partner robbed him of £80,000. The Revenue wanted £125,000. He tried to trade his way out of it. He tried so very hard. He worked later; he took on more work; he employed more people to generate more income; he cut down on expenses; he took no holidays; he kept his wardrobe and that of his family to a minimum; respectable smartness as opposed to current fashion.

But hard as he tried, he was unable to catch up. He knew this was known as the Law of Diminishing Returns. If you tried to do more, it cost more; if you work faster, quality suffers and in the end, business gets affected and the return diminishes. In a word, he was broke.

He resigned his practising certificate. He had been a priest before he became a solicitor. Then he married. Then his marriage failed. Now he was a failed priest, a failed husband and a failed solicitor. In the village they said he was a bankrupt who could provide little for his wife and child.

The seagulls broke from their feeding flock at the water's edge. The little stream spread itself wide on the strand carrying the drained bog water from the land, together with scraps of carrion, on which the gulls feasted, from the hinterland to the ocean. The wind was from the south-west, and the waves, some at least, wore white mufflers, heralding a gale. It cleared his head a little. The Angelus bell rang from the village chapel. It reverberated the angry ache of iron down over the rooftops covering the village under its mantle of pronouncement of noon and the traditional call to prayer and reflection.

'Angelus Domini nuntiavit Mariae,' he intoned to himself in Latin and stopped almost immediately. He stared out to sea and stood defiantly against the gathering squall. He would see how long he could stand here before something would happen. The pain in his mind was numbing. The stiffening wind provoked no feeling in him. In this nothingness, a greater good would come to him and flood him. If he stood here long enough, something would happen and he would patiently outwait God until it did. The Angelus bell stopped. A moody sky spat at him. Rain. God had sent him rain. It gave him the excuse he wanted. He would go to the pub and spend the £20 left from the dole.

He sat by the fire which the establishment maintained because of the ambivalence of the weather. He took a sip of his double whiskey. It made him gasp a wince. Feeling was returning. He put in the smallest drop of water to bring out the flavour. At Mass, the water and wine were mingled to symbolise the impending incredulous mystery. Interpretation was the basis of perception, or was perception the basis of interpretation? Like the drop of water getting lost in the wine and then bringing out the flavour. How symbolic. Water lost in wine. Man lost in God. And here he was, lost in a mess and now hoping to lose himself in drink. Was Man's purpose to bring out the flavour of the world?

What a mess, what a mess. He stared at the smoky reddening coals. The wind was rising steadily and draughting the coils of smoke from the bottom of the fire as if it was draining the grate up the chimney. A stick sparked and crackled. He took another sip in order to urge on the anticipated mellowness. He called for a pint of Guinness.

He stared back into the hypnotic fire. The meandering mind muddled on. The Jesuits had been good to him. He had got his Bachelor of Arts degree and had taught in New York while studying for his Masters. He liked the States. He fell in love with one of the female staff members. It was four years before he decided to leave the priesthood. He knew he was attracted to her before he left the priesthood. He convinced himself it was not on that account he had abandoned Holy Orders. It was the falseness. He was a red-blooded young man and the celibate life was false. It had been created historically for reasons of preserving power. It had been canvassed as mortification of the flesh.

The seminary taught him that there were four ways to preserve 'the grace' of celibacy: Humility, Mortification, Devotion to the State of the Priesthood and Love of God. The seminary said these disciplines required constant vigilance, constant practise and constant prayer. Nobody said anything about masturbation. He relied a lot on masturbation to relieve the tensions this process created. Grace does not jump to the command of man. How much of what he had been taught was bullshit. How much of it was true? How much of it was just a control mechanism? How much of it contained what the 'Jesus Man' had said? He found it difficult to call Jesus Christ by his name because of the way his belief in what he had stood for, had been used by those in authority to maintain their grip.

The authorities laicised him. But they pointed out to him, 'once a priest, a priest forever.' It did not follow automatically that you could marry when laicisation was permitted. That would require a separate application. Two years later, Marianne and he married in a civil ceremony. He came back to Ireland a year later, after his mother had died. She had been a widow for eighteen years.

They had one child who became the lasting meaning to his life. Ironically, after all they had been through with the Church, they called the child Helen – the mother of Constantine, the Roman Emperor who gave Christians their freedom.

Caesar achieved the expansion of the Empire by bloody conquest, followed immediately by peace treaties which the terrified victims accepted – Roman governance. It was known as Pax Romanum – the Peace of Rome. Constantine's political fortunes had been waning. In a stroke of genius, he claimed Divine inspiration through a vision of the Cross immediately before he defeated Maximillian for the crown of Caesar at the battle of the Milvian Bridge. He now achieved obedience through the Peace of Christ which replaced the Peace of Rome and became known as Pax Christi. It too was accompanied by Roman governance and organisation.

That's what he had been taught and that's what he had believed his faith to be. This was what he had sacrificed his life for – the utmost sacrifice for God in order to promote the love of Christ. After all, it was based on the Truth of the Gospel and the sincerity of its promoters. That's what he had believed even after he had left the priesthood.

But the Child Abuse scandals were just now breaking and he had stopped going to Mass. How could the Pope, the Curia and the bishops hide paedophiles in their ranks and at the same time outlaw contraception and abortion? Monsters had used children as innocent as Helen to indulge their sexual cravings. Who created these monsters? How did this happen?

The answer he believed lay in the answer to a different question: 'Who created our sexual nature and who brought in rules to frustrate it?'

He sipped his pint and let his thoughts drift further. What happened to these, at first, well-intentioned men? The Government had set up commissions for so-called child protection and for treatment of the perpetrators. If the engine of the car wouldn't work, why did they insist on filling it with petrol?

The poor little children, he thought – and then he remembered his own.

Helen became more than the 'apple of his eye'. She became iconic. When she contracted the measles, she hovered at death's door amidst medical rumblings of 'Rubella.' Marianne had stayed in hospital with her.

He reminisced, as he sipped, on that awful time and the deal he had made with God.

In desperation and at his lowest point, he drew on his limited reserves of Faith and knelt at the end of his bed. In his empty room, in his empty house, he shook his fist at Heaven, saying, 'Take my practice, take my marriage, take my house, take my reputation, but leave the child.' He beseeched in prostrate supplication, 'Take every damned thing I have but leave my child.' He had sobbed and sobbed. He had pleaded nakedly with God for the life and health of his only daughter. His emotions were at their barest. He had been at the utmost point of physical, emotional and spiritual traumatic confluence. His eyes watered at the memory. But the bargain had been kept, she had lived – and now payment was being taken, he was being taken, he was losing it all.

A voice in the pub intermingled with his day dreaming, 'It's paid for'. There was a pause. 'It's paid for,' the voice said again. The solicitor looked up from the fire as the barman placed the pint in front of him. The reality of the pub displaced his reminiscences. It took a moment for things to register. The barman pointed to James Lannigan, farmer and the benefactor of his pint, who waved to him as he disappeared out through the door of the lower bar.

He smiled to himself as he remembered Lannigan's case.

Lannigan had cause to be grateful. The father had died leaving him and his brother to fight over the farm. Lannigan, who was reputedly a member of the IRA, agreed to buy out his brother. Some felt 'pressure had been applied' but no one dared to say. If he was in the IRA, it didn't show. Lannigan had difficulty raising the money as the economy was struggling and interest rates had, in some cases, gone as high as 26 per cent per annum.

Another sip of the whiskey and his reminiscence continued – well he knew about borrowing. He had borrowed heavily to start his practice. He was now paying the price too. The bloody banks. They used to say a bank would only give you an umbrella when it wasn't raining.

They were so like the Church – monolithic and untouchable. They drifted with public opinion herdlike when it suited so as not to become isolated. Then they got the organisation to think and then work as a group and steer matters the way they believed they should. Sociologists called this 'Herding and Group think.'

Lannigan's farmhouse and shed burned down the night before the sale was supposed to close. He would never forget it. It was the day after Helen had come home from hospital with a clean bill of health. Had he the energy to tackle this difficult case in the wake of the good news on his daughter? The insurance company suspected the fire was a fraud to get money. They repudiated the policy. They didn't say they were suspicious of an IRA 'obligement'. They sifted through the proposal form that Lannigan had signed and found their reason. 'Material nondisclosure of an essential fact, a breach of the principle of utmost good faith'. This was the obligation to disclose all material risks truthfully and sincerely – like in a good confession – at the time the agreement for the policy was entered into. It was known in Latin as the principle of Uberrime Fides. The utmost good faith. And if you did not do it in good faith, you had a bad confession (he laughed to himself) – and your policy became void and, he sniggered quietly – they then would literally let you go to Hell!

The roof was repaired. However, the insurance company said emphatically they were not informed. There was an absolute binding legal duty to disclose everything. A mistake of omission was no excuse, accidental or otherwise. The courts applied the rule strictly and the insurers knew this.

'But the Broker knew,' said Lannigan. That was no use he had advised because the Broker was deemed to be Lannigan's agent at law.

'But Mr. Cartwright, the insurance inspector, from the insurance company filled out the proposal form for me when he called out. I told him there and then,' said Lannigan.

(Maybe they wouldn't be able to tell him to go to Hell after all!)

This was different. The insurance inspector was the insurance company. Could this be proved? Lannigan insisted he had told the insurance inspector, but the insurance company insisted he had not. A photocopy of the proposal form revealed that Lannigan had signed the form. The form asked if there had been repairs. Clear as day, the answer that Lannigan signed had indicated: 'None'. He had signed a document stating that there had been no repairs to the roof when clearly there had.

'He's a frigging liar. That wasn't there when I signed. What I signed was blank. They just don't want to pay,' swore Lannigan.

Lannigan's brother saw his opportunity and got a judgement against him for the amount of the purchase money for the farm with a view to having him evicted. Lannigan's only hope had been the insurance monies. This raised the insurance company's suspicions even higher. The brother procured a judgement preliminary to an application being made to the High Court to have him sent to prison for contempt for breach of the Court's Order that Lannigan pay his brother on foot of the judgement.

Leacy was enjoying his drink and his thoughts. Maybe he was not a complete failure after all. He ordered another pint.

Two fishermen came in and ordered two rums and blackcurrant, a large bottle and a pint. He opened a page of the paper and saw a heading:

'Bishop Calls for Review of Celibacy'.

He drank from his now fully black pint. The bishop was being honest he thought, but where would that get him except into trouble? The bishop has a paedophile cleric on his 'hands' and the story was only breaking. He had met the bishop once. The bishop was bright – but he did have problems. And Rome wouldn't wear this one. Celibacy be removed, me eye.

He remembered the rigmarole the Curia expected him to go through in order to marry Marianne. He baulked at being put through a process of semantic legalities. The Curia was not going to allow a stampede of their clergy out of the Ministry by permitting them to remarry once they got clear of their Orders. As often as not, an affair would have commenced whilst the applicant was in the priesthood. The Church had no notion of facilitating difficulties of this nature for itself. The goblins in the Curia did things at their own pace. They replied to letters and applications when it suited them. They were their own law. They were not interested in truth or good faith they were interested in making the law and they hid behind it. And when the law did not suit them, they changed the law to make it suit.

He took a gulp of whiskey and cooled it down with a few swallows of Guinness. The men at the counter stared silently at the mirror behind it.

The clock ticked. A turned-down radio played 'Don't Look Back in Anger'. He smiled at the irony. Now he was going through another process with another organisation founded on legalities. The Law Society and the Courts would have their way with him. He would have to attend meeting after meeting before they would decide his fate. The fault was his after all. He felt as if providence was telling him that one way or the other he would have to learn to live with laws, rules and regulations.

'There are doors, walls and windows,' he advised clients. 'You walk through doors, look through windows and the walls are there to protect you. If you get their functions mixed up, you end up in trouble. The law is that simple.' He had himself walked straight into a wall. He had misjudged where the door was. He had been unable to take his own advice.

'The young wan is making her Confirmation a' Sunday?' the fisherman with the pint addressed him.

The fisherman's information surprised him.

'She is, yeah,' he responded.

'Time flies,' said the Pint.

'Tempus fugit,' he involuntarily responded.

'Whass da?' asked the Pint inviting repetition.

'Ah, it's Latin for the same thing.'

'Latin?'

'That's right.'

Pause. Pause and stare.

'You used to be a priest,' said the Pint.

He hadn't intended getting into this. He knew from experience the simplest way was to play along, obligingly.

'A long time ago, too,' he replied.

'You did the right thing to 'lave,' approved the Pint.

'It's only a "hape" a bullshit anyhow,' said the Large Bottle.

'I must go for a leak lads anyhow, bullshit or not,' he laughed.

In the toilet he made up his mind to go back to the table, finish up his drink and go across the village to the hotel bar where he would have another drink before going back to the flat over the office where he now lived, and which he was trying to sell in order to pay his debts. The

Revenue had forced him into insolvency and he would do his best to come to a deal. But with interest rates as high as twenty-six per cent per annum, who wanted to buy?

In the hotel, Lannigan saw him. He came over to him at the table in the corner where he was sitting on his own. Even though it was daytime, the hotel lights were on. The painted-over embossed wallpaper glistened mildly under the wall-bracketed cupped electric lights.

'How are you?' enquired Lannigan.

He knew the enquiry was well-intended.

'Not great to tell you the truth.'

'Mind if I join you?'

Before the answer could be given, Lannigan was seated and had called Matt from behind the bar for a pint and two half ones.

Lannigan knew he was going through a hard time and told him that he was a good man who had helped many. Then as if there was affinity because of 'the big case' they had fought and because the story had become legend, Lannigan thought to raise his spirits with the memories of past glories. Leacy listened to the compliments and resolved not to become sentimental. Whiskey had that effect upon him. Lannigan wanted to tell the story to Matt of how he had been saved from jail on foot of the brother's judgement decree and how this man here had saved the farm for him. Matt left down the two whiskeys and the pint on the little table, lit a cigarette, and sat down with them. He mused to himself at the co-incidence of Lannigan's empathy with his earlier reminiscence.

Lannigan wanted to get him going, to get his mind off himself and his troubles, to try to draw him out. Maybe Lannigan was more sincere than he had believed. 'Actually, I had just been thinking about the case earlier,' he said.

'That feckin' insurance company. Christ, how you handled them – and caught them flat-foot.'

'Great minds, eh?' Lannigan said and laughed.

Lannigan told Matt he was sure the brother's case against him was going to put him in jail for contempt of court unless he came up with the purchase money, which he couldn't raise before the fire had started. 'Surely ta Jaysus I couldn't raise it afterwards. They wouldn't pay purely on a technicality. It was a lie. Made up it was. Go on tell him. You're better able to tell that stuff than I am,' said Lannigan.

He took a gulp from the whiskey and his pint and eyed Lannigan and Matt. He knew he would have to tell the story. He didn't mind. It had been a good case, but you had to be in form to tell a story like that. He slowly took more swallows from his pint.

He explained the case to Matt. Before an insurance policy would issue, an insurance form, called a proposal, had to be completed honestly and fully by a proposed insured. He repeated the requirement for scrupulous honesty in its completion as being a fundamental consideration to understanding the story. There could be no mistakes. It was expected that truth would be meticulously adhered to and they had a name for that.

'I'll never forget it,' said Lannigan to Matt,' 'the utmost good faith' they called it. Even if it was by accident something was left out, it didn't matter. Null and void says they. Null and void. But I knew me man here, Matt. I knew me man here. I'm sorry for interrupting you, go on.'

The whiskey had greased the wheels and the kick-start by Lannigan had excited his wit and his memory. It was just after his little daughter had been sick. He recalled being desperate about the case but he was so relieved about Helen not having the Rubella that he was able to give it all his energy and strength. He had believed Lannigan had told him the truth when he said he had told the insurance inspector about the repairs to the roof, but that the inspector had not written it down on the proposal form when he was told. At first, he was reluctant to believe the inspector had been deliberate in not writing it in. Maybe it was a question of sloppiness and the inspector had forgotten about it later when asked. Maybe the proposal form hadn't been sent in to head office by the inspector until after the fire. But most of all – and there was the rub – maybe the inspector filled it in incorrectly after the fire to avoid the insurance. Now here was the intrigue.

When he allowed his brain to imagine what might have been the case, he had a flash of inspiration. He had received a black and white photocopy of the proposal form from the insurance company when he first queried their refusal to insure. Maybe, just maybe, the original might reveal some gap or other which would reveal the form had been completed at different times. It was an outside chance but it was worth exploring.

Seventy-two hours before he was due to represent Lannigan in the High Court, he phoned Franklin, the solicitor for the insurance company, for permission to look at the original. By arrangement, he drove to the southern headquarters in Cork to examine it. When he read it, he could hardly believe his eyes, or Lannigan's luck. He had spotted something in the original proposal form that the black and white photocopy did not reveal. He telephoned Franklin and they arranged to meet next morning. A courier delivered the original proposal form from Cork to Dublin and the two solicitors met there at nine o'clock in Franklin's office. He told Franklin he had 'the goods' on the insurance inspector.

The Proposal form was divided into three parts – Public Liability, Employer's Liability and Fire Cover. The questions raised in each section had to be written in and signed by the insured. There was a place at the top of each section for each separate policy number to be filled in AFTER the proposal form was accepted by the insurance company.

Sure enough the policy numbers on each section had been written in by the inspector in his own hand in green biro at the top space marked at the top of each section and the answers to the section on fire were also written in green biro by the same hand. But the signature of Lannigan was in blue biro. And the answers to the questions in the first two sections was also in the inspector's hand but in blue biro as, again, so was Lannigan's signature. The green biro revealed the completion of answers to the fire section at the time the green biro was used to write in the official numbers for the policy when they were procured back in the office. The blue biro revealed the completion of the Employer's and Public Liability at the time of the blue-biro signature of Lannigan at his own premises when the insurance inspector called on the first occasion. The different colour of the biro ink had not been possible to detect in the black and white photocopy. And Lannigan had never been in the office. And therefore the fire section had been blank when he had signed it. What the inspector had written was not what Lannigan had told him.

It could have been written in after the fire, but he was inclined to give the inspector the benefit of the doubt on that. It didn't matter. The responsibility for the completion of the form had passed to the insurance company through the inspector once he had put pen to paper to answer the questions for Lannigan. Unwittingly, the inspector revealed the completion of the form had taken place in the office by filling in only the fire section with the green biro that he also used to write out the policy numbers. It had not been filled in while Lannigan was present.

Franklin told Leacy it wasn't that cut and dried but if he could make a saving for the insurance company, he would settle the matter. Leacy phoned Lannigan and told him the offer.

'Take hand and all, says I', Lannigan recounted.

Lannigan covered all of his expenses and the purchase price and had a little start-up fund in addition.

'What did I tell ya?' said Lannigan. 'A legal genius.'

'No doubt about it,' said Matt, 'best wan I heard yet. Calls for a drink on the house.'

Matt was entering into the spirit.

'The utmost good faith,' said Lannigan, 'and the two-faced hoors in complete and total bad faith.'

Matt poured a strong measure and two half ones.

'Down the hatch,' said Matt.

As they drained the dregs, the door opened and in came the two fishermen from the pub across the village. Matt went to serve them.

Lannigan looked away from the counter, smiled at him, and put his hand on his shoulder. He told him he was a good one, one of the few; he knew he'd be back bigger and stronger than ever. He told him to be careful. He heard that he had been hitting the hard stuff. Then he gulped his drink and was gone. As they bade farewell, he saw Lannigan hand some money to Matt and nod in his direction. Against the advice he had offered for taking the whiskey 'aisey', Lannigan was sponsoring a spraoi.

He was off again with his ruminations. How good was he really? Wasn't he a failure? A failed priest? A failed husband? A failed father? Wasn't there a pattern? He thought he was doing his best each time. He wasn't able for the 'two-facedness' of the Hierarchy. He eventually couldn't relate with Marianne. Being from the States, she was culturally different. Eventually, they ran out of common ground and understanding.

Had he been simply running away from his problems instead of standing his ground and fighting? His thoughts drifted on.

She had agreed not to take Helen back to the States where initially she had intended going after the break-up. However, as children are wont to do, Helen blamed him for the break-up and sided with her mother. It broke his heart. But what could you expect? There were stories of other women and he didn't deny them. He was lonely and he needed a companion from time to time. You couldn't expect a ten-year-old daughter to understand that. Maybe in time, but he doubted it.

The bank had refused to honour cheques and returned them. On the same day, he received a Petition for his bankruptcy. He certainly wasn't born lucky. He couldn't run away from this.

On that Friday afternoon, the Law Society faxed a message to him. He was to have his books available. He felt a cold chill in his soul when he read it. He knew he was in trouble. He spoke to a friend of his who was a lawyer and on whom he relied. He tendered the resignation of his certificate to practise. He had to let his staff go. They knew something was up. When he saw their tears, he, too, broke down. His tears gathered once more with the memory.

He cursed internally to himself because of the whiskey. He was glad his father and mother were both dead and had not witnessed it. He had lost everything, his practice, his reputation, his marriage. Now he was selling his office. Was this the price of Helen's health? If it was, it was still worth it. He had no doubt about that. Was it really a bargain he had made with God? Was it that he was disenchanted with life and the law and subconsciously wanted an out, and behaved recklessly? Maybe he had a death wish. Or maybe he had just been too well indoctrinated by the Church. Yet he still retained a fundamental belief in God. He sometimes thought that might be fear. But he thought not. It was just the way life appeared to go on no matter what.

In the slobbery way that life works, out of disaster there springs surprising new life. This restored his confidence in his belief in 'a real God' – not a theological concept, but a happening, living, surprising, unpredictable force for good. He ruminated some more. We are designed for failure, he thought. We feed ourselves only to die. Maybe failure is a type of paradoxical success – difficult though it may be to see it. Maybe the acceptance of it was all that was required. Was it all intended as a 'valley of tears' as the Hail Holy Queen at the end of the Rosary used to say? He did not say many Rosaries now.

'You didn't get far,' said the Pint.

He looked up suddenly and with rapier-like repartee quipped, 'You nearly beat me to it.'

'Going 'round in circles,' said the Pint.

'Just like life,' said the Large Bottle.

'*Rotha mór an tSaoil*,' he volunteered.

'Is that Latin, too?' said the Pint.

'No, it's Irish. It means 'the great circle of life' as you were saying.'

He paused for a little.

'You learn those things on the water too,' said the Pint, with reference to the University of Life in which he had been schooled at sea.

Interested in the remark, he picked up on it and asked them about their life as fishermen. At first, they moaned about the hardships. Then contradicted this by saying it was the only life for them. A man is the sum total of his own contradictions he thought to himself. What kept them going, he asked.

The Pint replied,

'You have to believe in something.'

He looked at the Pint and dared to ask, 'What should a fella believe in?'

Philosophically the Pint replied,

'You have to keep faith with yourself.'

There was a long pause. It was so long that the Pint, the Large Bottle and he became aware of the grandfather clock ticking in the corner as they each took a long swallow. He wondered to himself whether the Pint's remark was deep or shallow. What did it mean? And what had the Pint intended?

'Keep faith with yourself.'

He smiled. You meet angels on the lips of other people he had once been told in a catechetics class. He smiled to himself again, the Archangel Pint! What sort of feathers would you put in his wings?

'If you can't be kind to yourself,' said 'the Archangel Pint' taking another sip, 'you won't be kind to anyone else either.'

'Did you learn that fishing?' he intruded.

'Yes, indeed. Like the story in the Gospel 'They fished all night and caught nothin'– on nights like that you learn things like that.'

'Bejaysus' – he thought to himself – 'a philosophical Archangel'.

Maybe group thinking and herding were not confined to banks and churches. The notion of an Angelic Pint and a Midas-like Pint scheming market strategies and encyclicals tickled him and he spontaneously laughed out loud.

It was almost embarrassing. But sure fellas talk like that with a few drinks in them he told himself.

It was getting on in the afternoon. This time he was leaving. When he got back to the flat, he slept. He dreamt he was on a liner that was cutting a furrow across the Atlantic Ocean. The passengers were singing Auld Lang Syne. The sun was splitting the heavens.

On Sunday morning he collected Marianne and Helen for the Confirmation. The two Sunday papers carried the bishop's remarks on celibacy on their front pages.

'Bishop Wants Celibacy Banned,' proclaimed one of the tabloids.

'Bishop Carpeted by Rome,' yelled another.

The pressure of his situation was etched in the bishop's face. Newspaper attention of the type he was getting was not conducive to sleep – and he was drinking too much. Notwithstanding, he thuribled his way through the ceremony and the incense smoke and the seraphim voices of the schoolchild choir. He pondered on the upturned shining faces of those who would be anointed in their Christian faith, chicklets in a mossy nest, wide open beaks, unable to squawk, but yearning for the spiritual morsels Mother Church would give them to satiate the hunger inculcated in them and would sustain them in their journey.

The confluence of anxieties, including his own, betrayed on the bishop's countenance. It was also revealed in the compassion he had for Man's lot. The anxiety and suffering which permeated his sermon,

revealed itself in the bishop's demeanour of benign resignation to his per-
secution not alone by the newspapers, but also the demands of his superiors in Rome, the desire to enlighten his flock that all was not lost, and
the necessity to really believe things would work out.

The bishop finished his sermon:

'On the Last Day when the Pearly gates are flung open, the first group
in through the portals of the Kingdom of Heaven will be, I believe, the
members of the Travelling Community. Theirs is a special relationship
with God. It is, in my view, reflected in their lifestyle for which we in the
settled community, regularly condemn them. They know no boundaries;
everything is seamless – including, at times, notions of ownership. They
do, I believe, accept what life sends them, the good and the bad, and they
will see the gates open and they will drift in naturally, with or without an
invitation. This is, I believe, their natural and fundamental disposition –
a natural and inherent faith in their entitlement to be in God's presence
at all times.

'And likewise the little children here today whom I have confirmed
and who come here as of right to be confirmed in what they have been
taught and believe unquestionably, will, with their friends and peers,
gravitate innocently and naturally to the goal in which they have been
instructed, and which, with the innocence of children, they believe they
are justly entitled.

'At this point I will make a running burst and try to squeeze myself in
between the two groups.'

There was mild laughter from the congregation.

'Oh, there will be winks and nudges from those hanging around outside, 'Where does that fella think he is going? I could tell you a thing or
two about him.'

The congregation burst out in spontaneous laughter.

'And there skulking around outside will be the congregation to
whom I am addressing my remarks today. The Good Lord will come out
and ask, 'Are you not coming in?' and you will say – modestly and
politely of course – 'We don't believe we deserved it – we don't think we
have earned it.' And the Good Lord will reply, 'Did nobody ever tell you,
you don't earn it?'

'And you will look at him with surprise and say 'No'. It's then I'll come out and remind you all what I told you today. You will look at me as disbelievingly as you look at me now, and I will say, 'I told you that, on the day your children were confirmed. And you all thought I was giving a sermon.'

The congregation was aroused to impressive silence as he blessed himself and turned back to the altar.

As he looked at the bishop and pondered his words, which he found moving, Leacy thought of his circumstance and he thought of Helen. He had offered to give up all of his definitions of himself in order that she might live in the world while he lived in it. He could not bear the thought of a world without her and he would readily accept the requirement to shed all definitions of himself and submit himself to whatever pain this might cause in him. 'If only she would live.' She had lived. He hated the public odium to which he was being subjected and empathised with the bishop's position. He had dreaded her Confirmation because of the knowing looks and glances. He felt the shame, and the patronizing pity. However, when he thought of Helen, her innocence and delight, it dissipated and seemed to not matter at all.

The ceremony ended. Then came the photographer who took images of the families and the bishop in the churchyard. Wisps of cigarette smoke blew in the Sunday afternoon sun as boys in new suits and bridelets in white veils giggled and pranced to every trick and whim of wind gust and excitement induced by compliment after flattering compliment.

When Helen, Marianne and himself were getting their photograph taken, he complimented the bishop on his sermon and his courage in his statement. The bishop responded saying that at least it would keep the clerical abuse issues off the front pages for the day. His laugh was hollow and was simply his way to extricate himself without causing controversy.

Helen, Marianne and himself went to the hotel with a lot of the other Confirmation parties. They sat at their own table overlooking the harbour. The conversation was slow and, as usual, inevitably about the weather. There was mundanity about the thing, which he welcomed, and which continued until they were half-way through dinner. In the middle of the silence, Helen said:

'Do you not love us anymore, dad?'

He reddened. He looked at Marianne and back to Helen. Marianne was on tenterhooks but waited to see how he would respond.

'Of course I do,' he replied.

'Leave your dad alone and eat up your dinner,' said Marianne.

Helen looked at her plate. There was an awkward interlude. Helen was determined to make her point. She waited and then continued the ambush on both her parents.

'Do you believe in God?' she asked.

With slightly hurt and awkward indignation, he again replied, 'Of course I do.'

'Helen!' admonished her mother.

But Helen was going to get out of her system what she had been nursing.

'Am I going to die?'

They were both utterly disarmed by her candour.

Defensively Marianne rushed in, 'Of course not, darling. What's got into you? What would make you say such a thing?'

'Because I got Rubella when I was young and it might come back.'

'That's all behind you now, sweetheart. That's all over,' she comforted.

And then, with the outright frankness of the innocent, Helen said, 'But how do you know?'

Marianne was spellbound.

He had been taking in all of these matters and then very slowly and very deliberately holding her gaze evenly he said,

'By the life that's in your body, and in mine, I guarantee it.'

It worked. All emotions were quelled. Marianne's through shock, and Helen's through the conviction of his statement. She stared evenly back at him for a full minute. Her frozen expression dissolved into a smile, which gently came over her. She placed her napkin on the table in front of her. She got up from her chair, left her place walked over to her father and gave him a hug and a kiss on the cheek and with glorious understatement redolent of her true circumstance of innocence, said, 'I'm going to the lav!'

When she was gone, Marianne looked at him with daggers in her eyes.

'What sort of thing was that to say?'

He kept eating his dinner which infuriated her even more.

'A residue of the priesthood – or some other epiphany dare I say?' she sarcastically sliced.

This was a snide reference to his deal with the Almighty over Helen, which he had recounted to her in better times. It stung him deeply and he was unable to withhold his reaction.

'Once a Yank, always a Yank,' he bitterly rebuffed.

'I don't believe in superstition, as well you know, or black magic, or white magic.'

'Maybe that explains why there is so little magic between us now,' he said as he got up and went over to the bar.

'Go and hide in your whiskey with your women,' she hissed at him before he left the table and anybody could hear her.

The two fishermen were at the bar counter in their Sunday best. He ordered a drink of whiskey, a coke and the usual red wine for Marianne. Helen returned sporting a ten pound note given to her by one of her friend's parents. He felt bad because he had no money to give her for her friends. He knew Marianne would begrudge whatever he was spending on drink.

Lannigan, who was with another party, came over, and gave Helen a 'fifty.' He was deliberately patronising of Marianne. The feeling was mutual. He deliberately pulled Leacy up by the elbows and went over to the two fishermen at the counter.

'A great man, the bishop,' said the Pint.

'Indeed,' said Lannigan.

'Had his troubles too,' gossiped the Large Bottle.

'We all do,' he said.

'And that's not maybe,' said the Pint implying an invitation to reflect personal experience common to all.

'When you're in pain, you're in pain.'

'That's when you need big faith,' said Lannigan.

Lannigan looked at him. He smiled back a knowing grin, shook his head and laughing said,

'Uberrime Fides.'

The Pint looked up. 'Latin or Irish?' he twinkled as if he was one of the one's in the know.

'The utmost good faith,' translated Lannigan.

'The only type to have,' said the Pint.

He missed the pointed nature of the relevance of the remark but scored a goal without knowing it. In the aftermath of the quip and the stillness of the afternoon, Helen stared longingly at her father. He noticed she was ignoring her mother who was wearing a face that would stop a clock.

'The only type to have indeed,' he said as he excused himself to go back to his table.

He explained to his company, 'There's a young lady over here giving me the glad eye.' 'Work away,' said Lannigan.

'God bless,' said the two fishermen.

Notwithstanding the frosty snowstorm he was going to encounter from beside her, he made his way over to the 'apple of his eye.'

'Who knows what might happen?' he mused.

II.

The Passenger

The Passenger was reading a book on the train when the four of them got on.

The carriage was divided by an aisle, with tables and upholstered sprung-back seats facing a formica-topped table in each section. There were eight sections on either side of the passageway, each with a window. The windows reflected the profile of the passengers, in ghostlike fashion, on the flashing fields, trees and hedges.

The woman wore a dirty pink headscarf that was in a fashion not of the twenty-first century. George was more sober than Paddy who sat on the outside seat beside the passageway. He had a navy overcoat and a sun-tanned brown-red face which revealed the tincture of cider. He had consumed enough of it to make him a pinker shade of tan and well-mellowed.

The fourth, who had at least two days of stubble on his chin, sat next to the window beside the woman and opposite the other two. His chin held the trace of a wiped dribble. He appeared to be of dulled intellect.

'Sit down, can't you?' said Paddy.

'I'm tryin' to get me can. It's after rolling under de sate when de train pulled out,' said George.

Paddy got up. He was a little with five feet and had a curly red head and a look of the ageing cur. Unsteadily, the train pulled away while

Paddy eyed the passenger with a dribbling open jaw. He held the seat with one paw and wiped his other across the grey steel growth of unshaven face smearing the moistened glisten in the process. He crossed the aisle to the opposite table.

He sat down at the table opposite the Passenger and with a grin said, 'How a' ya?'

The Passenger looked up, put his book away, and replied warmly,

'I'm grand.'

'Where a' ya from?'

He told him, sedately.

'What part?'

He answered again, politely.

Giddy from being spoken to politely, the response was loud and rough.

'I'm a farmer. I owns a hundred an' fifty acres – yahoo ya boya – lave it there' (holding out his hand).

He reached forward, took the Passenger's clean, smooth, delicate hand that had cleanly cut nails, and shook it with his own big, dirty, unwashed, weathered shovel of a hand that had been more places than one would care to mention in polite company, and sat back down abruptly and coolly in the seat opposite the Passenger.

An awkward quietness came over the other passengers in the half-full railway car, like a wake room when a sympathiser calls. A woman three seats away looked up from reading her book and caught the eye of the Passenger. A recognition of his predicament revealed itself in a momentary flicker of sympathy.

The conversation continued,

'I farms a hundred an' fifty acres meseff. What do you do?'

'I'm a lawyer,' he said.

'A lawyer?'

'Yes.'

He took three gulps from the can and left it on the table.

'Yer a lawyer.' He smiled the grin of the lewd; wasn't he the brave lad not concealing either his guile or motive and not bothering or caring who noticed.

He became bolder.

'Whass yer name?' he intruded further.

'What's yours?' the Passenger half-heartedly asserted.

'I assed ya first,' parried the bould Paddy.

'There's my card.' The lawyer deferentially handed him a business card.

'Yer a lawyer.'

'I am.'

'Yer no jaysus good,' he insulted and took another gulp.

'I farms two hundred an' fifty acres meself. Me brudder has a pub. An, 'thass me wife, Josie,' he pointed at the woman who feigned laughter. He got up unsteadily and went over to her.

'Give us a kiss, Josie.'

'Sit down – can't ya.' She pushed him away.

'Lave it there.' He turned to the Passenger on his way back and sat down while he shook hands palms to thumb in the style of chums, with his obliging victim.

'I have hapes o' money,' he said.

'Good man, well done and more power,' said the Passenger.

George laughed, Josie giggled. Paddy persisted with his steady grating and unrelenting grilling:

'Have ya got a light?'

'I don't smoke.'

'Ya can't smoke here – don't ya see de signs,' said George.

Paddy got up once more and went back across the aisle to his companions and sat down with George.

'Give us a fag,' he said to George.

'Jaysus, will ya lave me alone,' came the weary reply,

'I'll box da head a'ya.'

He boxed him on the shoulder.

'Ah Jaysus, will ya lave me alone.'

'Next Stop,' announced the internal communications system.

'I'll take me coat off to ya,' said Paddy making a shape to get up again and began to take off his coat and stopped. He slumped back, got up again and annoyed his disgruntled companions, once more unsettled by his maliciously inspired seat changing. He lunged across the aisle and plonked down heavily opposite his easy placid victim.

'Ya bollix,' he said to the Passenger.

He stopped and grinned at George. Then they grinned together and laughed like hyenas – high-pitched, nervous and false at each other, and then Paddy leered at the Passenger who innocently smiled benignly.

'Lave it there,' said Paddy, and he again shook hands with the Passenger and slumped back into the seat with assistance from the train as it pulled out of the station. He rescued the cider can as it moved on the table as the train chugged forward.

'Were y'ever in court around here? I tink I seen ya,' said George.

'I was indeed,' said the Passenger.

'Wid you do work fur da high – ya know – do you do court for da low – you know – trubble an' stuff?'

'I work for whoever pays me,' said the Passenger.

'There's wan for ya,' said George.

'How much d'ya make in a day?' said Paddy.

'Don't be askin' the man his business,' said Josie.

'I'll ask him what I wants.'

'Lave the man alone,' said George.

'I never touched him.'

'Lave the gintleman alone,' said the woman.

Paddy put the can of cider down and it fizzled and then bubbled out of the can and dribbled down onto his clothes.

He looked down and then looked away ignoring it as if he wasn't bothered by the wet.

'You'll destroy de man's clothes – will ya stop goin' on,' asked George rhetorically.

'I'm grand entirely,' said the Passenger, patiently.

Paddy took his finger away from the top of the can.

The fizzing was finished.

'Were y'in Court today?' he asked.

'I was.'

'Where?'

'The City.'

'Did many get sent ta jail?' said George.

'A few,' the Passenger replied.

'How much do ya make a day?' resumed Paddy.

'How much do you make?' the Passenger answered.

George laughed and so did the woman.

'There's wan fer ya,' she said.

'Answer dah wan,' said George supposedly in triumph with his allies, Josie and the polite passenger.

'I thinks I'll have to take me coat off to him. He's trying to get wan up on me.'

'What age are ya?' said Paddy.

'What age do you think I am?'

'Ya looks forty-five.'

'I'm fifty-three,' obliged the Passenger.

'You're nine years older'n me,' mused Paddy.

'Let me in dere beside ya.' He rose from his seat.

'Sit down, yer grand where y'are.'

The other passengers started taking more interest when they sensed confrontation. He sat down again.

'Do ya know hurlin'?' he asked.

'I played it,' said the Passenger.

'We'll win a Sunday,' referring to the impending Leinster Senior Hurling final.

'You will if you're let,' said the Passenger defending his own county's team.

'Do you know anthin' 'bout hurlin' at all?' said Paddy rising up. This time he leaned forward again but this time his hand took hold of the Passenger's tie.

On the personal intrusion, the Passenger raised himself slowly from his seat and placed his hand down on the top of the intruder's head and with the strength of the lean and bony athlete, steadily but forcefully, he forced him back down with one hand on the seat, while steadily retrieving his tie with the other.

'Sit down there now, like a good man,' he said with a hint of concern that matters could get out of hand.

When they saw the height of him by comparison with the scut-sized Paddy, the woman laughed. George laughed. The woman who was reading a book looked up. Two men at the end of the carriage looked back out over the seats to see what was causing the laughter. They started to laugh at the incongruous scene.

'Stay down,' said the Passenger with firmness and latent strength.

'I knows yer bigger'n me,' said Paddy.

George and the woman were convulsed with laughter.

'Sit down' y'eejit,' said Paddy's deserting comrades.

The Passenger gathered his book and briefcase together.

Paddy sat down beside George.

'Give us a light?'

A lighter appeared in the hand of the one who seemed intellectually challenged and a flame flickered into life.

'Give it to us,' said Paddy as he struggled to get the cigarettes from the box.

'Lave the poor craythur alone,' said George.

'Yer always causin' trouble, Paddy,' said Josie.

'We're nearly home,' said George.

'I'll box de head a ya, when I get out,' said Paddy after he had taken a light and a drag from the fag.

'We're goin' without ya,' said the woman.

'We're goin' without ya,' Paddy said to George.

''Tis you she's talking to,' said George to Paddy.

'I'll box de head a'ya.'

The Passenger was looking out at the fading autumn evening. A crane was being driven into a field where the stubble was fresh.

He wondered what was the reason for bringing a crane into a field.

He wondered how long before the passengers for the next stop would start to collect their coats. He was going further on down the line. His fleeting thought on the manouvre of the crane disappeared with the flash of the vanishing countryside as the train sped on.

'I'll box de head a' ya,' said Paddy again.

George snarled. His patience was wearing.

'Listen here, Paddy. I'm hardy and ya won't bate me. I'll kill ya when I get out.'

Paddy hit him on the shoulder with a fist. George roared, 'Cut it out or I'll give it to ya.'

'Will ya stop Paddy, yer always causin' trouble,' said the woman.

'*Next Stop.*'

They moved heavily and droopily. They were dressed for a winter that was not yet here and they smelled of cider and the streets.

The other passengers went to the other door. Remaining glances were exchanged with the disembarkers. The train stopped. After they had gone, the Passenger moved three seats away. 'Drunks,' he thought to himself.

As the train pulled away, a beer can rolled down under the seats. It spun, fizzed and spilled before hitting the Passenger on the heel. In an aware and conscious demeanour of responsibility, he stooped down to pick it up. His wallet fell from his inside pocket onto the floor. His driving licence fell out on impact and opened. There opposite his photograph was the Court endorsement that revealed he had been disqualified three weeks previously for being drunk while driving.

12.

The Confluence

I

I have been asked by Dr. Byrne to make a statement setting out my history and my beliefs and feelings before and up to my attempted suicide near the standing stones in Whitechurch last August. I am to make this statement dealing with the issues that were pressing upon me coming up to that date which resulted in my subsequent admission to hospital. I am told this is an important step on my way to recovery. I have already done my first step in the recovery unit for alcoholics and I am to only barely touch on its history and then write it more or less for context. This statement is focused on dealing with my depression and to see whether the triggers of my alcoholism are located in my depression or whether my depression is otherwise located within my own psyche and history.

I am also to indicate as I am writing what feelings (if any) I may experience and in particular I am to give as much detail as possible of any dreams or hallucinations or subconscious matters that I now

observe in hindsight and I am asked to volunteer my
own observations.

I am presently sitting out on the veranda of my residence which is located
in Ballysop near Whitechurch in County Wexford. I am aged forty-nine
years and I am a single man. I studied for a B.A. in Maynooth College
where I trained for the priesthood. Whilst there, my emphasis in study
centered around early and medieval Irish history. I have a diploma in psychology. As a consequence, I am very interested in archaeology and local
history and in my spare time I write articles occasionally for local history
journals and magazines.

I left the seminary and became a lecturer in the arts faculty off cam-
pus in the local Institute of Technology. I lecture in history on a part-
time basis and run a public house in Whitechurch, County Wexford,
two miles from where I now sit. The dairy farm on which I was reared
has been in the family for generations; it is my heritage and means a lot
to me. The public house is now heavily in debt. My father was born here.
His mother, my grandmother, was also born here. My parents were second cousins. I often wondered if that close relationship had affected me.
Her name was Sutton and the farm has been in the family since the time
of the invasion of the Normans. The leader of the invasion was
Strongbow and his uncle, Harvey de Monte Mariscoe, was given all of
the land in this area. Supposedly Roger de Sutton, a lieutenant of
Harvey's, was brought to the top of Sliabh Coillte and offered all of the
land that he could view from where I am now sitting, and writing with
my fountain pen. The parish was also called 'Sutton's Parish'.

As you look due south, you can see as far as Hook Head down to the
Celtic Sea. You can see the confluence of the Three Sister rivers where
the Barrow and Nore come down from New Ross and join the Suir coming down from Waterford at the Great Island Generating Station where
there are now two giant chimney stacks, before it winds its way down and
out through what is known as the Waterford Estuary down past Nuke
and Ballyhack and Arthurstown on the Wexford side, Passage and
Woodstown on the Waterford side before it sweeps out past Duncannon

and Broom Hill on the Wexford side and doubles back towards Creadon Head and Dunmore East, before finally bidding farewell to Hook Head as the current aids the parting ships off out into the Celtic Sea and the wider world.

As I have said, the mountain is a very special place for me, not simply on account of the fact that my grandmother settled it on my parents in a marriage settlement giving them or 'the survivor the right to appoint such child or children, or the children of their children, of the family as they or the survivor should by deed or will appoint'. As I was the only child, it was plain my mother would give it to me after my father died a few years back and she did. Leacy was our solicitor and he advised a power, called a Power of Revocation, be reserved to her the power to revoke matters in case I went to the bad. I had a row with him about this at the time.

He insisted it was the appropriate thing to do at that time and said it was not a good idea to live ahead of your time and if you lived synchronised to your time all problems could be worked out. When you tried to buy or sell time you had not lived, you could end up with unpleasant surprises. The Cistercian monks in Dunbrody who founded a monastery there compliments of Harvey de Monte Mariscoe in AD1200, had lived with this commercial philosophy. They called the system 'credit-sale'. They sold next year's sheep this year. One year they had a failed flock and they got caught out. They went broke. The same often happens to people with mortgages. They forget life can change and so does income and expenditure. Leacy was right. This is what happened to me. I took a chance during the so-called Celtic Tiger years.

The Power of Revocation was farseeing because I have ended up in financial difficulties and now there is a snag. Because I spent most of my time running the public house and a new building development enterprise I entered into with a friend of mine, O'Loughlin, we, quite separately, leased the land and the milk quota to another dairy farmer and the rent and all the entitlements are paid into my bank account directly. The bank holds the title deeds by way of security. My mother was required to sign the lease because she had this Power of Revocation, and because the lease was on the property, the bank wanted to retain the title documents so that when the lease was finished and I came to either sell or negotiate a new lease, the bank would be the holder of the deeds and would be able to dictate whatever terms were necessary for them. It was cleaner for the bank that way.

In the meantime, my poor mother got ill and is now resident in a local nursing home. She suffers from Alzheimer's. Be times she is good and be times she is bad. She has lucid moments when you least expect and then she would dazzle you with her brightness.

I am now living on my own at the top of Sliabh Coillte. The farm is known as The Seven Wells of Oisín. I have some of the wells on my land but not all of them.

Oisín went to Tír na nÓg (the Land of Youth) with Niamh Cinn Óir. The legend says he spent three-hundred years away with her and it seemed like only a day and when he came back he saw some weak-limbed men trying to lift a stone that one of the Fianna would have lifted with one hand. He left his true love in Tír na nÓg for the day only under the strict order that he not dismount from the steed on which he was travelling. When he stopped to give the men a hand he stooped from his saddle to lift the stone with one hand but the girth broke under him and he fell to the ground and immediately turned into a very old man. '

I am stopping writing now for a moment because I want to get a quotation from a book that I was reading which I think throws some light on my thinking.

I have the quotation:

A myth, therefore, only makes sense if it is translated into action – either ritually or behaviourally. It is comprehensible only if it is imparted as part of a process of transformation. Myth has been aptly described as an early form of psychology. The tales about gods threading their way through labyrinths or fighting with monsters were describing an arched type of truth rather than an actual occurrence.

– Karen Armstrong

I don't want to get too bogged down in the myths and legends but they came very much alive for me when I was putting the rope around my neck down in the field with the standing stones, and an understanding of their imagery goes to the root of my dreams and psychology. I have already been asked if I thought that place was haunted and I must honestly say I don't know.

I regard myself as a spiritual person but I have been greatly affected by the Church's failure to deal with child sexual abuse and consequently have lost my confidence in their ability to tell the truth. The attitude of the Church to sex and sexuality affected me also and does have some bearing on my issues.

I have met a local girl who is Presbyterian and is the daughter of the bank manager who loaned me the money for the development. The banks are now suing for repossession of the public house. They are also suing for repossession of the farm. We ran into trouble with the development once the bank stopped lending to purchasers to buy. The building company myself and O'Loughlin were involved in, has been wound up and the bank have possession of the sites. None of them are being sold. O'Loughlin is a great friend of mine. I call him Luchtleanamhnaigh (pronounced Lucktlanoonig). It was the Irish name given to the Vikings and the O'Loughlins are descended from the Vikings. He also plays the guitar. I play a harp and we often play together for the entertainment of customers particularly when other musicians call. The music is very important to me and I use it a lot to express my feelings. I used to be very socially awkward and playing music helped. I have a girlfriend now.

The girl, with whom I am now great, the bank manager's daughter, is Hazel.'

I need to make a cup of coffee now as my hand is getting sore from writing with the pen. I am deliberately writing with a fountain pen as I want my thoughts considered and composed and sometimes my mind races but the fountain pen slows them down. I think this is one of the things that has caused my difficulties. My mind races a lot.

I knew the philosopher and writer John Moriarty and so did Leacy, my solicitor. He spoke to me about this stuff. Moriarty had been a professor at the University of Manitoba in Canada lecturing in English literature. The rat race was too much for him and he left and came back to Connemara where he earned his livelihood digging gardens with a spade, and writing books. I would regard him as more of a mystic than a philosopher, and a very spiritual man. I met him by accident about twenty years ago when Leacy asked me to give him a lift down to Waterford. He made a great impression on me and when Leacy called out to see me after the bank served the High Court summonses on me last August, he reminded me of some things he had told us. I will get the coffee now.

The winter has been hard and there was a lot of snow before Christmas. I found it peaceful in the aftermath of my coming out of hospital and recuperating. Now it is early spring but the evenings are still quite short and I will have to go inside shortly. It is cool enough and the light on the veranda allows me to keep writing as the dusk is falling. It is too cold for moths but it is not freezing.

'I like Sliabh Coillte particularly because of its name. It is worth taking a little time about that. As I was saying earlier, there is psychology in the myths and legends of Ireland. The locals say the name means The

Wooded Mountain. I believe this is incorrect. I have a book entitled Bardic Poetry inside written by the famous Irish scholar, Osborne Bergin, and when I was reading it one night I discovered what I always believed to be the case. The word for wood in Irish is spelled c-o-i-l-l (pronounced keel), the word for lost in Irish is c-a-i-l-l (pronounced kyle.) My mother, who was born here and her mother, my grandmother, always called it Caillte (pronounced Kylecha). Osborne Bergin revealed that Sir Samuel Ferguson had made a mistake in a poem by James Clarence Mangan called 'A Winter Campaign'. Apparently they made a hames of the Irish translation by mistaking the word *lost* for *wood* i.e. they mistook the word 'Caill' for 'Coill' and made the same mistake by translating the word as 'wood' instead of 'lost'. I believe the correct name of the mountain is 'The Lost Mountain'.

Why would a mountain be called the Lost Mountain? This bugged me a lot which probably reveals an intensity to my nature which is probably worth noting at this point. I have picked this up from my friend Leacy, the solicitor, who told me this when he was going to look into saving my property from the banks. He said he would focus his concentration on the issue and he passed a remark about problems that were difficult. He said problems were ugly. His exact words were 'there is nothing so ugly that the application of intense and brilliant light will not beautify'. That is exactly what I believe myself. I followed the mystery of the name of the mountain like a detective with a clue pursuing the answer to a crime. It became very exciting and it also ended up with an experience in the field of the standing stones where I experienced an intense and brilliant light.'

The light I am now depending on almost completely is coming from the veranda as the daylight has almost disappeared from the sky and I am beginning to get a bit cold but I want to finish this part before I go inside.

I want to explain something now that is, I believe, deeply significant in this story and I am sorry for being so longwinded but I think it is really worth understanding the mythology, as I was saying earlier, in order to understand the psychology.

In the course of my studies I became aware of and have known for a long time the importance, historically, of the confluence of the Three Sister rivers. Its location is visible to me from where I am now writing in the dusk. I can see in the distance way down at the river are the two red lights that are on the top of the Power Station chimneys located at Great Island at the confluence.

The Island has a causeway joining it to Ballyedock. It took its name from Mileadach as it was described by the seventeenth-century Irish historian, Geoffrey Keating. Prior to that it had been referred to in the *Book of the Invasions of Ireland* (*Leabhar Gabhála Na hÉireann*) by another seventeenth-century historian called Michael Cleary (Micheál O Cléirigh) who was involved in writing the *Annals of the Four Masters*. He wrote down what he compiled from seventh and eighth-century manuscripts which referred to traditions about the first invasion of Ireland and I am setting out very briefly what that said. The account was originally pagan but was converted by the Christian scribes (Cleary was a Franciscan lay brother) to accommodate the necessary ingredients to show how the Irish would be saved by God. According to the Old Testament, only those descended from Abraham were to receive salvation.

The recorded Irish mythology states in *The Book of Invasions* that the first invader of Ireland was Cessair and she landed with forty-nine women and three men. The men were Bith, Ladrann and Tuan. Cessair was supposedly a granddaughter of Noah who built the Ark. She apparently advised that an idol be made and then departed leaving her grandfather, Noah, and the rest of her family. She sailed the seas until she landed in Ireland. She supposedly later drowned in the flood. Ladrann was the first recorded death which, according to the *Annals*, was caused by either 'an oar through the buttock or an excess of women'. The causes might have been related! But Tuan, it appears his name was also Fintan, survived by changing his shape to a boar, a stag, an eagle and a salmon.

They had landed at Mileadach, which according to the myth, was then called 'Bun Suaimne'.

They were sun worshippers and this is what is significant. There is a graveyard adjacent to a beautiful garden where Mileadach was. It is right opposite Ballyedock which in the Irish translates as Baille Aod Oc and Mileadach as Mil-aod-oc. The graveyard is the remains of an old Celtic enclosure and contains bullaun stones, the real proof of it. It also has the smallest high cross in Ireland. In the same way, the pagan myth of pagan Ireland with its sun-worshipping practices and symbols were subsumed into Christianity and merged. The Cross of Christ superimposed on the sun gave us the powerful symbol of the Celtic Cross. Cessair was given a pre-Christian heritage.

The Celtic enclosure at Kilmokea was also converted and the name Mil-Aod-oc was converted to Mo-aod-oc giving us the name Mogue (Maodog). It was then converted to Aod-an and Aidan. Aidan is the name of the Patron Saint of the Diocese of Ferns. The place is called after the Church of Maodog now called Kilmokea. This reveals the evolution of the place, like its people, from pagan to Christian by a process of cultural ingestion and a merged evolution. And here is the big psychological point: change did not really go to the core but it came from it. The internals might require changing quickly in order to live but only if it was deeply worthwhile would the change last. What will be bound on earth will be bound in Heaven.

When all of these things began to come together I knew there had to be a provenance that was magical and I discovered it in the midst of my turmoil last August in more ways than one. Just prior to the 'apparition' in the field of the standing stones, I was drinking heavily at the time, and it came to me one night in that flash of inspiration that arrives immediately before you get drunk. Kilmokea, and the line of the standing stones and the top of Sliabh Coillte were all in a straight line. What astonished me was my discovery that this line travels from a line of fifty-nine degrees at the top of Sliabh Coillte. It exits at two-hundred and thirty- nine degrees at Kilmokea, which is near the sunset. I have more research to do on it, but when it struck me that August evening, I could see that it was the only way to understand the topography of the landscape, and what I believe is the sovereignty of the countryside. Its identity and how that is all tied up in me has to do with understanding, how it was viewed before man developed it, and this reveals the atmosphere and sacredness of the place. And that is why *Sliabh Coillte* is the *Lost Mountain* and why Whitechurch or *Teampall Geal*, is *The Temple of Brightness*. But it only comes to life when you begin to understand the gods they worshipped were the sun, who supplied the bountiful harvest, and Lugh, who excelled in intelligence. In order to live with life as it changed, challenged and frightened, his inspirational deeds in legend gave them hope and a way to live, a culture, a way to explain life to themselves and give it meaning inspired by these heroic exploits as something more than a way to survive. It gave them a way to live with dignity and pride, a path to their destiny of excellence and greatness where happiness was neverending.

Where the standing stones are located resonates with the festivals and bonfires of extravagant festivals of light where there were few inhibitions and less control than there is nowadays. I suspect the pressures upon me that night came face to face with the reality of the freedom I once had, and that there was an internal explosion of reality within me as I came face to face with what the rat race had turned me into, and what the nature of the place in which I was living was forcing out of me. I suppose it was also represented in my having received a High Court Summons that day and phoning Leacy who came out and brought Moriarty with him who fortuitously was passing and was looking, once more, for a lift to Waterford. When they arrived out in the afternoon there were few enough about, and that was possibly why we started to drink.

I am tired now and I am going in and I will see how I am feeling after I make some supper for myself and whether I will wait until the morning to write more.

II

It is half past seven in the morning. I got up at seven o'clock and had a shower and shave. I have eaten three slices of brown bread and had a cup of tea. I have some coffee brewing if I need it. When I was eating my supper last night I remembered I had to go to a meeting of alcoholics anonymous. The meetings are good for me. I have come face to face with the notion of a higher power in my life. I had been a good practising Catholic until the sexual abuse cases damaged my belief in the Church leaders. How could they perform the cover-ups they were doing and at the same time claim to be preaching the truth about something else. Anyway, when you are in a religion you become plagued by doubts as to whether what you are believing in is true or false. And when you are out of a religion you become plagued by doubts as to whether the religion you came out of might, in fact, be right after all. This time I have come in contact with a force that is keeping me away from drink in a way that I did not believe I could. The bond amongst the members is based on honesty and humility. There is nothing put on. I slept well after I came home and I got up this morning and read a bit of the bible as I normally do since I came back from the hospital. I only read a little bit. When I was younger I used say the rosary but I gave that up too. I met a priest in the hospital when I could not sleep and he told me to try saying it and not to think about it when I was trying to go to sleep. He told me to keep saying rosaries until I got to sleep and he guaranteed me I would never finish the second one. He was right.

I am at last in touch with my feelings and that says to me I have got over the last bout of depression. I know this because before I started writing this morning, I read back over my notes so that I would be able to continue without having it disjointed and I wanted an unbroken stream of consciousness in order to nakedly expose myself for the purpose of an accurate diagnosis of my condition. I left off at how Sliabh Coillte could have got its name as the Lost Mountain because at the time of the flood, Noah's granddaughter landed at the confluence of the Three Sister rivers. This mountain could have been like Mount Ararat was to Noah as the first mountain that revealed itself after the flood. It certainly dominates the landscape which has its first Christianised flood based on the Irish version. It was essential for the scribes to link the Irish to the arrival of mankind in Ireland, their predecessors, with Abraham's descendent, Noah who survived the flood. You see, salvation according to the bible came through Abraham, and Noah, as we were all taught, after the flood, landed on the mountain lost from view and indicated only by the dove who returned with the sprig of leaves. The mountain was Ararat and every culture had such a mountain. Some say Ireland's Mount Ararat is called Ard Éireann up in Laois – maybe they're right. However, this mountain has all the mythological provenance– and the traditional phonetic pronunciation of the name – the lost mountain. Anyway, it's what I believe.

The Three Sister rivers are called The Barrow, The Nore and The Suir and my grandmother told me that on Halloween, the feast of Samhain, after the sun sets behind Kilmokea, if you listen closely you can hear the Three Sisters whisper the names of Éire, Banba and Fodhla, the three names given to the sovereign Goddess of Ireland, the spirit of Ireland. I can recognise sovereignty romantically by the smell of the fresh air here on the mountain and the smell of the river in the valley below where the three standing stones mark exactly the half-way point. The Temple of Brightness was located somewhere in that bowl which the earth formed like a saucer in the middle of the earth in the valley below.

I suppose it is the expression of these innate deepest feelings that over the passage of time came to be recognised as fundamental recurrences for which no human decision could claim responsibility and responsibility for this is given to a higher power that had to be named for identification purposes. The Ancients called them gods and named them and recognised different attributes, such as constancy (sovereignty) or, at the opposite side of matters, demi-gods which were regarded as deformities of soul whose perversions were represented by grotesque deformities, such as monsters with one eye – like the monster of the enemy, Balor of the Evil Eye, who was leader of the demonic race, the Formorians, but was killed by the Champion of the divine race, the Tuatha Dé Dannan, by none other than his own grandson. What a paradox human nature is. Your hero is related to your enemy. How sophisticated of the Ancients to represent the positive and negative sides of our nature in such a subtle and nuanced manner by ascribing the versatility of personality to our demons with such colour and artistry.

The first and tallest of those standing stones has a head on it like Crom Dubh. He was the most recent of the pagan gods to replace Balor who was around, supposedly, at the time of Cessair. He had an evil eye that slew all who fell under its gaze. It took seven men to lift the lid on the eye. I know seven is the traditional magic number like in the seventh son of a seventh son or in the case of the farm, the Seven Wells of Oisín. The atmosphere here is about Balor and his grandson, Lugh. Balor was evil and Lugh was good and the house where I am writing has something to do with these ancient gods and I am only now beginning to appreciate it. August is called after Lugh; in the Irish – Lughnasa. Intuitively I knew the place had this magic spell and I was initially not very keen when they turned one side of the mountain into an arboretum. However, it made the magnificent views available to everybody. It is great that all this can be shared with all the people except so few of them are aware of its truly rich heritage. What a pity.

Moriarty used to talk about Lugh. At a deep level Lugh was the sun god who enhanced life with intelligence. At a shallower level, he could do tricks and magic and was the progenitor of the Leprechauns. He was the god who saved the fairy people, the Tuatha Dé Dannan – the followers of the goddess Ana. Ana was the earth mother and the old pagan Irish were pantheists. They believed everything was part of God and was God. They treated everything with a sense of wonder and believed in the magical properties of the earth. By comparison I have often felt that scientific analysis has drained a lot of the beauty of our perception from us. I also believe science proves that the Celts were right. Was it not from the world that man emerged from the slime of the bogs and marshes, first, as an amphibian until eventually, over millions of years, he developed a back bone and got up and walked? Moriarty also had another take on it. He believed humans were the dream of the world and the dream had come to life. He also said that it was the job of the poet to bring the dream to reality, to make sovereignty real. To bring the spirit to life meant it had not alone to be believed, but it also had to be acted on. Which brings me back to that day in August when Moriarty himself and Leacy called out to the pub following the service on me of the Writs for Possession.

It was about three o'clock in the evening. There was nobody in the pub, and I started drinking a pint of lager and reading the paper. The last customers had been at lunchtime and they were the remains of some American tourists who had been visiting the John F. Kennedy homestead less than a mile down the road from Whitechurch in Dunganstown. Leacy would only have a coffee because he was driving. I poured Moriarty a whiskey. Moriarty knew I was in financial trouble because Leacy had asked him to come with him saying that I was under a bit of pressure. I am quite open about my affairs. Maybe I have a boundaries' issue or maybe it is something to do with bravado. Maybe that is something I should look at. In any event, Moriarty told me to try to stay in touch with myself and be as real as possible. We drifted away from the subject as Leacy mentioned something about a delegation of bishops coming to Ireland from the Vatican to collect information on the child sexual abuse issue and what a nonsense that was, he said that he would still sue them all because he knew they would never tell the truth unless they were forced to.

I poured Moriarty another whiskey and he pleaded with Leacy to be careful, that the Church had eyes and ears everywhere and they could be very vindictive. It surprised me somewhat as I knew Moriarty was a very spiritual man and in the nineties, I was present when he gave sermons for Lent in the Seminary I had previously attended. He used the figure of Lugh in those sermons, especially the story of how he gained access to

Tara, as an example of how we discover ourselves. Entry could not be gained to Tara unless you had a craft or skill that was not owned by anyone within. Having announced to the sentry at the gate all of his several crafts and skills which entitled him to the name Sam-il-danach, entry was still forbidden him because for each craft he had mentioned there was someone within with that skill. This was where Lugh excelled. His brilliance lay in his ability to turn obvious disadvantage into advantage by cleverness, by trickery but always by the application of intense and brilliant light manifested in clear and simple wit.

He responded by asking if anyone had all the skills. Of course they hadn't, so immediately he was admitted. As I said, Lugh was regarded in tradition as the father of the Leprechauns. The Leprechauns were always pursued by mortals for their pot of gold, but the mortals were always outwitted. Aren't the Irish known throughout the world for their wit and their luck?

Living life happily is a matter of accepting ourselves as we are and understanding our ability to change and adapt to the challenges we meet, he told Leacy. Then pointedly he told me that I, too, would need to change my shape and I reacted by taking exception to being asked to change myself. He told me it was not myself that should change. I would always be myself. The DNA in me would never change. The soul in me would never change. This was because I owned my sovereignty, my belief in myself, because I knew where I was from and who I was. All I needed to change was my shape. I did not get it. At the mention of Lugh, I told him of the discovery I had made the previous night about the axis line from Sliabh Coillte through the standing stones down to Kilmokea. He was fascinated.

He wanted to see the standing stones. We went out the door of the public house and down the road a couple of hundred yards to the gate of the field where the standing stones were. The corn had only recently been cut and the gate was open. Then he did a remarkable thing. He told us to wait at the gate and he took off the jacket he was wearing and handed it to me and said to me very dramatically:

'Hold that. This is holy ground. Stay where you are. I am going forward alone.'

At first I thought he was a bit touched – a bit daft, but I could see he was utterly taken by the sacredness of the spot he was in. Leacy had looked away. I knew Leacy was not a cynic and he certainly was not a sneer but he was a little bit taken aback as well, a bit embarrassed I would say, and was afraid his reaction would be revealing of bemusement to say the least.

Moriarty walked down the gently sloping field to where the standing stones were. About twenty yards behind there was a Fulacht Fiadh. These were old eating places which were used in the Bronze age and later for cooking and were always located near a river. A stream would be diverted in a kidney shape by way of spur, and meat would be emptied into a hole into which the diverted water would course. When the stones were heated they would be put in with the meat which would already have been dressed and then it would be covered over and cooked.

As Moriarty was walking down the field, I spoke with Leacy about my more pressing legal problems. It was then he told me he would give some intense thought as to how the banks' case might be handled over the next few days. He thought it was going to be difficult. He must have noticed how anxious I was because it was then he reassured me and spoke to me about what Moriarty had said of Lugh and how you deal with problems. 'There is nothing so ugly that the application of intense and brilliant light will not beautify,' he said. The application of intense and brilliant light, he said, always brought solutions. I knew him to be good at his job and a great friend but I knew him to be honest as well. What he said at first about it being difficult really scared me and increased my anxiety. But he insisted the solution to the problem was always found within it, it was simply a question of looking at the problem patiently and intently. He really had taken Moriarty's philosophy to heart and was applying it directly to the problems, and the rat race in which he worked was delivering plenty of them to him on a daily basis. And now I was delivering another to him as well.

I looked at Moriarty removing his shoes, placing his hand on each of the standing stones and pausing, as if draining the energy into himself back from 5000 B.C. and the Beaker people who put them there. He was standing at the tallest of the stones, the Balor – the Crom Dubh – the

most powerful – the most evil stone looking towards the mountain, its
back to Kilmokea. He then put his shoes back on and made the sign of
the cross. What a complex man I thought.

As he was coming back up the field, Leacy asked me about Hazel and
I almost broke down. I told him we had not spoken for six weeks and I
was afraid things were going very badly for us. I told him this matter
would not help and he told me neither would the drink. I knew he was
right. The Presbyterian ethics of herself and her father despised my
drinking. I knew I was making matters worse and equally I knew I could
not stop.

When we got back to the pub, Moriarty was so energised there was a
radiance from his countenance. My humour was more sombre but he was
so enthused about the place it lifted my spirit in a bitter-sweet way as I
knew I was about to lose it all.

Leacy asked me to play the harp and reluctantly I pulled it out. It was
gone past five o'clock when I started to play the Culan (Culfhionn).
Moriarty was fascinated with the harp and had never before heard me
play. I had a painting of Denis Hempson, the 18th century harpist, hanging on the wall and I drew his attention to it. He studied it for a while
and then remarked at the cross expression that was on his face. I told him
that Hempson had been born in 1690 and that Bunting, the folklorist
and music collector, had the picture made at the Harpers' Festival in
Belfast in 1803. Bunting had asked Hempson to play a tune from the
time of the old Gaelic Order before 1690 and the tune he played was
'Faigh an Gleas'. ('Fetch the Instrument'). He could only play the first bit
as it upset him greatly because of the memories it recalled for him. Leacy
wittily remarked that Hempson was entitled to have a cross face on him
if he had lived in three centuries, but Moriarty observed he must have
had a great overview of life and I gave a smart Alec reply that he must
have had an overdose of it anyway, at which they both laughed. He then
took down from the wall a glassed and framed printed extract I had from
the Enactments of the Parliament of 1297. It was hanging on the wall
and was the legislation that forbade the wearing of hair in the Irish fashion down the back which was called the Culan (Culfionn) and where the
title of the tune and its provenance had come from. The tune was based

on a song in which the words recount how the lover missed her sweetheart and was no longer allowed to wear the Culan. They looked at the enactment, passing it from one to the other, and I played. It was the eleventh extract in the enactments for that year – AD1297. The extract was printed as follows:

[11] Also, in modern times, Englishmen, as if degenerate, wear Irish clothing and having their heads half-shaved, grow their hair long at the back of the head and call it a CULAN, conforming to the Irish both in dress and appearance. As a result, it frequently happens that some Englishmen are killed and taken to be Irishmen, although the killing of Englishmen and Irishmen requires to be punished in different ways: by such killings, a cause of enmity and rancour is generated among many people and the kindred of both the killer and the person killed are often by turns struck down as enemies . . .

Moriarty came back to me when I was finished and held my hand earnestly and told me that the awful thing the English tried to do was to rob us of our sovereignty, to make us live the way that suited them and their ways, but what suited them was not the same as what suited us. He said the Normans never tried that – they grew with us, but the English were different, they tried to change us. But how do you change the engineering of a man's mind or a man's soul or a man's body? Sovereignty was where ourselves, and the place we belong, unite. Those were his actual words and they still ring in my ears. 'Sovereignty is where ourselves, and the place we are, unite.' And, in a very real and meaningful way I was experiencing that connection. I could feel the attempts being made by the banks to disunite that and force me out. Sovereignty is like a man's home, I said. He agreed, and to reinforce the point, he told me another of his many stories.

He told me the story of Big Mike's son who roamed the world for thirty years looking to find himself. Moriarty had committed it to a compact disc and though I had played it many times before he came, I have to say it was great listening to him tell me once more. He also told me the same story on the day I first brought him to Waterford to the Retreat

Centre in Gracedieu to where he was then travelling. The story was recited the same way each time by him and I knew it was coming from the core of his being and what a great thrill that was to hear someone so genuine, articulate the truth.

Big Mike's son had been to the Outback in Australia and couldn't find himself. He had been to the Tibetan Monks where the Dalai Lama reigned and had spent time there and couldn't find himself. He had visited Native American Indians, and had seen voodoo in the Pacific and Africa and still had no joy. When his father died and he came home, at the risk of bringing a curse upon the fishing fleet in his village, he put out to fish with them in his late father's fishing cot. And one night in the dark when fishing, it all came to him. Suddenly, he now knew what he was searching for was deep within himself – it was his own sovereignty and he could only find it in his own place, in his own solitude.

It was too close to the bone for me – too much for me – and I broke down. I said it was a sin against humans that banks would be allowed to take a man from his home and evict him.

Memories of Foley's Fort and the evictions of 1897 three miles up the road in Ballykerogue immediately came to mind. It made national headlines in that time. Leacy remarked how he had often used it against financial institutions by telling them that on the basis that no one would buy a farm from which anyone had been evicted, they should try to negotiate instead. But I insisted there should be a law against that, there were other ways banks would have of getting their money but evictions were wrong and they were cruel and they were a breach of fundamental human rights. I recall Leacy saying that there were unenumerated rights in the Constitution of Ireland and given the types of changes that were taking place in the law I might yet have a point and maybe it should be included as one. I remember protesting vehemently that it should not be left to the Courts, that it was a matter for Government. Perhaps it was this outburst that provoked Moriarty, but at that point he taught me the big lesson. He told me I should learn from the land, learn from the history and learn from the mythology. I should learn from Lugh and change my shape and then with the clarity of mind of the genius in him, he recited the song of the Wandering Aengus from start to finish to make his point.

'I went out to the hazel wood because a fire was in my head,
I cut and peeled a hazel wand, and hooked a berry to a thread;
And when white moths were on the wing,
And moth-like stars were flickering out,
I dropped the berry in a stream
And caught a little silver trout.
When I had laid it on the floor I went to blow the fire aflame
But something rustled on the floor and someone called me by my
    name:
It had become a glimmering girl with apple blossom in her hair,
Who called me by my name and ran and faded through the brighten-
    ing air.'

It was at this point I again became tearful because I thought of Hazel and the love that I had for her, and still do, but I hid my upset as he continued.

Though I am old with wandering through hollow lands
    and hilly lands
I will find out where she has gone, and kiss her lips
    and take her hands
And walk among long dappled grass, and pluck till
    time and times are done
The silver apples of the moon, the golden apples of the
    sun.

                                            – W. B. Yeats

    I think I will get a cup of coffee now as I am becoming a little bit upset again with the memory of it all and I hope I do not find it too difficult to recall what happened next. I know they left sometime later that night and the next I remember is my bar manager, Matt, locking up after the night and I putting away the harp.

When I was taking my break with my cup of coffee and dreading the thought of what I have to face into now by recalling the memory of that night on the 1st of August, I thought I would fortify myself with a little spiritual reading. I do this now since I started on the AA programme – which is really a programme of living which leads you back to yourself and that, I suppose, is what I am doing now in writing my thoughts and feelings down on this paper for analysis so, I suppose, this has now become part of my process, too. One thing struck me that I read from the book I am currently reading. It said that most people are not really unbelievers as such. They appear to have rejected only the picture of God they were given for a different reason in a different time and place, mostly as children, and when they shook off the things of the child, they never replaced them visibly. I was intrigued to read about a Russian mathematician called Dr. Ivan Panin, a genius with figures. As a young man he was an active nihilist and participated in plots against the Tsar. He died a Harvard scholar and a citizen of the US in 1942. He was a firm agnostic, and when he converted to Christianity his fame at that stage was so huge it carried national headlines. By accident he discovered a mathematical code in the Bible, it was a complex code of numbering, the pursuit of which which he dedicated his life. The numbers ingrained through the Bible was a sort of inherent water-mark, if you like, a type of literary DNA, where numbers are a type of literary seal to block counterfeiting. A Bible in numeric appears to be God's watermark – a type of seal of authenticity. The sixty-six books of the Bible were written by thirty-three different people who were scattered throughout various countries of the world and the Bible was written over a fifteen-hundred-year period with a four-hundred-year silence. Yet the books are found to be a harmonious record, each in accord with the other. When he tried to rationalise this, Dr. Panis pronounced:

'If human logic is worth anything at all we are simply driven to the conclusion that if the facts I have presented are true, a man could never have done this.'

That's all very well and comforting for a man who is driven to despair and looking for a meaning in life. But could it be true? It is also a consolation to discover an insight he had which he shares with us: two men pleased God, one who serves him with all his heart because he knows him, and one who seeks him with all his heart because he doesn't. I suppose I didn't. I suppose I fall into the latter category. I have been strongly drawn to Thomas Merton, the American writer and Trappist Monk, who died following an electrocution in Thailand in 1968. One thing he wrote which makes this current exercise relevant for me :

'Without a more profound human understanding derived from exploration of the inner ground of human existence, love will tend to be superficial and deceptive.'

I suppose the depth of my feelings and my upset on that day in August literally vomited themselves up through me and perhaps I can see how an analysis now in the cold light of day some months later could be really worthwhile and illuminating.

Today is Valentine's Day and the campaigning for a general election is underway. They tell us this is the most important election for some time and maybe they are right. Because of the mess the country is in and because the Government have signed up to a four-year deal with the International Monetary Fund and the European Central Bank, I think the immediate result will make little difference. But it will give the country a four-year period of retreat to consider what they really want to do. To a great extent we have given over the power of our own determination to others outside of us. Leacy was furious about it and insists that our sovereignty is shed. He points to Article 282 of the Lisbon Treaty which was passed last year 2009. He was completely against it. It says that the European Central Bank is independent of all the member states and is free from their influence. They now tell us what we can and can't do when it comes to money, more or less. This affects me in two ways. First, I am a developer who sold houses on the basis that the banks would lend money to my customers to buy from me. The banks couldn't lend half quickly enough and we couldn't charge half enough. We wanted to get rich quickly. I wanted to get out of debt fast. Secondly, now that the bubble has burst, the banks who misread the situation and created the problem blinded by their own greed, now want all of their money back as quickly as possible with as high a rate as possible. The Irish banks played their way out of the game and now it is the Central Europeans who are calling the shots. You could see the way the last government started behaving in a giddy fashion towards the latter end of its time in office how they had lost all sense of their sovereign integrity. Once they knew the responsibility was taken from their shoulders, they gave up their ability and our right to control our own destiny. It would have been hilarious if it had not been so tragic.

I realize I am spending a lot of time before I come to the point of what happened on the first of August. You see I am afraid of who I will meet in my heart when I go back in my mind. Anyway here goes:

When Leacy and Moriarty left the pub that night, Matt left shortly afterwards. I took down the Parliamentary Enactment of 1297 about the Culan which Moriarity had put back on the wall after he had read it. I poured myself a double Jameson. I always drank doubles – ' do nothing by halves,' was my motto.

The English tried to change us into something we were not I thought to myself as I re-read the framed Enactment. Then I thought of the High Court Writs. I would be forced to the road. I remember thinking the Seven Wells of Oisín would become a synonym for evictions, the same as Foley's Fort had in the 1800s. A pain like a fire came into my head and I thought of Moriarty and the Wandering Aengus and the Hazel Wood. Then my thoughts went to Hazel and how this would drive a further wedge between us. I started to ruminate that these were changed times. Nobody would buy Foley's Fort so they brought the battering ram. They wouldn't need a battering ram this time. Some money-grabbing, unscrupulous disconnected foreigner, caring little for community or tradition, would put in a bid and bide his time. The foreigner would later sell it on for a handsome profit when the markets regained their confidence and when people would again slip into the vicious circle of once more borrowing, and once more paying high interest rates while slaving away their lives to meet usurious interest rates to satisfy bankers in Dublin and Berlin. They wouldn't care about his inheritance of his grandmother's farm, nor the three standing stones, nor the Seven Wells of Oisín, nor care a fig for the sacred atmosphere of the Lost Mountain, or any other place for that matter, lost or found.

I was ruined. The more I thought about it, the more I thought about Hazel and how these pressures had driven me to drink and alienated her further from me and her father as well. Not alone had I failed to repay the bank but I was now a waster, a ne'er-do-well, a feckless fool whose head was stuck in the clouds or in a book. I had fanciful notions of an ancient pedigree that was far from the reality of where sound and sensible people worked and lived, decently, honestly and soberly. And paid their debts. Hazel's love was the only one in my life. She has great interests in history and mythology. She got it from her grandfather who was a Presbyterian Minister. We met in the Wexford Historical Society, a most unlikely venue for romantics and my field research fascinated her as it brought all of the myths to life. Moriarty used say, I remember, that a poet had a duty to bring the reality of men's thoughts which were bedded in them into the light of day. I think I said that already. But I could feel I was losing the determination to fight. I could feel I was giving in to drink and the more I felt this, the more I needed drink. She told me she could not stand my drinking and she issued an ultimatum and stormed out the door. I know now that my pride got the better of me and I have learned this from going to the meetings. Nobody was going to tell me what to do. I could not give in to being manipulated just to avoid a row.

'Work hard and drink hard,' the Luctleanunaigh or Luchtleanamhnaigh used to say. She thought he was a bad influence on me. I was a bad influence on myself and nobody else.

I remember getting up and getting more drink and deciding I wanted to compose a backing for The Song of the Wandering Aengus. That moment of brilliance that I had been drinking for was beginning to come. I remembered the nineteenth-century journeyman poet Red Mick O'Brien who composed 'The Ballyshannon Lane' one hundred years after the Rebellion of 1798:

'I paused for a while beside the stile of the courtyard in Courthoyle

'Twas the month of June and the silvery moon o'er rebels' graves did sail

Near Jack Keating's gate, where I chanced to wait, my thoughts drove me

insane

I prayed for the dead and through Raheen fled through the Ballyshannon

Lane'

I had been plucking on the 'D' string of the harp when it all came together in a confluence. The confluence. Where the Three Rivers met. The confluence where Éire, Banba and Fodhla met in sovereignty. The confluence where Bith, Ladrann and Tuan arrived with seven times seven women and three men. Where the three of us, Leacy and Moriarty and myself, had met and where the three standing stones stood in The Temple of Brightness.

And then there was the inspirational flash of Moriarty reciting the poem and the trout changing to the girl and Lugh, the Samildanach – the shape-changer galloping into the battle – the second battle of Moytura – to defeat and replace the demonic with the divine. To change evil into good. Change!

Change! Change! Change!

Change! The poem was telling me.

Change! Moriarty and Lugh were telling him.

Change! The poem was telling me.

But the rebel pedigree and the rebel songs said fight. Fight!

Fight! Fight! Fight!

More voices were screaming at me, flee. Flee!

Flee! Flee! Flee!

And then my conversation with Moriarty fought back through the turmoil,

'You are saying I should trade myself in for someone else?'

And Moriarty's keen and deliberate exhortation which echoed and reverberated back to me.

'Change your shape, not yourself. Change your SHAPE, not yourself.

YOUR shape, your SHAPE.'

Moriarty's eulogy to my dying spirit came back to me about how the Irish ended up on the fringes of Europe as a result of all of the wars and battles that were fought there, and immigrations from Central Europe, not unlike now, resulted in all of the invasions into Ireland away from the controlling power of those at the centre and the attractive idyll that the prospect of fleeing brought. The ancestors of the Irish threw all of that power to one side and resumed the natural progression of their own development by sailing to the furthest extremities to practise it away from the hardness of argument and judgement. The clarity of thought excited me. I had the psyche of an Irishman not a foreigner and then I remembered Moriarty's parting benediction to all. The head must serve in order to let the heart rule. Not the other way around which is what happened.

Socrates, Aristotle and Plato – the supposed great minds of the Western world – may yet turn out to be the corner boys of history.

The argument is not King – simple kindness is King.

The world and life are not arguments to be won. The world is a place to survive and live joyfully – not under sufferance of some oppressor.

Humility is the heart and soul of wisdom.

Sometimes you fight.

Sometimes you flee.

But you always change because life is a continuum of change.

I challenged him that he was proposing a revolution but he looked at me sanguinely and said:

'No, there is an older and more fundamental reality. One that says that your soul is eternal.

But bodies can and do change their shape – if you let them.

Be humble and listen to what your solitude is telling you from within.'

But now that Moriarty and Leacy were long gone and I was helping myself to another drink, the doubts returned. Wasn't this all piseog and fairy tale though? Could you imagine bringing notions of this nature to a legal forum? Couldn't you just imagine making a legal submission?

'I know you want to repossess my farm but actually it's an ancient enchanted Temple and the pub is a Palace belonging to the Ancient Kings of Ireland of whom I am a direct descendent and on that account I would be obliged if you would tell the banks to go back to their masters in Berlin and let me go back to Mileadach and Cessair where it all started and let me get on with living out the rest of Irish History in peace and tranquility and I'm sorry the auld housing development didn't work out quite so well as all had hoped and expected. But, sure you know yourself – what the hell – you win some, you lose some'

What a successful defence that might be.

'Oh, and by the way, I'm going to change me shape!'

The humorous tangent I had run off on began to lose its funny side, as I slithered back into glumness. Depression. I pondered a bit more on the thought of the trout shimmering and changing into the shape of the beautiful girl, Hazel. I slithered down some more whiskey.

And then I grimly remembered – I am a man in debt. I have no money, therefore I am fucked. That was rational thought. That was reality. These thoughts banged around in my head as I clattered and collided with the bar stool and the harp that I was trying to put away. I supped some beer and I recall knocking over the bar stool, which I straightened. Looking back now I can see the progressive nature of my disease. I used never get drunk so quickly and I convinced myself I was not that bad. I remember going out the door and deciding that tonight I would walk home the mile and a half to the Seven Wells of Oisín. I remember meandering along the road and thinking about Hazel and the mixture of joy and depression that welled up and down, up to bitter sweetness and down to black depression. I remember crying. I am crying now as I remember back but I must keep writing.

My situation looked desperate. What was the point? How could I face my family and my friends and all those who had relied on me? I remember looking up at the moon's pale surface through the skeagh thorn bushes. I remember stopping at the gate into the field of the standing stones which had not been shut. In the field there was a light surface fog about two to three feet over the ground and with the moon shining on it, it looked like something out of a fairy storybook. The standing stones were like three sharks' fins on a flat ocean. Pointed. Sticking up out of the fog, as fins above the sea surface. I remember going towards them. They were now an island in an ocean of fog, with gaps of stubble showing through here and there. The last I remember was putting out my hand to the tallest of the standing stones – the stone that represented Balor – the big one with the awkward head – and as I leaned forward I remember falling headlong down – down – down. I fell down between the stones into the grass, head over heels tumbling down, down, down.

I will now write what comes into my head as I have been doing and I am not sure what of this I remember as having happened or simply the way it seems to me now. My breath is coming in staggers.

I groped around in the scutch grass where the blade of the combine harvester had kept away from the stones. There was a rope – I saw it. Dark thoughts came to me. The height of the trees at the Fulacht Fiadh in the corner of the field beckoned to me like palm trees on a Pacific island paradise in the light of the yellowing moon. I wanted them to help me and went towards them with the rope. I can't remember my thoughts. I can't remember my feelings. I remember throwing the rope, and throwing the rope, as it missed. I remember railing at the tree and sobbing and falling backwards and sideways. I staggered into the stream and back out and fell and cut my knees on a stone – I held my knee and felt exhausted and tried to get up but I fell back down and I remember hitting the ground with my fists and cursing everyone, whoever ate in the Fulacht Fiadh, whoever walked in the field and whoever placed me at the centre of the universe. I began to feel something. I was an isotropic man in the middle of the universe where there was no perspective. I was a man floating in a pool in the dark in the middle of the night not knowing where was up or down, in or out, north or south, east or west. Suddenly I saw a vision of single-file, long-cloaked, grey-bearded, armed warriors, poets and kings, come from behind me into my body and out of it, and as they came into my body I could feel my stomach begin to churn, and as they came out of it, I heaved and retched and vomited out all of these ancient heroes in my pedigree, entombed within me over centuries, layer upon layer of years of breeding all encased within my mortal coil, now being forced into existence, and out of existence, all at the same time, all coming into confluence in me, and dispersed out of me in a paradoxical birthing, and still birth, in grotesque and macabre umbilical connection and disconnection, all at the same time. I was exhausting myself. I could feel the life going out of me. I had no reason to live. The rope was around my neck and I was climbing and falling and I remember ringing the bell rope. I was pulling on it to ring the bell, but each time I pulled, I just felt pain and I could feel I was suffocating and I kept pulling and pulling and then I was shivering, shivering. Then the shivering stopped and I went limp and I began to float and float. I was floating on the fog which was swirling and swirling and I was swooning and swinging from the umbilical bell rope that was ringing and ringing and my body went limper and limper and I found myself drowning in the fog and then there was dark. Dark, dark, dark. Then there was cold. Cold, cold, cold.

It was then I saw the blue sparkling light. At first it appeared like a beautiful flickering star, and its beauty took me. It began to slowly spin and then rapidly, and then in a surge of magnificence it exploded into sheer and brilliant light. I was blinded and called on God. I cried out, 'O God! O God!' But as spontaneously as the words were uttered, there formed in my eye, without effort, without pain, without suffering, a vision of a beautiful woman – a most beautiful woman, but then again she looked worn and haggard, with a babe in arms. She looked up and saw me and smiled the most beguiling and beautiful smile such that her wan face became radiant and her visage changed to that of beatific vision. It was Hazel. But then her countenance darkened once more as the scene changed yet again. A dark and gathering cloud changed into a gigantic being with an evil face, one which was distant from me but one which I recognised – it was the face of unrelenting demand with the aspect of red tooth and red claw, its demeanour was vicious. It had one eye. That eye was closed. From the dregs of my scholarship and learning, the image was becoming a reality and I knew I was looking at Balor of the Evil Eye. This was evil incarnate and the face initially was unclear. I knew I recognised the personality which was the direct contradictory opposite of the spéirbhean of Irish mythology, the beautiful muse – who was holding her strong boy child. Was this Eithne, the daughter of Balor who married Cian who gave birth to Lugh who killed Balor at the second battle of Moytura? Was I Cian, the husband and lover of Eithne? Her beauty was not receding but regarding Balor without fear, not challenging him defiantly but maintaining a strength of presence and inner peace. Then the face of Balor revealed itself as that of Hazel's father, the bank manager, and all the banks were represented in him. The child in Hazel's arm became uneasy and writhed and as it writhed it grew and wrestled from her arms, the child changed into a golden-haired boy and leaped to the ground, released the cord from around my neck and, by a trick of magic, turned the cord that now strangled me into a weapon to save me by magically turning it into a slingshot. This was the magic and philosophy of Lugh to turn disadvantage into advantage. However, immediately seven men, who were under cover and bearing bank logos on their tunics, leaped from where they were concealed in the mountain heather, each from one of the Seven Wells of Oisín and rushed forward to lift the lid of the Eye of Balor in order to release the shaft of lethal light that would slay all in its path. Spirals and circles spun around the face of Balor which resonated a fear within me which turned to loathing and revulsion as the dread and threat of him moved forward. My strangled windpipe sucked in the air which rushed through my ears. The monster would now destroy me as the lid commenced its upward journey lifted by the seven men over the ball of the eye. As its exposure was commencing, a shot from the sling shot of the golden-haired boy found its mark in the dark-centred pupil of the evil eye and split the skull wide open with a shattering thunderous cacophonous explosion of penetrating sound that burst open the vision as the Taidhbhse of the Second Battle of Moytura came to the end of its repetitious enactment in the slaying of the grandfather of evil by his golden grandson of innocence and youth. And the female form of Hazel from Eithne turned towards Éire, Banba and Fodhla as the Three Sisters, The Nore, The Barrow, and The Suir whispered their names as she hauntingly repeated a mantra,

'Depend on us for we are you. Depend on us for we are you,' and the spéirbhean of sovereignty, passed into the day as gently as she had come into the night.

There was nothing left except a deep dark blue sky and the sound of voices and rough feet on grass. I remembered someone pressing on my chest to respirate me in the manner paramedics do in films as the last of my retching and vomiting trickled from me. I was lying there in wasted fashion.

I believe it was seven o'clock when they found me at the bottom of the field, shivering, bathed in sweat blood and vomit. I heard afterwards they said I was "jammering and speaking gibberish into the ground like a man who had lost his reason".'

I must pause now. It is now five o'clock in the evening of Valentine's day. I have taken the afternoon to recover but I want to finish this. I need to finish this. I feel wasted and tired. I am drinking a cup of coffee and I have slept for two hours already. I am not going to try to analyse all that happened other than to say the reality is that there are marks on my neck from the rope and that is a very harsh reality with which I have to live. I found it hard to swallow for a few days after I came into the hospital. The unit was good for me particularly the group therapy. I think I cried everyday for three weeks. The Librium kicked in early but I found detoxing very hard at first.

What have I been able to learn from it all? Mainly I think I discovered a side of me that has a passion for life that frightens me. The bottom line is I don't want to change from who I am but things are changing around me and I have to change with them and it seems that though I heard everything that was said, I was unable to listen to it and believe it.

Leacy called to see me when I was in hospital. He is a good man and one upon whom I can rely to do what is best for me. I always knew the reality was that the pub would have to be sold, but, sound man that he is, he is negotiating for me with the bank from a position of strength. It is hard to believe that a position of strength could be found in the landscape of disaster that somehow turned out to be my life. When I said this to him he told me it was my innate self was the strong position and that was what Moriarty was referring to as my sovereignty. The deep part of me was the farm alright and not so much the land and the income from it but the place where I call home and associate with being alive and which has helped form my values and my identity that keeps me together. Stuff like this has no place in commerce; it is not unlike a woman's entitlement to not be thrown out of her house or home because of a profligate husband, or a man for that matter, by an arrogant wife. Mostly men of my generation were the title-holders but people are beginning to see that differently now. I am a man of my generation inherent with all of the prejudices with which I have grown up. I notice it now and again and try to change just like I tried to retrieve my obvious prejudice there now about married men being the owners of the property where they live with their wives and family.

Leacy had his flash of inspiration – his moment where the ugliness of what the bank was doing was subjected to the concentration of his intense and brilliant light and, not unlike my own metamorphosis, it yielded strange results which are still ongoing. He found a loophole. My mother's Power of Revocation over the title to the farm meant that she was entitled to revoke the settlement of the property on me. He said it was clearly obvious, because the bank had thought not to disturb her at the point during the Celtic Tiger years when things were going well, (that would never be done) and could not now as she was suffering from Alzheimer's. But people with Alzheimer's have moments of perfect lucidity and know perfectly well what is going on and can be perfectly clear at times. But where would the property go once taken back from me? This was a vexed question of law as to how she could pass it on because the deed said it had to remain in the family. There might be a way around this in ordinary circumstances. But when you're insolvent, you can't change your title in order to defeat your creditors – that is fraud.

This raised a whole issue for me which is probably relevant and that is about emotional security and control. I suspect the extreme feelings I was experiencing had a lot to do with that and I think that is where Hazel came in as well. Leacy told me he would have to think longer about it, but he felt we were on the right track and if we were, life would help. I asked him to see Hazel.

I have spoken very little about her and her influence in my life which probably says more about me than all I have written. I think maybe I am too self-centred and maybe this is coming out in me now as a result of the new programme I am following at the meetings. I know that since I came into hospital she was very concerned and quickly I began to see how much a part of my life she was and how much I wanted to marry her and raise a family. I have often wondered how her face ended up as the face of the spéirbhean in the vision, I know from my study of mythology that the Goddess of Sovereignty came to life and beauty when her true love came to her, and became worn and haggard when that love was threatened, and I recall again that aspect of the hallucination in the field of the standing stones. I also understand that the evil represented by Balor was the threat that came from the banks, which her father also represented, and is more than likely why his face was that of the evil Balor. I wondered for a long while about the golden boy who leaped from Hazel's arms and I am still afraid even mentioning it to you from fear you may think I have become insane. I know I am not insane and I know you do not think I am insane but I find it very difficult to explain some matters in the story I have written. I suppose the best thing is to simply keep writing out the facts and let the rest of it explain itself because I find I am still afraid to do so.

Shortly after I had seen Leacy in hospital, I asked him to ask Hazel to come to see me. She had sent text messages enquiring after me, and I had responded, but they were only messages and nothing personal. I don't do personal stuff in text messages or on the phone. The second time Leacy came to visit me and told me about his brainwave. I started getting a lot better and his news encouraged me a lot. I asked him if he had spoken with Hazel and he told me he had spoken to her only briefly. I was disappointed but I phoned her next day and she agreed to come to see me after I told her I was more and more determined about the drink and that I knew I had a big problem.

I was three weeks in the hospital and a week into the unit when she came. I was going through a rough time, and as I had no family, I asked her if she would come in for me to the group meeting on the family day. This is a big group meeting. Everybody else has a family who does it. Reluctantly she agreed. On the following week when she came, she followed the protocol of the rest of the families in the group who recounted for the entire group the hard life that had been meted out to the members of the family of the alcoholic by each of them. These meetings were very difficult for me.

The families had all been told it was important not to spare the patient and you will recall my telling you about the awful experience it was for me. I knew she was upset by my drinking but I never expected she would be so upset or so hard on me. It seemed to do her a lot of good and she agreed to come back the following week also.

The second week was much more difficult, not because of what she said at the meeting but what she told me afterwards. She asked that we have a one-to-one meeting with the group psychologist after the business of the day. I agreed. Other couples who were going through a rough time in their own relationship, did this. They were mostly people who were married. I was not expecting what she told me and I was glad the psychologist was present. She told me she had agonised over the entire situation and she was glad I was doing so well. She said she was really proud of me for addressing it but she would have to break off the engagement. Though it was already broken off anyhow, I was still shocked. I was numbed and was unable to speak. It was then that she told me for the first time she was four months pregnant. She burst out into tears and all I could do was cry and cry and cry with her. It was then that the real devastation that I had caused came home to me with force and brutality. It was her tenderness and sensitivity that penetrated my thick hide and, not unlike the slingshot to the Eye of Balor, burst me open inside. I know that hallucinations are all part of yourself like dreams are, and I know that much as I would like to characterise them as being the responsibility of somebody else, I know they are all about my own issues. It took me a long time to leave her and it was the first time since I went into the hospital that I felt I really needed a drink. Isn't that funny, the very last thing

I needed was a drink and here it was the first thing that suggested itself to me? The hospital facilitators were very good. When she left she agreed to come back for the last day the following week, two days, before I would be allowed home.

For the entire week I thought of nothing else except the hurt and the damage I had caused to everybody else but it was then I learned I had caused most of the hurt to myself. I knew once I had accepted that, I was really starting the road to recovery, and that was the first time I began to understand I really had lost myself and I really needed to claim that back. When I told Leacy that weekend he called up to see me, his eyes lit up. He apparently saw an opportunity to defeat the banks in their claim on my home. The pregnancy of Hazel opened up an opportunity.

A transfer of the farm from my mother to my child would leave the banks with nothing to charge their judgement on. I told him there was no way was I going to jeopardise anybody further with my problems especially Hazel and most especially our child. He was surprised at that. I had already told Hazel of how he proposed dealing with the banks on the Power of Revocation and she thought that was great even though her father was the bank manager. Then the depth of everything struck me. The bank manager's own grandson would actually defeat the banks in their own malicious, insidious, acquisitive pursuit. Life indeed seemed to be coming to the rescue. Could I really participate in it – would it not be just too – what's the word – too venal – too facile – too mercurial – too cheap? If she could think like that, did it really mean she loved me? For the first time I began to feel secure. I knew I was thinking about myself again. It was really my own security with her I did not want to jeopardise. I am beginning to go in on myself and start confusing my motives.

When she came back the following week, I still did not mention it particularly when she told me she had a scan and they were able to say that the child she was carrying was a boy.

It is too much for me to take on board that in some way at some deep level all of this connection worked itself out in the field that night in August 2010. I refuse to believe that at some deep level I was aware Hazel was pregnant with my son and that, in a paradox of paradoxes, this innocent was going to defeat its grandfather's bank in taking what they claimed and was not rightfully theirs. When I got out of the hospital and got back to the Seven Wells, Hazel had the place tidied up for me and there was a fresh bouquet of flowers waiting for me on my arrival home. I drove home myself as I was well able and back to full strength, well almost to full strength, at that stage and I wanted to ease myself slowly back into what I was going to do. Beside the vase of flowers was an envelope with a welcome card beside it and on it was written a poem by Amergin, the first poet of Ireland and the poet of the Milesians, the last of the Celtic invaders she had last spoken to me about in hospital. I read the poem.

I am the Wind that blows over the sea;
I am the Wave of the Ocean;
I am the Murmur of the billows;
I am the Ox of the Seven Combats;
I am the Vulture on the rock;
I am a ray of the Sun;
I am the fairest of Plants;
I am a Wild Boar in valour;
I am a Salmon in the Water;
I am a Lake in the plain;
I am the Craft of the artificer;
I am a Word of Science;
I am the Spear-point that gives battle.
I am the God that creates in the head of man the fire of thought.
Who is it that creates in the head of man the fire of thought?
Who is it that enlightens the assembly upon the mountain, if not I?
Who tells the ages of the moon, if not I?
Who shows the place where the sun goes to rest, if not I?

I had told Hazel everything and had told her that I really did not know what to do, but I had let her know what was going through my mind and all I really knew was that I really loved her and she was the only one I trusted. She had been my anchor but that now I had to find myself and I could not hand over decisions to anyone. I could learn from the hospitals and the standing stones' experience and from Leacy and Moriarty, and I could even learn from Lugh. It was then she struck me dumb. 'Do you know Lugh was a god to the Tuatha Dé Dannan – but they moved on in time too and were replaced by the last of the Celtic invaders – the Milesians, or had you forgotten?' She was telling me I had been too wrapped up in myself. She was telling me I had been too tuned in – too introverted. It was time to move on – to move out. It was now time to leave the hospital. And then when I arrived home the card that was waiting for me was by the poet of the Milesians.

I cried then and I am crying now as I write these last words. I don't know how things are going to work out but I know how important it is that I don't know. It is only by being myself and fighting for what I believe in that it will happen.

I know if I fight for what I believe in there is a good chance things will change for me in that direction and that appears to be also how I will change my own shape. But then, I have to let things happen too – and I will have to work with them as well. Maybe Hazel and the baby and me will work out – and, maybe it won't – but I hope it will. Maybe she will hope for the same. Maybe our thoughts and feelings will bring us to the same place – in confluence. Maybe they already have.

These are my thoughts and feelings as they have come to me and I have related them for you as best I can. This is the place for me to finish I believe.

Signed: Roger Sutton
Dated: August 25th

I hear a car and see the lights coming up towards the house. I will put down my pen now. It might be Hazel. I hope it is.

Before you leave the stories in this book you should know . . .

Always, at the end of a show in the parish hall, the person responsible for putting it on came out on stage after the curtain dropped, and thanked the parish priest for the use of the hall. This was right, proper and moral and entirely what was to be expected in a civilised village. Because I was well reared, I am now doing the same.

The lives of hundreds, perhaps thousands, of people have provided the background, the provenance, the content and the material for the research, writing and production of *Sacred Cows Silent Sheep*.

Everyone of them is a part player on the stage of our society in which politicians, bankers, teachers, guards, lawyers, priests, judges, travellers, public servants, altar boys, nuns, doctors, jugglers, movers, shakers and others too motley and numerous to mention play a leading role for good or for bad, are represented in this book. I thank them all. In one church every one of them is a sinner. In another church, having endured what they have endured, they are saints. I therefore thank the cute hoors, the hypocrites, and the backstabbers, those who are daily communicants and those who are lapsed Protestants. I thank those who are atheists and have given up on their lack of beliefs and those who have now lapsed and are back as Catholics again. A few of them do good where they can. A few of them do bad when they are let. The rest of them come to me for representation.

I hope this book has inspired, consoled, vexed, entertained and provoked your thought processes and maybe inspired you to belief and action or affliction and depression. At least I hope you have not been unmoved. Most especially I would like to thank you for having taken the trouble to read this far.

I thank Lillian for her endurance beyond what normal human living would require. Thank you to the six other Kennedys of Duncannon, Patrick, Brian, Niamh, Gráinne and Niall and my eldest Sinead who has emigrated to Gorey where she resides with Padhraig and the two dedicants of this book, Ciaran and Cathal.

Michael Freeman, my editor, was a source of annoyance, frustration, bemusement, amusement and every other emotion betwixt. He is responsible for all the mistakes. I will only take credit for what you believe to be good within these pages. I salute Brigid, his wife, for her remarkable bravery and perseverance.

Margaret Cullen from Wexford typed and typed and typed and more especially observed, cajoled and challenged. I am truly grateful for her assistance throughout this marathon.

Helen Ashdown of Clonleigh, Palace, sub-editor and Paddy Whelan of Ballinruane, Ballycullane, researcher gave valuable assistance in their criticism and production of editorial. They challenged the depths of what I could give. The dynamic of passing drafts to and fro has caused depth of reflection and input from other than the author and peppered the text with nuance I could not have imagined alone. Great credit is due to them for work which is unseen but makes all the difference.

My secretary Mary Bradley and Denise (Dinjo) Doyle who typed when the pressure was on, and gave out when the pressure was off, had the craic with me, jeered me and encouraged me to the end. Rosemary (Prunella) Whelan, whose incisive wit and slicing humour peeled away the prospect of any fat developing on me, kept me on my toes at all times. (She thought the book should be about her!)

Media adviser Peter O'Connell, vice president of Publishing Ireland, arranged an interview for me with Oprah Winfrey. It didn't take place. I don't think she was up to it.

Declan Lyons, author, editor and communications adviser, from

Arthurstown and Glenageary held the manuscript up to the light and found errors of fact and conundrums of meaning which I dutifully ignored (They needn't think they're going to come down here from Dublin and tell us what we have to do).

Seán O'Keeffe, managing director and Dan Bolger of the editorial staff at Liberties Press painstakingly formatted all sixty-six thousand words of the manuscript into perfectly laid out pages. (There are actually sixty-six thousand, seven hundred and sixty-three words. Count them if you don't believe me!)

Sinéad Molony, independent professional editor, who with such incisive clarity and professional perfectionism having fasted for forty days and forty nights found two mistakes which have made all the difference. (We said we'd leave them in!)

Sinead McKenna of Sin É Design, Dublin designed the cover and in the process tried to recruit me for a paramilitary organisation with links to the Far East. (I nearly tried that once).

Clara Phelan, assistant editor with Liberties Press with perspicacity and gimlet eye eradicated useless adverbs and adjectives and put them all neatly, correctly, adverbially on the long, white, smooth silk like, beautiful sheets of paper. (We didn't let her read this piece!) Longingly, lovingly, dutifully, I therefore thank her for making the long smooth, silk white pages look so well.

And then to those others ... The members of Hal's Ceili Band, Peter Daunt-Smyth, Clare Doyle, Dr. Kevin Byrne, Mary Rowe, Eddie Rowe, Dave Walters, Willie Waters, Paddy Molloy, Padraig Molloy, Mick Kent, Sean Murray (when he arrives), Mick Finn (even when he doesn't), King Tom who keeps the rhythm sweet, Liz Cassidy and the Sundance Sid (her husband) and Ned Wall who hasn't been back for a while.

The jamboree of emotions provoked by insults, criticisms, good music and flat notes where there should be sharps, counter balanced by the juxtaposition of the geography of the players in arrangement around the bar stools and tables in the Strand Tavern in Duncannon every Thursday night provokes mirth, myth and amusement among those visiting longing to stay and those resident longing to leave. At this hour of my life, it is the closest I can get to playing Junior Hurling again.

The card school of Richard Tobin, Dick Power, Mattie Molloy and Peter Dunning, Brian Stafford (before he left), Brendan Chapman (who always takes up his trick), Seamus Cooney (who never misses a trick), Pat O'Connor (who always wins the money). Notwithstanding that the last two are from a colder climate in a neighbouring parish, the hospitality and warmth extended to them has kept them returning to the Fort Conan Hotel on a Sunday evening with the odd interruption by the odd broken leg.

My thanks also to the Sliabh Coillte Heritage Group of John Flynn, Danny Brennan, Mairead Cairbre, Dick Shannon, Noel McHugh and Bill Hurley who encouraged me in my interpretation that the Great Flood myth emanated from Kilmokea. Of greater significance is the legend that Noah's granddaughter Cessair landed there with forty nine women and three men as explained in the last story. According to John Flynn who, when he heard this, stood up, pulled open his waistcoat, put out his chest and said in the words of Lord Denning, 'This is a vista too appalling to contemplate.'

The proprietors and staff of Roche's Bar, Duncannon who, in ease of this struggling author, have augmented the finances of my various children from time to time for the purpose of maintaining a third level education and a broader education behind the bar.

The staff in Monart Destination Spa provided me with a refuge and haven when one was needed – which was often – and supplied pots of coffee (even more often).

Fr John Nolan gave me permission to denigrate the church from time to time without fear of excommunication. (I hereby return the compliment, Pope!)

The members of St. James GAA Club (men and women, young and old) who proved that sovereignty survives in spite of adversity and that successes fought for in the past are harbingers to a brighter future, notwithstanding the rigorous test to which the club insists its members pass through annually.

The clergy (men and women of undoubted belief), a hierarchy (of questionable belief), The Pope (who doesn't really believe in me) and the Almighty Himself, for my irreverence for which, I know He will readily forgive (and a good job too) deserve thanks.

Liam Stafford B.L. advised me not to mention him.

An t-Uachtaráin, the Taoiseach, the Cabinet, both Houses of the Oireachtas, the Courts and all the ombudsmen, the Civil Service and all those in power (including the former Fianna Fáil party) the present Fianna Fáil party, Sinn Féin, the IRA and the Green Party, the Blueshirts, the Reds under the Beds (not SIPTU), all of the ombudsman's committee for the rights of everybody's rights and its various sub-committees, Amnesty International and the Duncannon Tidy Towns Committee.

All of the above have been considered in no small measure (and a bigger measure than they could imagine) to the amalgamation of thoughts, experiences, existential considerations and other associated day dreams that manifest themselves in a process known as my thinking, from which this book has delivered me from future turmoil and torment. A special word of thanks to the Tuatha De Dannan.

Sutisa Yaetong from Thailand, Erika Tyschenko from Lithuania, Adam and Anna Zabrowska from Poland and the rest of our exotic citizens from other communities with their scintillating differences who have transformed Ireland into a shimmering emerald of dazzling variety with a new and unique perception which helps challenge Sacred Cows and Silent Sheep in a beautiful and more involved way.

In the consideration of the extraordinary wider world, I thank the following: John F Kennedy (lately deceased) for implying that he was related to me (notwithstanding the absence of forensic evidence the veracity whereof will be challenged by me at an appropriate time), Pope John XXIII for starting the Vatican Council, Pope Paul VI for continuing it and the deceased Archbishop of Dublin who tried to stop it. Her Majesty the Queen for visiting us last year in the sure and certain knowledge that all of us will return the compliment and give her a shout by calling over there one of these fine days. Barack Obama for feidearing ar linn and Simon Bolivar who claimed Irish association, not unlike many the dacent president of an American country, before him and since. All of these have their place in this book and their influence on me as I am sure they do on you.

I reserve the last and special thanks for our leaders in Europe. Long may they stay there. May they long benefit from any money they may give us. We thank them from the bottom of our hearts. Now that we have duly acknowledged our sincerely felt thanks in that respect, let not the matter of the few bob we owe them come between us and a good night's sleep. If there is a bit of luck coming our way we won't be behind the bush giving what we can spare. If they operate under the mistaken belief they were acquiring an interest in the country I am sure they will understand issues of this nature from time to time internationally, have occasionally been sorted out by a war or two, but as we all know, sure we're well past that now.

It only remains for me on behalf of the cast and the whole ensemble to wish you all a very good night and a safe journey home. Would the last one down at the back of the hall turn off the light in the porch on the way out and pull the door after you.

Good Night and God Bless